"What I need is a make-believe wife, Roxanne. A woman who can play the part of my fiancée, and, if necessary, marry me.

"The marriage would be annulled later—and you would receive a generous settlement. You could then live your own life—abroad should you wish it—or perhaps have a nice house in the country, where you could entertain your friends."

Roxanne was stunned, speechless at first, and then firm in denial. "That is ridiculous, sir. I do not know how you could suggest such a thing. You do not know me—and I do not know you. Even if I agreed, it would be wrong to deceive your grandfather so cruelly."

Luke frowned. "Last night, you said it could be a business arrangement. What is different about my proposal?"

"I meant a young woman of good family who would marry without love for the sake of a home and children—a lady who would be content to remain at home in the country, while you lived as you pleased in town. Is that not the way many marriages are arranged?"

"Yes, of course, but I explained how I felt about that—the distress and misery it can cause. A proper business arrangement, where the lady in question is paid a sum of money and understands her position from the start—that should not cause unhappiness at all, should it?"

* * *

***Make-Believe Wife***
**Harlequin® Historical #317—October 2011**

## Author Note

Roxanne is escaping from the gypsy who wants to make her his woman. Her friend has protected her but now she is alone—and, worse still, she has no idea who she really is. Roxanne hopes to reach London and become an actress. But on the way, she discovers a man called Luke Clarendon.

Luke is fleeing from his conscience when a fall from his horse makes him unable to walk unaided. When the beautiful and mysterious girl brings back his errant horse and helps him to reach safety, he makes her an outrageous proposal. If she will pretend to be his fiancée and perhaps, for a while, his make-believe wife, he will help her to become an actress and give her enough money so that she will never be at the mercy of Black Bob again.

Can Roxanne trust her heart not to become involved with this arrogant but charming man or will she wish they had never met?

This is a fun story that I hope my readers will enjoy. I love writing books for you and very much enjoy readers' comments through my website. I think the digital age is bringing many new readers to me and I look forward to hearing from any of you, as well as from my already established Harlequin Historical readers.

# Make-Believe Wife

ANNE HERRIES

TORONTO NEW YORK LONDON
AMSTERDAM PARIS SYDNEY HAMBURG
STOCKHOLM ATHENS TOKYO MILAN MADRID
PRAGUE WARSAW BUDAPEST AUCKLAND

ISBN-13: 978-0-373-30626-8

MAKE-BELIEVE WIFE



This edition published by arrangement with Harlequin Books S.A.

For questions and comments about the quality of this book please contact us at Customer_eCare@Harlequin.ca.



www.Harlequin.com

**Printed in U.S.A.**

***Available from Harlequin® Historical and***
***ANNE HERRIES***

*The Abducted Bride* #135
*Captive of the Harem* #145
*The Sheikh* #157
*Rosalyn and the Scoundrel* #166
*A Matter of Honor* #173
**A Perfect Knight* #180
**A Knight of Honor* #184
**Her Knight Protector* #188
***Lady in Waiting* #202
***The Adventurer's Wife* #208
††*Forbidden Lady* #209
†*An Improper Companion* #227
††*The Lord's Forced Bride* #231
†*A Wealthy Widow* #235
†*A Worthy Gentleman* #243
††*Her Dark and Dangerous Lord* #249
‡*Marianne and the Marquis* #258
‡*Married by Christmas* #261
‡*Marrying Captain Jack* #265
*The Unknown Heir* #269
*Ransom Bride* #276
††*Fugitive Countess* #279
*Bought for the Harem* #285
*The Homeless Heiress* #292
*Secret Heiress* #297
*Bartered Bride* #303
‡‡*A Country Miss in Hanover Square* #312
‡‡*An Innocent Debutante in Hanover Square* #314
‡‡*The Mistress of Hanover Square* #316
*Make-Believe Wife* #317

*Banewulf Dynasty
**The Elizabethan Season
†The Hellfire Mysteries
††Melford Dynasty
‡The Horne Sisters
‡‡A Season in Town

*ANNE HERRIES*

lives in Cambridgeshire, England, where she is fond of watching wildlife and spoils the birds and squirrels that are frequent visitors to her garden. Anne loves to write about the beauty of nature, and sometimes puts a little into her books, although they are mostly about love and romance. She writes for her own enjoyment, and to give pleasure to her readers. She is a winner of the Romantic Novelists' Association Romance Prize.

# *Prologue*

'Damn you, sir. I have had enough of your wild behaviour,' the Earl of Hartingdon thundered at his grandson. 'I shall not tolerate the disgrace you have brought upon us.'

'Forgive me,' Luke, Viscount Clarendon, said and looked contrite. 'This should never have come to your ears. Rollinson was a fool and a knave to come prattling to you, sir.'

Tall and almost painfully thin, yet with a commanding presence, the earl's bushy white eyebrows met in a frown of disapproval.

'Do you deny that you seduced the man's wife?'

Luke hesitated. The truth of the matter was that he had no idea whether or not he had seduced Adrina Rollinson. The evening in question was hazy to say the least. He had been three sheets to the wind and, when he'd woken to find himself lying next to the naked and undoubtedly voluptuous beauty, he had hardly been given time to wonder before her husband came storming into the summerhouse to demand satisfaction.

'I can only tell you that I have no memory of it happening, sir.'

'What sort of an answer is that, pray?' the earl demanded. 'You puzzle me, Luke. You have had every advantage and yet you insist on carrying your wildness to excess. If you cannot recall making love to a woman like Lady Rollinson, you must have been drunk.'

'Indeed, that I shall own,' Luke said instantly. 'I would not call the lady a liar, but I doubt I was capable of making love that night.'

'I suppose your taste is for whores?'

'I do not know what you may have been told of me, sir, but I assure you I have done nothing of which I am ashamed.'

'Indeed? I know that you have bought a house and intend to set up your mistress in Hampstead.' The earl's top lip curled in scorn. 'You are a disgrace to your family. Thank God your parents did not live to see what you have become.'

'Perhaps had they lived I might have been otherwise.'

'Are you blaming me? Impudent pup!' The earl's eyes darkened with temper. 'Well, sir, I have done with you. It was in my mind to make you my sole heir, for although the estate is entailed, the patent allows the title to pass through the female line and my fortune is my own to dispose of as I wish. However, I have a cousin who would restore both honour and fortune to the family name.'

'Horatio Harte, I presume? I wish you joy of him, sir.' Luke's temper was barely in check. 'Good afternoon. I shall not trouble you with my presence again.'

'I did not give you leave to go.'

'Yet I believe I shall. You have never liked me, sir. I have done things of which I am not particularly proud, but I am not the rogue you think me.'

'Come back here!' The earl's voice rose petulantly. 'You will hear me out. I shall give you one more chance, but you must marry a decent girl—one with perfect manners who knows how to behave in good society. I need an heir I can be proud of before I die.'

Luke turned at the door, denial on his lips. He would marry when and whom he wished and meant to say so, but even as he began the earl made a choking sound and sank slowly to his knees before collapsing in a heap on the floor.

'Grandfather! Someone, give me some help in here.'

Luke rushed to his grandfather's side. Rolling him on his back, he saw that his colour was slightly blue and acted swiftly in untying the tight starched cravat at his neck. He felt for a pulse and discovered a faint beat and yet his grandfather did not appear to be breathing. He was for a moment unsure of what to do for the best; then, recalling something he had once witnessed a vet do for the foal of an important mare, he opened his grandfather's mouth and made sure there was no obstruction in the throat. Then he pinched the earl's nostrils and breathed into his mouth. Luke repeated the action three times and noticed that a more natural colour had returned, though he had no idea if his actions had helped.

A voice spoke from behind him. 'He has had one of his attacks, my lord. He will recover in a moment.'

'He just keeled over. I thought he was dead or dying.'

'Milord has had one or two close calls, sir. Nasty little attacks that the doctor can't quite make out.'

'Why was I not told?' Luke rose to his feet. The colour was back in the earl's cheeks now.

'He did not wish to bother you, sir.'

'The stubborn fool—' Luke began and stopped as he heard a sound. The earl had his eyes open. He was staring up at them.

'Don't just stand there, fool. Help me up, Marshall.'

'You should have told me you were ill, Grandfather.'

'Stuff and nonsense! It is nothing. As you see, I am perfectly fine now.'

Luke and the butler helped him to his feet and assisted him to a sturdy mahogany elbow chair. Luke felt his body trembling and realised how thin and frail his grandfather had become. When had this happened? Why had he not noticed?

'Forgive me, sir. Had I known you were ill…'

'What? Would you have mended your ways?' The elderly man's eyes gleamed. 'Want to make amends, eh? You know my terms. Get yourself wed and give me an heir.'

'I am sorry you are ill, but I shall not make a promise I cannot keep. However, I will promise not to become so drunk that I do not recall with whom or where I go to bed.'

'Not enough,' the earl growled. 'Leave me to Marshall and come back when you have a wife.'

'Grandfather, that is unfair,' Luke protested, for he was genuinely upset by the news of the earl's ill health.

'Unless you oblige me I shall not leave you a penny—and, what's more, I'll tell the lawyers to cut the allowance you receive from your paternal grandfather's fortune.'

'You cannot do that, sir. I have commitments...'

'To your mistress, I suppose? Well, the choice is yours, Luke. The terms of the Marquis's will state that I can limit your income until you are thirty if I so choose. I have never done so, but now I shall make a change. I need an heir soon, Luke—and I want you to give me a grandson. Marry well and everything will be as it was. Turn your back on me now and you'll find yourself short in the pocket. Show me that you intend to settle down and make me proud of you.'

Luke hesitated, a grim set to his mouth. Had he not just witnessed his grandfather's collapse he would have told him to go to the devil and bought himself a pair of colours while he still had the money. Yet despite his harsh words, there was something vulnerable about the earl, something that made Luke realise that deep within him he cared what happened to the old devil.

'I must have time to think this over, sir.'

'Yes, of course, and to find a suitable girl—but do not take too long, Luke. I may not have more than a year or so left to me.'

Luke inclined his head and left, feeling his temper surge as he curled his nails into the palms of his hand.

He ought to walk out and never return. The lawyers would probably tell him that the earl was lying through his teeth—yet if it were the truth Luke would be in trouble.

He had made a promise to his best friend and nothing would make him break it.

# *Chapter One*

Roxanne glanced back over her shoulder, listening for the sounds of pursuit, but all she could hear were birds calling one to the other as they flitted between the trees and the occasional snuffle of a small animal in the undergrowth. The woods themselves held no fear for her, but she was afraid of being made to return to the camp.

She had been walking for hours without stopping, but now she was hungry. She was fairly certain that no one had followed her. It must be safe now to stop and eat some of the food she had packed. Placing her larger bundle on the ground, Roxanne spread her shawl on the dry earth and sat down, opening the cloth that carried her bread, cheese and the preserved fruit she had brought with her. Sofia had always kept a jar of dried fruits on her shelf, because she said figs, dates and apricots were good to eat in the winter when they could not pick fruit from the hedgerows.

She missed Sofia so much! Her friend's sad death had left her alone and in fear of the future. She had no one who cared for her and no one to care for. She was not sure which felt the worst, because she had enjoyed caring for her friend in her last months when she became too feeble to care for herself.

Blinking away her tears, Roxanne rose to her feet and gathered her bundles. Sofia had been one of a band of travelling players, almost a mother to her, and she had given Roxanne so much, even her name.

'If anything happens to me you should go to London,' Sofia had told her only a few days before she died. 'You are a fine actress, my love. You could find fame and fortune—and perhaps marry a man of substance and be the lady I believe you truly are.'

Roxanne had begged her not to talk of dying, tears stinging her eyes, but after her death it had become clear that Roxanne could not stay with the band of travelling players with whom she had lived for the past five years. She was in danger and her only choice was to run away before *he* returned to the camp.

She had made up her mind that she would get to London if she could, though it would mean walking for many days, perhaps weeks. Before she reached the great city, she would need to find work for a few days to earn her food.

Lost in thought, she was startled as she heard a loud cry and then a horse came crashing through the trees towards her. It was saddled, but without a rider, its reins hanging loose, and she realised that someone must have fallen.

Instinctively, she ran in the direction from which the cry had seemed to come. She had gone only a few yards when she saw a man lying on the ground. His eyes were closed and his face looked pale. Her heart caught and for a moment she thought he was dead. Dropping her bundles, she knelt by his side and touched his face. He felt warm and she drew a breath of relief. His fingers were moving and he was still breathing, though seemed unaware of her. He must have been knocked unconscious by the fall from his horse.

She hesitated, then unwound his white stock from his neck; taking out her precious store of water, she poured some of it onto the fine linen and began to bathe his face. His lips moved, a groan issuing from him, then his eyes flickered open and he looked up at her.

'What happened?' he muttered. 'Who are you?'

'My name is Roxanne. I think you fell from your horse. It came rushing at me through the trees and I heard your cry.'

'It was the fox,' he said and pushed up into a sitting position. His dark grey eyes fixed on her face. 'It started up just in front of us. I tried to stop, but I was riding hard and the stupid horse reared up in a fright.'

'The horse was startled. They are nervous creatures, sir. If you were riding too hard, the fault was yours.'

'The devil it was.' His slate-coloured eyes narrowed, became intent and suspicious. 'What is a lady like you doing alone in these woods—dressed like that?'

Roxanne hesitated, for to tell him her true story was too risky. She did not know him and should use caution.

He was undoubtedly a gentleman and Sofia had warned her to be careful of the gentry, for they were not to be trusted.

'I was with a band of travelling players, but I had to leave. I am trying to get to London to find work as an actress.'

'Are you indeed?' His gaze was unsettling. 'I see you have water, Miss Roxanne. Will you give me some?'

'I used some to bathe your face, but you may have a few sips.' Roxanne handed him the stoneware flask and he lifted it to his mouth, drinking deeply. 'Please leave some. I may not find a stream to refill my flask for hours.'

'I passed a stream not far back,' he replied. 'But if you are making for London you are walking in the wrong direction.'

'Oh…' Roxanne frowned as he handed her back the bottle. 'Perhaps you could—' She broke off as he attempted to stand and shouted with pain. He swayed and would have fallen had she not caught hold of his body and supported him. 'Where does it hurt?'

'My right ankle,' he groaned. 'I think it must be broken. If I sit down again, could you take the boot off for me?'

'Do you think that wise, sir? The boot will probably have to be cut off if your ankle is broken—and a doctor should do it. Sofia would have known how to treat you, but I do not have her skills.'

'Who the hell is Sofia? Is she with you?'

'She was my dearest friend and she died recently.'

'Sorry,' he muttered, his face white with pain. 'I

have a knife. Cut the damned thing off and bind the ankle with the stock. It will have to do until we can find an inn and a doctor.'

'We—are you expecting me to go with you?'

'How do you imagine I can get anywhere alone? Or were you planning to go on and leave me here?'

'Your temper does not help your cause, sir. If you will sit, I shall attempt to do as you ask—and, no, now you mention it, I was not planning to abandon you.'

His eyes narrowed in annoyance, his mouth set hard. 'You speak in the tones and manner of a lady, yet you say you are an actress. You must be a clever one.'

'Sofia said I could play royalty to the manner born,' Roxanne said, helping him to lower himself to the ground so that she could attend to his ankle. 'She was once a courtesan and had both royal and aristocratic lovers in her youth so I imagine she would know how they behave.'

'She sounds quite a remarkable lady?'

'She was wonderful.' Roxanne hesitated, then ran her hands down the length of the boot. Not yet! She would not tell him too much too soon. 'It is difficult to tell while this is on, but I think you may have a break just above your ankle. It will hurt too much if I try to pull the boot off—have I your permission to cut the leather? I dare say it may have cost a great deal of money.'

'I have other pairs; just do it.' He thrust a hand into his pocket and brought out a silver penknife.

'I think I have something better.' Roxanne opened her large bundle and took out a long thin dagger. 'The blade is very sharp. It will slit the leather easier than your knife.'

'Good grief, what are you carrying a dangerous thing like that for?'

'I am a woman travelling alone. I needed to be sure I could protect myself.'

'Remind me never to try to seduce you when I'm drunk.'

'Are you in the habit of seducing women when drunk?'

Roxanne's eyes held a sparkle of amusement as she glanced at him and then back at the boot. It was long and tight fitting and obviously the best quality. She inserted the knifepoint into the leather and began to slit the length of the boot. Her patient groaned once or twice as she worked, a muffled cry escaping him as she finally drew it from his foot.

'Damn!' he muttered as her fingers began to explore his ankle and the region above. 'It hurts like hell.'

'I think there is a small break just above the ankle,' Roxanne said. 'The flesh is not torn, but there is a bump where there ought to be straight bone—it might have been worse.'

'You cannot feel the pain,' he muttered fiercely.

'I am certain it hurts, but I shall bind it with your stock and use the last of the cold water. That may stop the swelling from becoming too bad, but I am not an expert, sir. If we can make you comfortable enough to ride your horse, it will be much easier for you to continue your journey.'

'Supposing we could find the damned creature.'

'I dare say it will not have gone far. I will look for it after I've bound your ankle.'

'You'll go and leave me here.' He looked angry, as if he believed she would simply walk away.

'I promise I shall not. All I have in the world is in these bundles. If I leave them with you, I must return.' She finished her work and rose to her feet. 'Try to rest until I return with the horse.'

'And if you cannot find it?'

'I shall return and try to help you, though it may be best to fetch help. Wait patiently if you can. I shall not be long.'

'Damn you,' he muttered through clenched teeth. 'You're made of iron. You should have been born a lady, you belong with the starched-petticoat brigade.'

'Sofia always said I was from good family.' Roxanne smiled. 'Lady or not, I shall not desert you, sir.'

She walked back the way she had come. The horse had been in a blind panic, but once it stopped its mad flight it would stand and wait to be reclaimed by its owner. She must just hope that it had not injured itself because she needed it to be strong enough to carry them both and her bundles.

Luke cursed as he reached into his coat pocket and took out his pocket flask, which was still half-filled with brandy. His ankle was hurting like the devil and the girl had been gone too long. If she did not come within a few minutes, he would have to try to find help himself. If he ignored the pain, he might hobble far enough to find a farm or a woodcutter's hut. He was attempting to rise when he heard a rustling sound and, a moment later, the girl appeared through the trees leading his horse.

'I thought you had decided to leave me after all,' he said a trifle sulkily. 'You were gone a long time.'

'Your horse was not sure he wanted to come to a stranger. He was a little shy at first, but we have become friends now.'

She led the horse to Luke. 'I think he will carry us both and my bundles, sir. If not, then I can walk beside you. I do not think you capable of riding hard this time.'

'Impertinent wench.' Luke scowled at her and then laughed. 'You remind me of my Great-Aunt Dorethea when she was young.'

'Indeed? I'm not sure whether I should be flattered or insulted.' Roxanne's brows arched. 'Do you think you can mount if I hold the horse?'

'Flattered. I admired her. Give me your arm, Miss Roxanne. I need you as a crutch.' Holding on to her arm, Luke levered himself on to his left foot. He hobbled towards the horse, then, as she held its head steady, took hold of the saddle and belly-flopped over it, using the strength of his arms and body to pull himself into a sitting position. Beads of sweat had gathered on his brow by this time, but he controlled his desire to yell out with pain. Roxanne had fitted her bundles round the pommel of the saddle; then, with an agility that surprised him, she took his outstretched hand and swung herself up behind him. 'You've done that before?'

'I've been riding horses barebacked since I was thirteen or so. We did an act that involved my having to jump up on to a moving horse.'

'You are full of surprises, Miss Roxanne. I thought you a lady at first, but no lady of my acquaintance could do what you just did.'

'A lady might not have been near when you fell,' she reminded him. 'I may not be a gentlewoman in the sense you mean, sir—but I will thank you to show me the proper respect. I am not a lightskirt and shall not be treated as one.'

Luke glanced over his shoulder. 'How do you imagine I would treat you if you were a whore?'

'I have no idea how a gentleman behaves with a lady of easy virtue, though Sofia told me that gentlemen are invariably the worst. I only know that I did not like the way Black Bob looked at me.'

Luke was intrigued. 'Who is he and how did he look at you?'

'He is the leader of the troupe and looked at me as though he could see through my clothes. He told me that now Sofia was dead, he would claim me as his woman—so I ran away.'

'You have run away from your people?'

'Yes. He had to go somewhere on business and so I took my chance while he was gone.'

A rueful laugh escaped Luke. 'And you ran into me. Well, Miss Roxanne, I must thank my lucky stars that you did. If you help me as far as the next inn, I shall return the favour by hiring a coach to take us both to London.'

Roxanne stiffened. 'I told you, I am not a whore—and I shall not be your mistress.'

'Have I said that I wish you to be? I am merely repaying a favour, miss—and if you have any sense you will accept my offer. A girl who looks like you will have offers enough, I dare say, but most of them will not be to your liking. If you are to become an actress you will need patronage, and you may as well accept mine as another's.'

Roxanne's breath caught. She almost wished she had walked away from him in the woods. He could surely manage now he had his horse.

'Put your arms about my waist,' he instructed. 'Hold on tight, Miss Roxanne. My ankle is painful and we had best find an inn before I pass out and you have to cart me there in an unconscious state.'

Roxanne did not reply. She put her arms about his waist, holding him tightly. She did not fear him, as she did Black Bob, but if he were to fall unconscious she might have difficulty in getting him safe to an inn. Perhaps the feel of her at his back would keep him awake long enough to reach the nearest inn. She hoped that he would not fall senseless, because she had no idea of where she was headed and the sooner he reached a doctor the better.

Roxanne could have no idea how very aware Luke was of his passenger, her full breasts pressed against his back. He had noticed her perfume as soon as he became conscious and found her bending over him. It was light and yet sensual, unlike any he had smelled on the ladies he met either in society or in the world of the *demi-monde* he sometimes frequented. She was different, unusual, and he'd felt intrigued from the first.

Roxanne was a woman most men would notice, her figure not willowy slender, but athletic—statuesque, might be a good word. She reminded him of the marble figure of Diana the Huntress he had commissioned for his country house, which stood in a fragrant corner of his garden, but warm with life and passion instead of white and cold. He could imagine what the leader of the travelling players had planned for her and the thought brought a frown of anger to his brow.

Damn the man for his impudence!

Clearly, her friend Sofia had been a person of influence, protecting the girl as she grew to womanhood, but once she was dead, Roxanne was at the mercy of any rogue who saw her. Luke did not know why that thought made him angry, but his protective instincts had been roused and, in thinking of her and ways to make certain she was protected, he was able to fight off his pain.

He cursed himself for riding carelessly as a wave of faintness washed over him and it took all his willpower to stay in the saddle and hold on to the reins.

'I could take control of the horse if you wish, sir. He would respond to me, as he did earlier.'

Roxanne's words jerked him back to reality and her arms about him helped fight off the faintness. He must stay awake, because he needed to be in command. She must not be allowed to slip away when they reached the inn. He could not lose her yet; he needed her help.

'I can manage,' he growled. 'It cannot be much further.'

'I pray you are right,' she said and her arms tightened about him, as if she would save him from falling.

A sharp wave of desire shot through Luke, bringing him to his senses more surely than any words. He laughed deep in his throat—it was like him to want the unobtainable. Luke had met with little resistance in his adult life; the ladies were usually more than willing to share his bed—or even entice him into the summerhouse. It was ironic that the first one to evoke such a strong response in him for an age had placed herself out of reach.

Roxanne had made it clear she would not be his mistress and in all honour he could not use his charm to persuade her after all she had done. However, it would not suit him if she were to run away. He might never see her again, and that thought was sufficient to stave off both the pain and the faintness. An ironic smile settled over his lips. She had already shown herself compassionate; perhaps the best way to keep her with him was to plead his need of a nurse or helper to see him home.

'Hold me tighter,' he said. 'The pain makes me faint. I beg you, do not desert me, Miss Roxanne. In this state I am helpless and at the mercy of unscrupulous rogues—men who would see me dead as soon as look at me.'

'You have enemies?'

'An enemy,' Luke improvised. 'You accused me of

riding too hard, but I was trying to escape from him when the fox startled my horse.'

He justified his lie to himself. His enemy was the bitter anger that had been festering inside him since the interview with his grandfather. The Earl of Hartingdon's unfair accusations and his outrageous demands had smouldered in his brain, making him careless.

'Will you be safe when you reach London?'

'Yes.' Luke waited, holding his breath. 'Once I am home I shall be perfectly safe, but I need help lest I lose consciousness and lie ill by the wayside.'

'It is true that not everyone would help if you became ill of a fever. I know that men like Black Bob might take advantage and rob you.' Roxanne seemed to hesitate, then, 'Very well, I shall not abandon you. I will see that a doctor is fetched, and, if you are ill, stay with you until you are home. I will nurse you and care for you should you need it. However, you must give me your word not to take advantage, sir.'

'You have my word as a gentleman,' Luke said. 'I am Luke Clarendon, a man of independent means and of good family. You may trust me, Miss Roxanne. Watch over me until I am fit again. I shall reward you by taking you to London—and I will introduce you to the manager of a theatre.'

'Very well, it is a bargain,' Roxanne said and her arms clung comfortingly to him once more.

Luke smiled. He did not think she would break her word for she might have done so in the woods. If he could delay their journey for a few days, she might come to like him—and once they were in London, he would find a way of keeping her with him.

# *Chapter Two*

The inn they came to a little later was a small posting inn, not one of those Luke had frequented in the past, but decent in appearance; its yard was swept clean and the groom who came running to help respectful and eager to serve.

'Mr Clarendon has had a fall from his horse,' Roxanne said and slid down from the saddle unaided. 'He cannot walk without assistance. We need a room for him and one for me—and a doctor must be called at once, for his ankle is hurt and he is in great pain.'

Luke moaned as he slid down from the horse and his injured leg jarred. The action had caused the pain to intensify and he swayed as the faintness swirled in his head. Roxanne and the groom rushed to his aid, managing to save him from a further fall. The groom shouted for help and another two came running.

'Ned, take the gentleman's horse—Jeremiah, help

me and then fetch the doctor. Mr Clarendon is in pain with his ankle.'

The two grooms supported Luke towards the inn, which was a modest building, with whitewashed walls, a thatched roof and small leaded windows. Luke glanced over his shoulder and drew a sigh of relief as he saw Roxanne was following with her bundles. His whole leg was throbbing now and he felt very faint. Indeed, he might have fallen had the grooms supporting him not been strong men.

He was supported into the inn. A large portly man came to greet them, his knowing eyes going over both Luke and then Roxanne.

'Would you be needing a room for you and the—lady, sir?'

'We need two rooms,' Roxanne said. 'Mr Clarendon has hurt his ankle. I think there may be a small break. One of your grooms has gone for the doctor. However, I shall be nursing Mr Clarendon until we leave.'

'And who might you be, miss?' The landlord's brows met in a frown.

'I am Mr Clarendon's new governess,' Roxanne said in a clear firm tone. 'He has employed me to teach his nephew. My horse was lost in the woods; it ran off and we could not waste time looking for her. My name is Miss Roxanne Peters.'

Luke glanced at her, resisting a grin. It appeared that she could spin a tale as easily as he. The landlord looked uncertain whether to believe her, but was galvanised into action by a moan of pain from Luke.

'Take the gentleman up to the best chamber,' he

commanded his minions. 'The governess can have the smaller room two doors down.'

'Thank you, landlord,' Luke said and glanced back at Roxanne. 'Follow us up, Miss Peters. I shall want you in attendance when the doctor arrives.'

'I shall be with you in a moment, sir.'

The landlord had gone before them. He gestured at the room that was to be Roxanne's, leaving her to make her own way while continuing further down the passage.

Roxanne went inside the small room. There was a narrow iron bedstead with a white counterpane, blue curtains at the window and a small chest of drawers. To a girl who had been used to living in a caravan it was perfectly adequate. Roxanne dumped her bundles on the floor, took the key from the inside of the door and locked it as she went out, pocketing it safely. Her possessions were not valuable, but they were all she had and she could not afford to lose them—nor did she wish the landlord to go poking his nose into her things.

Walking quickly to the room where she had seen them take her employer—she had decided that the best way to go on was to act the part of an upper-class servant—Roxanne entered and saw that the landlord was standing by the bed. Both the grooms had gone.

'Thank you,' she said. 'I can manage him now.'

The landlord turned, his eyes narrowed and not exactly friendly. Roxanne felt a prickling at her nape. Mr Clarendon seemed barely conscious. She had a feeling that had she not been here to protect him, he might well have been robbed of his possessions. Perhaps she was wronging the landlord, but she was not sure he was honest.

'Right. I'll send the doctor up when he gets here.' He looked at her hard. 'I'll be wanting five shillings a night for this room, two for yours—food and the doctor extra.'

'Yes, of course. You will be paid. Mr Clarendon is a respectable man and we should not dream of running off without paying you.'

'You better hadn't. Jake Hardcastle never forgets a face—and I reckon I've seen yours before, but I can't recall where. You weren't a governess then.' He leered at her. 'If I don't get paid one way, I can take my dues another.'

'Will you please leave us.' Roxanne's manner was haughty, more the great lady than a governess. 'After the doctor has been we shall want food—perhaps some good chicken broth and fresh bread.'

He inclined his head, but made no other answer. Leaving the room, he paused to look back as Roxanne bent over the bed.

'Mr Clarendon,' she said, placing a hand to Luke's forehead. He was feeling warm and a little damp. She thought perhaps he had started a fever. 'Do not worry. I am here. I shall not leave you.'

The sound of the door shutting soundly made Roxanne look round. The landlord had gone and when she turned back, her patient's eyelids fluttered and then opened.

'Has he gone?' he muttered. 'The place looks decent

enough, but that fellow is a rascal. I don't trust him. You won't leave me, Roxanne?'

'Miss Peters. I am your employee, remember?'

A wry laugh was wrung from his lips. 'You will make a damned fine actress, Roxanne. You reminded me of a strict governess I once had—she frightened the life out of us all, except the earl.'

'The earl? Who is he?'

'Oh, just someone we lived with when I was young. He isn't important.' Luke moaned and beads of sweat appeared on his brow. 'I am sorry to make so much fuss. I wouldn't have thought a broken bone could be so painful. I do not recall it hurting this much when I broke my arm as a youngster.'

'You had to ride here and be manhandled up the stairs. I have not been trained to set broken bones and the bandage I applied may have made the pain worse. When the doctor comes he will rebind it and give you something to help you sleep.'

'Will you sit with me while I sleep? Or perhaps you should keep the money with you? I do not trust him.'

'Nor I,' she admitted. 'Do you trust me with your gold?'

'What choice have I?' Luke reached out to touch her hand as she frowned. 'No, that was badly put. Yes, I trust you, Roxanne. It is odd, but I feel I have known you for ever. I know you will not desert me, for you have given your word.'

'Then I shall put the money somewhere safe.'

'It is in my coat pocket, in a leather purse. I do not

know exactly what is there but it should be enough to see us safely back to London.'

Roxanne examined his coat and found the purse. She opened the strings and counted the gold, holding it out on her hand so that he could see.

'You have ten gold sovereigns, sir. I think it should be adequate for the journey, don't you?'

'You did not need to show me. I told you, I trust you. Now put them somewhere safe.'

'Yes, I shall.'

Roxanne turned her back on him. Lifting her skirts, she located the secret pocket sewn into her petticoats and added the gold to her secret treasure. It felt heavy, making her very conscious of its presence, but she would become accustomed to the extra weight.

She turned back and saw Luke staring at her.

'It is the safest place I know. My bundles could be searched or snatched.'

Luke nodded, his eyes narrowed and thoughtful. 'You are a resourceful woman, Roxanne. I wonder what your secret is—what you are not telling me?'

'Why should you think I have a secret?'

How could he know? No, he could not. He was just testing her.

'I shall not pry,' Luke said and yawned, closing his eyes. 'You keep your secrets, Roxanne—and I shall keep mine.'

Roxanne turned her head. How had he sensed that she was hiding her secret? She had not told him about the day Sofia found her wandering, all memory of her previous life gone. Nor had she told him about the jewel she carried in her secret pocket. Sofia had told her she had been clutching it tightly in her right hand when she was found and refused to let go for days. She also carried a lace kerchief with the initials R. P. embroidered into the corner in red. Sofia had said the name Roxanne suited her. They had never bothered with a second name and she had used Peters when the innkeeper asked, because it was the first to come to her mind. She had once done some sewing for a Lady Peters and been given a gold sovereign for her trouble.

Sofia had hidden the ruby safely and Roxanne had forgotten its existence until her friend reminded her as she lay dying. Sofia had said she should sell the jewel, but Roxanne was not certain she had the right to do so, for she did not know whether it belonged to her or someone else. Had she stolen the jewel and run away from her home—or her employer?

Why had she refused to let it go for days?

She hesitated, considering whether she ought to tell Luke Clarendon the rest of her story, but the moment had passed; she heard the sound of voices outside the door and then it opened and a man entered. He was dressed in a shabby black coat and knee breeches, the battered hat he deposited on the chest having seen better days. However, his linen looked clean and he nodded his head respectfully as he approached the bed.

'The gentleman took a fall from his horse, you say?'

'Yes,' Roxanne replied. 'He has been in considerable pain since.'

'I shall examine him,' the doctor said and bent over Luke, pulling back the covers. He unwound the stock

Roxanne had used and ran his fingers over the swollen ankle, frowning and nodding to himself. 'I think this may be a case of dislocation rather than a break. Your employer has been lucky, miss.' Hearing a moan from the patient, the physician turned his gaze on him. 'This may hurt a bit, sir. I am going to...' He pulled Luke's leg out straight, making him yell out with pain as something clicked. 'Yes, I thought so. It will be painful for a while, but I shall put a tight bandage on and visit again tomorrow. You will need to rest for a time, but in a few days it should start to mend. You had dislocated the bones just above your ankle and the ligaments will be inflamed, but I am sure the bones themselves are not broken.'

'I pray you are right,' Luke muttered between gritted teeth. 'It hurts like hell now.'

'Yes, I dare say it may.' The doctor dipped into his bag, brought out linen bandages and rebound Luke's ankle and above to his calf. 'That should help the damage to settle and it will heal naturally. I'll give you something for the pain.' He delved into his bag again and took out a small brown bottle. 'This will help you sleep, but it is dangerous if you take too many doses. You will have to measure it—just four drops into a cup of water every six hours. Miss Peters, is it?'

'Yes, that is my name,' Roxanne lied and took the bottle. 'Is this laudanum?'

'Yes—have you used it before?'

'A friend of mine used it sometimes. I know that it must be handled carefully, sir.'

'Then I can trust you to look after our patient.' He

glanced down at Luke. 'You will sleep soon, Mr Clarendon—and there should not be a fever, but if it happens you may send for me again.'

The physician took his leave. Roxanne carefully measured the drops into a glass of water. She helped Luke to sit up and he took the cup, gulping it down and draining the lot. Then he lay back against the pillows with a sigh.

'I was selfish to ask you to sit with me. You should go to bed and rest.'

'I shall sit here by the fire for a while. The doctor says there will be no fever, but I want to be sure you are peaceful. You were warm and sweaty earlier. I thought you might take a fever, but perhaps now you can rest you will soon feel better.'

Roxanne sat down by the fireplace. Someone had lit the fire when they brought Luke Clarendon up and it was just beginning to draw well. Her room had no fire and she might as well sit here in comfort—but she would lock the door first, just in case she dozed off.

Roxanne woke with a start. The fire was still burning so she could not have been asleep long. She got up quickly and went to the bed, bending over Luke. He appeared to be sleeping peacefully and when she placed a hand to his forehead, he was only slightly warm.

If he had not made a sound, what had woken her? She went to the door and stood with her ear against it, listening.

'Is anyone there?' she asked softly, but received no answer. 'What do you want?'

Another sound alerted her and she turned swiftly towards the window, just in time to see a man's face looking in. Someone must have fetched a ladder to try to gain entrance that way after realising the door was bolted on the inside. Instinctively, Roxanne bent down and retrieved the iron poker from the fireplace. She approached the window, raising her arm high, making it clear that she was ready to repel any intruder. For a moment she stared at the face looking in. The features were coarse and common, unknown to her. Aware that he had been spotted, the man hesitated and then disappeared. Roxanne looked out and saw the top of his head hurriedly descending the ladder, which he then picked up and ran off with towards the stables.

Roxanne's legs felt slightly shaky as she sat down by the fire once more. She had not known the man attempting to enter by way of the window, but she was certain the landlord would. Her instincts had been right. Their host was a rascal and it would not be safe for her to leave Luke Clarendon alone while he was in a drugged sleep.

For a moment she wondered if the doctor had been in with them, but Luke seemed to be easier now and she thought the physician had known his job well enough. She shivered and bent down to place another log on the fire. If Luke were well enough to hire a carriage of some sort, they would do better to move on as soon as they could.

'Have you been to bed at all?' Luke asked as he opened his eyes and looked up at her. She had been applying a cool cloth to his brow. 'That feels good, but I do not have a fever. My mind is quite clear now. I think I slept for a long time?'

'Yes, you did. I stayed with you all night. There was an attempt to gain access through the window, but it woke me and I faced the intruder down with the poker. He ran away, back to the stable.'

Luke's mouth thinned. 'In league with the innkeeper I imagine? Some of these fellows are rogues. Not content with their pay, they will rob the unwary.'

'He must have thought you were alone. I am afraid I have wasted two shillings of your money. I did not use the room I asked for at all.'

'Well, you should go there now and rest. But first, give me my pistol—it's in my coat, the inside pocket—and then ask the landlord to bring food and drink, Roxanne. I doubt he will try anything in broad daylight, but if he does I shall show him I'm no fool. I shall enquire what kind of transport is for hire—but if there is none available here we shall go on together on my horse.'

Roxanne fetched the pistol from amongst his things and handed it to him. Had she known it was there, she might have used it to protect them instead of the poker the previous night.

'Are you sure you can manage to move on so soon? The doctor said you should rest and he would come again today.'

'My ankle feels sore at the moment and there is some pain in my calf, but the excruciating pain of yesterday has gone. I would rather leave if I can manage it.'

'If we can hire a chaise of some sort, will you leave your horse here?'

'I doubt I should see it again. I shall pay the man for the hire of his vehicle and change at the next posting house, but take my horse with us.'

'I confess I cannot wait to see the back of this place. Had I not been with you, you would certainly have been robbed as you slept.'

'I should not be the first vulnerable traveller to die in his bed at the hands of rogues calling themselves landlords.' Luke frowned. 'I have much to thank you for, Roxanne. It seems as if you have saved me from my own folly more than once.'

'I have done nothing any decent person would not,' she said, a faint flush in her cheeks. 'Travelling with you will save my small store of money and I shall reach London sooner.'

'I might not have reached it at all without you.'

Luke's gaze was so warm and so intent that her cheeks flamed and he laughed as he saw her discomfort. 'Now I have embarrassed you. Forgive me, Miss Roxanne. I have not forgotten my promise. I shall not try to seduce you—at least until our bargain is at an end.'

'You should not try it at all, sir. You will be disappointed. I have no intention of becoming your mistress—or any other man's.'

'So you say.' Luke smiled lazily. 'You are far too beautiful to remain untouched for the rest of your life, Roxanne. Someone will persuade you to part with your innocence—I should prefer that it was me.'

'I think you must have a fever, sir. You hardly know me—and you should know better than to mock me.'

'I was not mocking you, Roxanne. Believe me, there are not many women who make me feel the way you do—but I shall not tease you, because I might frighten you away. I may be able to leave this place soon, but that doesn't mean I am safe until I get to London.'

'Are you thinking of your enemy?' Roxanne looked concerned. He might be arrogant and too sure of his power to charm, but she did not fear him, as she had Black Bob. 'I thought it was one of the landlord's rogues trying to rob you last night, but your enemy may have followed you here to try to kill you.'

'No, I do not think so.' Luke frowned and wished he had not spun her such a tale. 'He might want to punish me, but he would not kill me.'

'Oh—then I dare say it was not he.' Roxanne looked thoughtful and he wondered what was in her mind. 'If you truly know a theatre manager who might give me a trial, I should be grateful.'

'I shall help you, as you have helped me,' Luke promised. 'Whatever else I may be, Miss Roxanne, I am not ungrateful. One day I may try to make you my mistress, a position you might find to your liking if you gave it a chance, but it shall not be while we journey together.'

Within two hours, they had left the inn. The groom who had first aided them the previous day was driving a chaise, which was in reasonable order, with Luke's horse tied and trotting behind. Roxanne sat beside Luke on the seat facing forwards so that they could see the groom's back. He had told them his name was Harold and seemed likeable. Hopefully, he was honest, but they would only need his services until they reached a well-known posting inn a few miles further on the London road. Roxanne was not sure what Luke Clarendon had said to the innkeeper, but though he had looked at her in a surly way when they left, he had not spoken to her disrespectfully. She had previously returned Luke's gold to him and he had paid for their lodging and the doctor's fees.

Roxanne was certain their host had added extra to the bill for himself, because his charge of two guineas for the doctor's visit seemed extortionate to her, but Luke had paid it cheerfully.

'It was worth treble for the relief he has afforded me,' Luke said. 'I am still in pain, but it is bearable now.'

'I am glad to hear it.' Roxanne was thoughtful. If Luke Clarendon was capable of travelling alone now, she ought to leave him and make her own way. He had offered her help, but she was uncertain of the price she might be asked to pay.

Sofia had so often warned her to be careful of gentlemen, especially those who smiled and promised her help or a fortune. This man was charming and handsome, but she did not quite trust him.

Well, he might attempt seduction, but she did not believe he would force her—the way Black Bob would have had she stayed with the travelling players. Luke Clarendon was a gentleman, after all.

Roxanne knew that his warnings were valid. If she

became an actress, she would be offered protection by various men—perhaps the manager of the theatre himself or gentlemen who came to watch her perform. If she gained admirers, she might follow in Sofia's footsteps and become the mistress of an aristocrat or even royalty. It was not what Sofia had wanted for her or what she planned for herself, but it might be impossible to avoid some such relationship.

Why not a man she had already begun to like?

The thought had wormed its way into her mind against her will. Roxanne did not wish to become any man's mistress, but if it was inevitable— Her thoughts were interrupted as Luke glanced at her.

'You look pensive, tired. Why do you not lean your head back against the squabs and sleep for a while? I think we may trust Harold. Relax your guard and rest.'

'Yes, perhaps I shall.'

Roxanne leaned her head back against the squabs, closing her eyes. When Luke Clarendon looked and spoke to her in that way her defences crumbled. He was such an attractive man and she was beginning to like him all too well.

When she woke an hour or so later, the chaise was drawing into the yard of what was clearly a prestigious inn. She discovered that she had been leaning against Luke's shoulder and apologised, her cheeks warm.

'Forgive me, sir. I hope I have not made you uncomfortable. Does your leg pain you very much?'

'It is sore and, yes, a little painful,' he said. 'I shall

live, Miss Roxanne—and you did not make me uncomfortable at all.'

The groom had brought the chaise to a halt. One of the inn's employees had come to open the chaise door and let down the step. Seeing that Luke was carrying an injury, his breeches split and opened to allow for the bandages, the man offered his hand, helping him to descend. Luke did so slowly and carefully, his flinch of pain not going unnoticed by either the ostler or Roxanne.

'I have suffered an accident, as you see, Johnston,' Luke said with a friendly smile at the man who clearly knew him. 'If you would have someone care for my horse and ask someone to give this kind fellow something to eat before he goes on his way again. Please help me inside yourself.'

'Yes, sir, of course,' Johnston replied and signalled to his minions, who came running and were given curt instructions to see to the horses.

Roxanne frowned as she thanked Harold for bringing them here safely and gave him a shilling of her own money for himself.

'I'm sorry if you weren't treated right at the last place,' he said and pulled his cap. 'I heard what happened, but I didn't know until I was told what you did, miss. You were right brave.'

'I do not think you belong at a place like that, Harold.'

'No, miss, nor don't I,' he agreed. 'I stayed because it were better than being on the road, but when I take this rig back I shall give me notice and look for work elsewhere.'

'I am sure you will find it,' Roxanne said and inclined her head before following Luke into the inn.

When she entered she saw him in close conversation with a man who looked to be the landlord. He was a very different man from the last one they had met; portly and pleasant-faced, he smiled and nodded at her in a friendly way.

'This gentleman has told me he owes his life to you, miss. I know there's more than one who should be grateful to you. My wife will take you up to a nice comfortable room and look after you. I dare say you are very tired.'

'I slept a part of the way here,' Roxanne replied. She looked at Luke, her fine brows raised. 'Have you asked our host to fetch a doctor, sir? I think your leg may need further attention—just to make certain it has been properly treated.'

'Don't you worry, miss. His lor…his honour is in good hands now.'

Roxanne heard the change in the landlord's tone and his hasty correction. What had he been going to say? It was clear that Luke Clarendon was well known and respected here—but how was he normally addressed?

She frowned as the landlord's wife came to greet her, curtsying respectfully. 'Come this way, miss. We are always glad to have his lordship come to stay—' She clapped her hand to her forehead. 'There, if Sid didn't tell me I was to call Lord Clarendon his honour. My tongue runs away with me, so it does—but everyone knows who he is so why not say it openly?'

'Why not indeed?'

Roxanne felt her cheeks getting warmer. What a fool she was not to have made sure of her facts for a start. He had told her his name was Luke Clarendon and she had assumed his title was plain Mister. He must have been laughing at her behind his hand.

Luke Clarendon was an aristocrat and therefore not to be trusted. Sofia had told her that they were the worst of all and warned her never to lose her heart to a member of the upper classes.

*'If you do, he will use you and then abandon you. Take notice, child, for I know of what I speak.'*

Roxanne felt her stomach knot with a mixture of anger and disappointment. For a short time she had begun to think that perhaps Luke really liked her—so why had he not told her he had a title from the start?

He had pretended to trust her, but he hadn't trusted her enough to tell her who he really was. She felt the sting of tears, but blocked them out. There was no sense in crying. She didn't know Lord Clarendon at all and, after listening to Sofia's opinion of the aristocracy for years, she was sure she did not wish to. Her friend had warned her that they were all the same: proud, arrogant and ruthless.

*'They know how to be charming and they will smile and tell you they adore you, but underneath they are cold and heartless. They will not marry out of their class—and they toss you to one side when they are finished with you. The English aristocracy are the worst.*

*Some foreign royalty are kinder and more generous. Never trust an English gentleman, Roxanne—particularly if he tells you he will always love you. Just take what you can from him and move on before he does.'*

Roxanne kept her anger in check as she followed the innkeeper's wife along a hall and into a room. It was large and comfortable, well furnished and, with a fire burning in the grate, warm.

'This is next to his lordship's chamber,' she said. 'He always has the same one when he visits on his way to stay with the earl.'

'Who is the earl?'

'Why, his grandfather, of course.' The woman gave her an odd look. 'I thought you would know that, miss, being a cousin of his lordship.'

'Yes, of course. There is more than one earl in the family.'

Her quick answer banished the other woman's frown. 'So there will be,' she replied and laughed, her large bosom shaking. 'Silly me. Now, is there anything more you need, miss?'

'May I have my supper here, please? Just something light—and I would love a cup of tea.'

'Yes, of course you would. You ladies love your pot of tea and bread and butter—but I've a nice pie cooking and some chops for his lordship. His lordship is partial to a nice chop or two.'

Roxanne inclined her head. She was so angry that she barely knew how to answer. One part of her mind was telling her to walk out now and make her own way to London. If Harold had not left, he might have taken her a bit further before returning the rig to its owner. Yet if she did that she would not have the chance to tell Lord Clarendon exactly what she thought of him and his lies.

The warmth of the fire was enticing and Roxanne's feeling of annoyance faded as she moved closer, holding her hands to the flames. There was nothing to stop her moving on alone, because *Lord* Clarendon was amongst friends and would be properly cared for. Her instincts told her that she might be laying up trouble for herself if she stayed here and yet she was seduced by the thought of a warm bed, the fire and some hot food.

What harm could it do to travel on with him, even if he had not been entirely honest with her?

It was good to be in a house again instead of the cramped conditions in the caravan… Now *where* had that thought come from?

Try as she might, Roxanne had never been able to remember anything about her previous life. Sofia was convinced she had run away from her home, that she was the child of gentry, but had been in some terrible danger.

*'Something happened to you, my love,'* Sofia had told her. *'You were frightened and ill. In your fever you spoke of many things, of places you'd seen and people you knew. For weeks you woke crying and screaming, frightened of a dream, but you could never recall it. It is the reason I did not try hard to find your family. If you ran away in such distress there must have been a*

*reason—and I would not give you back to people who might ill treat you.'*

Had Roxanne's family mistreated her? Sofia had burned her clothes, because she said they were not fit for use and could tell them nothing about her past, except that they were of good cloth.

Roxanne shook her head. If her family had wanted her, she would not have been wandering the roads alone and in such a state. It hardly mattered where she had come from. Sofia had been like a mother to her, giving her all the love she instinctively knew had been missing from her previous life. A wave of grief swept over her, bringing tears to her eyes. She dashed them away with her hand, determined not to give into foolishness. Sofia was gone and she must manage alone.

Faced with walking the rest of the way to London alone or travelling in a chaise with a gentleman, who was truly in no condition to ravage her, she thought she must be sensible and choose the latter. If Lord Clarendon tried to seduce her as he recovered his strength, she could leave him and go on alone.

Removing the black-velvet cloak that had been Sofia's, a relic of the days when she had moved amongst gentlemen of fortune and their mistresses, Roxanne sat on the edge of the bed. Her dress had also belonged to Sofia when she was a young woman; though old-fashioned, it was of good cloth with a low, dipped neckline, in which Roxanne had sewn a frill of soft cream lace for modesty's sake. Amongst her things was a silver hand mirror that she had inherited from her friend, an ivory comb and a bristle brush. She took them out and then tidied her dark red curls, glancing at herself once before replacing them securely in her bundle.

When she heard the knock at the door, she gave permission to enter, but was surprised when Lord Clarendon walked in.

'I thought it was the innkeeper's wife, my lord,' she said and raised her head defiantly. 'Why did you not tell me you were the grandson of an earl? I should not have called you Mr Clarendon had I known your title, sir.'

'It hardly matters. Hartingdon is about to disown me anyway.'

'Why?' Roxanne asked. 'Is he not your grandfather?'

'He brought me up after my parents died, but I was a nuisance. He did not truly wish for the trouble of a young boy and I was left to the care of servants. When he was forced to discipline me, he was harsh. As soon as I inherited my father's estate I left Hartingdon and have visited very seldom since—and yet…'

Roxanne sensed his hesitation. 'You are troubled over something?'

'Hartingdon is an old man. He fell down in some kind of faint while I was visiting there recently and—to be honest, it distressed me. Had you asked me a week ago if I cared a damn what happened to him, I should have said no but now…' Luke shook his head and laughed ruefully. 'I am a fool. His health changes nothing. And if he makes that popinjay Harte his heir… it is not my affair.'

'Why would he disown you?' Her clear eyes disconcerted him and he dropped his gaze.

'He wishes me to marry a suitable young lady, someone with good manners who will not disgrace the family.'

'Why should he imagine you would marry anyone other than a respectable girl?'

'Because he has been told that I have a string of mistresses and it is true that I have found pleasure in the arms of whores. I have found them kinder and more generous than young ladies of my acquaintance.' He frowned. 'I dare say it was my fault that he was ill.'

'You are blaming yourself, are you not?'

'Yes. I thought he was going to die. It shocked me and I realised I did not wish for it.'

'You care for him,' Roxanne said and nodded, looking at him curiously. 'Why do you not do as he asks and marry a suitable girl?'

'Because the only ones I know bore me to tears. I would make him happy if I could, for I believe he may not have long to live—but to marry a woman I could not love is a life sentence. Even for his sake I could not do such a thing.'

'No? I thought men of your class often married for land or money?'

'If one is in difficulty…' Luke glared at her. 'My father was forever having affairs. He broke my mother's heart. As a consequence they quarrelled and…the chaise he was driving went off the road into a ditch filled with water and they were both killed. I was thrown clear and survived. The last thing I remember of that day was my mother screaming at him, crying because he had broken yet another promise. I would not wish to make any woman that miserable.'

'How terrible for you. I think I understand why you feel as you do.' Roxanne frowned. 'If the earl does not have long, could you not let him believe you mean to marry and then…?'

'Break it off?' Luke raised his brows. 'I should be a fine rogue to dash a young lady's hopes, should I not? Society would throw me out and I should deserve it.'

'Yes, it was a foolish idea, though if she knew and it was a business arrangement it might be possible,' Roxanne said and then changed the subject hurriedly because she had been outspoken. 'I have asked for my supper to be brought here. Did you want something, sir?'

Luke was staring at her. He looked as if he had been struck by lightning. 'What did you say—a business arrangement? What exactly did you mean?'

'It was mere foolishness.' Roxanne's cheeks burned. 'I meant nothing—did you want something of me, sir?'

'I'm not sure,' he said and looked thoughtful. 'I came to ask if you would dine with me down in the parlour, but perhaps I shall have my meal brought up to my room, too. You have given me food of another kind, Miss Roxanne—something to chew on for a day or two until I am certain of my own mind.'

Now what did he mean by that? Roxanne would have asked, but her supper arrived and Luke walked away with a nod of the head.

## *Chapter Three*

The sun shone through the small leaded window the next morning, bringing Roxanne from her bed with new energy. She had been up for some minutes when the innkeeper's wife entered bearing a can of hot water and was grateful for her thoughtfulness.

'Thank you. I was about to use the water left from last night and this is a kind thought.'

'His lordship would expect it, miss. Would you like to eat your breakfast here? His lordship is having his in the private parlour. You could join him, if you wish? He has bacon, devilled eggs, kedgeree and also cold roast ham, besides the toast, of course. You could have the same unless there is something else you would like?'

'If I could have some bread or rolls with honey, that would do very well. I shall come down as soon as I have washed and tidied myself.'

'Of course, miss. Whatever suits you.'

Roxanne thanked her and she went away. Despite

some fears about the future and her present situation, Roxanne had slept well and was feeling refreshed. She was ready and downstairs in a very short time. In the private parlour, Lord Clarendon, as she was trying to think of him, was drinking coffee and reading a news-sheet. He looked up as she entered and smiled. She realised not for the first time that he was very attractive and her heart did a funny little skip.

'Ah, Roxanne, did you sleep well? I trust there were no untoward incidents to disturb you last night?'

'None at all, sir. I slept perfectly and feel much refreshed this morning.'

'That is excellent news. I, too, am feeling less strained. I have been thinking about our situation and would like you to consider a suggestion that I believe might suit us both. Am I right in believing that you need to find work almost immediately?'

'Yes, that is so,' Roxanne replied and sat down just as the innkeeper brought in some warm soft rolls in a covered dish, also butter and a pot of dark honey. 'Thank you so much.'

She took a fresh baked roll and spread it with honey. Their host poured her a bowl of fragrant coffee, adding a drop of cream, and then left them alone together. Raising her clear eyes to Luke's, Roxanne questioned, 'I am not certain of your meaning?'

'It is a little difficult to explain. Have you been honest with me, Roxanne? From your story I think you honest and of good character—is there something I should know that you have not told me?'

'I do not see why you should need to know anything

about me, sir.' She hesitated, then, 'I will tell you that I have no memory of my life before Sofia found me more than five summers ago. I was in great distress, near to starving and out of my mind with a fever. I had a kerchief with the initials R. P.—and that is why Sofia called me Roxanne—and Peters was the name of a lady I once did some sewing for. It fits and might be my name, but I do not know the truth.'

'Good grief! So you have no idea who you are?' He frowned. 'That could complicate things…'

'What do you mean? What can my past life mean to you?

'Perhaps nothing, perhaps much.' He glared at her. 'What else have you kept from me?'

Roxanne thought of the ruby but decided she would not tell him everything just yet. 'I do not see what difference it can make to you.'

'It is in my mind to do as you suggested last night—but I should not wish for an unpleasant surprise. I do not want an irate brother or employer turning up on my doorstep causing trouble.'

'I fear you have lost me.' But she was beginning to feel an odd churning in her stomach and her suspicions were aroused. He could not be suggesting what she thought?

'You want work as an actress and you assured me that you can play royalty or the aristocracy to perfection. What I need is a make-believe wife, Roxanne, a woman who can play the part of my fiancée, and, if necessary, marry me. The marriage would be annulled later—and you would receive a generous settlement.

You could then live your own life, abroad should you wish it—or perhaps a nice house in the country, where you could entertain your friends.'

Roxanne was stunned, speechless at first, and then firm in denial. 'That is ridiculous, sir. I do not know how you could suggest such a thing. You do not know me—and I do not know you. Even if I agreed, it would be wrong to deceive your grandfather so cruelly.'

Luke frowned. 'Last night you said it could be a business arrangement. What is different about my proposal?'

'I meant a young woman of good family who would marry without love for the sake of a home and children—a lady who would be content to remain at home in the country while you lived as you pleased in town. Is that not the way many marriages are arranged?'

'Yes, of course, but I explained how I felt about that, the distress and misery it can cause. A proper business arrangement, where the lady in question is paid a sum of money and understands her position from the start—that should not cause unhappiness at all, should it?'

'No, not if the lady was content with the arrangement.' Roxanne saw the slightly excited, expectant look on his face. 'I am not a lady, sir. I told you, I do not know who I am—and I have lived with travelling players for some years. I have appeared on various stages about the country and might be recognised.'

'That might be a drawback, if you had played in London—but I think you have not?'

'No, I have never played at a large theatre. Sometimes we were employed by a provincial theatre, but often we set up on village greens or in the yard of an inn, as travelling players have for centuries.'

'Black Bob is not your relation—or your lover?'

'Certainly not!' she cried indignantly.

'Then I see no reason why you should not oblige me.'

'Do you not?' Roxanne pressed a spotless white napkin to her mouth, then laid it by her plate. 'I am grateful for the bed and my food, but I think we should part company now. I will find some way of reaching London alone.'

'You promised you would not abandon me. We still have one more day on the road.'

'You are perfectly safe now. These people are honest and they know you. Besides, I do not think you are in pain now.'

'I am not in as much pain as I was, but if I wanted to get down from the chaise on the road I could not do so without assistance. If my idea upsets you, I withdraw it. Last night I thought you willing. I misjudged the matter. Forgive me, but allow me to take you on to London and find you a place to stay and at least an interview with the manager of a theatre.'

'I see no reason why you should do anything for me. I have done very little to deserve it, sir.'

'Apart from saving my life twice?' Luke grinned at her. 'Say you are not offended, Roxanne. I assure you that my motives are not those of greed or wishing to deceive—except in a kind way.'

'A kind way?'

'I should like my grandfather to die with an easy mind. Is that so very terrible?'

'No, and if the young lady were willing I should not entirely condemn the idea—but I am not a lady. You would be lying to him if you presented me as a lady of good birth.'

'Supposing I merely said you were a young lady of good character—would that be a lie?'

'No.' Roxanne met his searching gaze. 'I am untouched—if that is what you mean. Sofia kept me safe. She believed I was of a good family and she wanted me to become a lady. She did not wish me to follow in her footsteps—but a lady is born, not made. I could live quietly, perhaps in Bath, as you suggested, but without patronage I should not be accepted.'

'Supposing I could find a lady who would sponsor you? Supposing you found yourself able to mix in company—would you then consider becoming my fiancée or, if necessary, wife for a short time?'

Roxanne hesitated. She hardly knew why she was resisting. Sofia had kept her jewel safe, telling her that she need not work on the stage. The chance to be accepted into society, to live as a respectable young lady, was something that might never come again. If she refused and insisted on finding work as an actress, her future was inevitable. In the end she would be trapped or persuaded into taking a protector.

'I might consent to a long engagement,' she said and then wondered if she had run mad. 'I think marriage might be a step too far, but if you were to introduce me as your fiancée and explain that we could not marry until…my father returns from India, it might serve.'

'Is your father in India?'

'I have no idea who my father is or even if he is alive. It was a game Sofia invented. She said I was the daughter of an English lady and an Indian prince. She was once the mistress of a maharajah and liked to tell me tales of India. I think her stories were so vivid that sometimes I saw the prince in my dreams. She said it would take away the bad dreams and she was right.'

'Your friend was a remarkable lady.'

'She taught me so much and I loved her. Sometimes her stories seem real to me, but I remember nothing beyond waking and seeing Sofia smiling at me.'

'It must have been terrifying for you.'

'Yes, at first, but Sofia helped me through the dark times when the nightmares came.'

'You were lucky to have her.'

'I think had she not found me I should have died—but you do not need to tell your grandfather lies. Surely there must be a young woman of good family who would oblige you?'

'I do not wish to make a marriage of convenience.' A tiny nerve flicked at his temple. 'My mother made such a marriage and was desperately unhappy. I would not inflict that pain on anyone. I truly do not wish to harm anyone.'

'Then…' Roxanne sighed '…perhaps we might have a business arrangement if you wished for it.'

'I begin to see how the story might work,' Luke said, his gaze narrowed. 'I could say that you were the daughter of an employee of the East India Company. You have not heard from your father for some time and, while consenting to an engagement, could not marry until he replies to your letter. If necessary, we could always kill him off at some future date.'

'Do not joke about such things.' Roxanne twisted her napkin in her fingers. 'I feel that we are discussing a wicked trick and I am not sure that I could carry it through. If the earl were to discover the deceit he would be devastated—it might lead to his death.'

'Why should it be discovered?' Luke's cool gaze intensified. 'You are an attractive young woman, Roxanne—but your clothes do not do you justice. Dressed as a young woman of good family you will look very different. No one is going to recognise you as an actress—none of my friends or family will have seen you on the stage. An engagement may be broken. If something goes wrong, we can end it and my grandfather will understand that these things happen. However, he may not live for many months. After his death, you will be free to go wherever you please. Is it too much to ask—to make an old man happy?'

Roxanne considered, then, 'No, that part at least is commendable. Yet I still feel it wrong to deceive him. Could you not bring yourself to make a marriage of convenience to a young lady of your own class, my lord?'

'I fear it is out of the question. If you will not accept, I must forget the idea. Grandfather has given me an ultimatum and if I do not abide by it… He has threatened to disown me and—make life extremely difficult for me and the people I support. Besides, his cousin Harte is a pompous fool and not fit to stand in Grandfather's shoes.'

'What happens to you if the earl disinherits you?'

'I lose the earl's title, his estate and fortune—but do not imagine I care for his money. I have sufficient of my own…or I had. He has told me that he can withhold the inheritance I had from my paternal grandfather until I am thirty if he chooses. I do not know if it is an empty threat. I must speak with my lawyers in town. It would be deuced awkward. I have commitments to some people that I would be loath to break.'

'What kind of commitments?' She saw his quick frown. 'That is not my business. Forgive me. It is just that I would be certain what is in your mind concerning this arrangement.'

'My suggestion stemmed from your own, Roxanne. Forgive me, I should not have mentioned it. After all, you hardly know me. I might be a ruthless rogue out to rob the old man of his money.'

'No, I do not believe that,' Roxanne replied. 'You must allow me a little time, sir. I shall complete the journey to London with you—and then we shall discuss this again, perhaps in a few days.'

His gaze fastened on her face. 'Yes, of course. We have another day on the road and then I shall take you to a place where you can stay until a decision is made.'

The journey was completed without incident. They were obliged to get down from the chaise once so that Luke could relieve himself. He had not lied when he told her he would need assistance to hobble into the bushes at the side of the road and leaned heavily on her arm. From the grimace on his face, she thought that he was still in some pain. She turned her head modestly and ignored the sounds from behind her, waiting patiently to help him back into the carriage when he was ready.

Luke shot her an amused glance. 'You play the part of a long-suffering wife to perfection, Roxanne. If you chose, you could easily fool Grandfather or anyone else into thinking we had been married for an age.'

Roxanne looked at him disapprovingly. 'I know you are jesting, but I do not find the suggestion funny. Marriage would not be an option. Even an engagement seems so deceitful when there is no intention on either side—but I do understand why you wish to please him.'

'He gets so distressed over the smallest thing,' Luke told her. 'I fear a fit of temper may carry him off. Once, that would not have concerned me, but now—I find I should not like to be the cause of his death.'

'You really believe that your refusal to marry may cause the earl to die in distress?'

'Yes.' Luke's expression was serious. 'You are right to accuse me of levity. It has always been my way to make light of things—but it shocked me when he had that turn. I thought he was going to die, and, had he done so, it would have been my fault.'

Roxanne nodded, but made no further comment. Luke sat back with his eyes closed and the remainder of the journey was accomplished in silence. However, he stirred himself as they approached the heath and told her that they had reached Hampstead.

'There has been a highwayman waylaying travellers hereabouts for some months, but last month they caught him and I dare say he will hang. The house I told you of is nearby. It is being prepared for someone—a lady and child. At the moment she is staying with friends in the south of England, but in another week or two she will take up residence. She will not mind if we use it for a few days.'

'You intend to stay there with me?'

'Not to sleep, but I must visit often. You have my word that I shall not take advantage. If you are to play the part of my fiancée, you will need to know certain things and we must dress you accordingly.' He smiled at her. 'Can you trust me, Roxanne? You must know that I would not harm you after all you have done for me?'

'I hardly know you—and I have been taught not to trust gentlemen of your class.' Roxanne was thoughtful. If the house had been prepared for a lady and child, she was probably his mistress and perhaps the child was his. He would surely not attempt to seduce her in the house he had bought for his mistress? 'Yet I believe you to be a man of your word.'

'That is something.' Luke was unsmiling as the chaise came to a halt. 'You may help me down if you will, Miss Roxanne—it is best I address you formally now. Mrs Mills is the caretaker here for the moment and will respect you more if she thinks you a respectable young lady fallen on hard times.'

'What do you mean to tell her?'

'Just what I intend to tell everyone.' His grey eyes were intent on her. 'You do not know who you are. Yet I am certain you came from gentry—and you suggested India, which may be the truth for all we know.'

Roxanne climbed down from the chaise and gave Luke her hand to steady him. He winced as his injured leg touched the ground, but immediately recovered and took the arm she offered. As they approached the front door of the modest red-bricked villa, it opened and a woman of some forty-odd years stood in the doorway, looking at him expectantly.

'Mrs Mills, I am pleased to see you again,' Luke said with the easy charm that had drawn Roxanne to him. 'This is not Mrs Fox, who is to live here, but a lady who has done me the honour of accepting my help.'

'Lord Clarendon, how good to see you,' she said and dipped a curtsy, her curious eyes on Roxanne.

'This is Miss Roxanne Peters,' Luke said without batting an eyelid. 'I have brought her here for a few days, because she had nowhere else to go. Her best friend has recently died and she is alone. Roxanne's father is in India and she is having difficulty in managing. She needs somewhere to stay for a little while—until we can settle things with the earl. In confidence, this lady is to be my fiancée.'

'Then you *are* planning to marry.' Mrs Mills looked surprised and pleased. 'Well, sir, I am sure the earl will be glad to hear your news.'

'We must hope so, Mrs Mills—but you know my grandfather.'

'Indeed, I do, sir, and if you will forgive me, I thought him a harsh guardian after your dear parents died so tragically.'

'I dare say he did his best,' Luke replied, a little nerve flicking at his temple. 'If you will be so good as to look after Miss Roxanne for me, I have business to attend. I shall return later to dine with you, Roxanne.'

Oddly, now that he was leaving, she wished he would stay. She offered her hand and he took it, bending his head to kiss it briefly.

'Until later, dearest,' he said and her heart jolted. He was playing a part, but for a moment she felt something so sweet and delicious that she wished their game was not merely make believe.

Roxanne nodded, turning to watch as he left before following the housekeeper up the stairs to her room.

'Such a kind man,' Mrs Mills was saying and she realised that she had not been listening. 'Always thinking of others. People try to paint his lordship black, but take no notice, Miss Peters, he has a good heart.'

'Yes, I am sure you are right,' Roxanne said as she was shown into a bedchamber. 'What a lovely room.'

'And this is the guest room. It's as I was saying, no expense spared for the widow and her child. Mrs Fox is a fortunate young woman if you ask me.'

'Mrs Fox is the lady who is to live here?'

'She and her son, the poor lady. Such a sad tale—but my tongue runs away with me and his lordship would be cross with me for tattling. I shall leave you to rest, Miss Roxanne—please ring for tea in the parlour when you come down.'

Roxanne looked about her at the pretty satinwood furniture, the silken hangings of green and white and the crystal trinkets with silver tops on the dressing table. If this was the guest room, Mrs Fox's room must be something special. Clearly Luke had deep feelings for the widow.

Was Mrs Fox his mistress? The thought troubled Roxanne. If he had feelings for the lady—and he must, for he would not otherwise have provided her with a house and Mrs Mills to care for her and her son—why had he brought Roxanne here?

If he already had a son, why did he not produce him as his heir and marry the boy's mother? It would surely solve all his problems.

Luke had told her he did not wish for a marriage of convenience. Was that because his heart belonged to a woman he could not marry?

Perhaps the earl thought Mrs Fox unworthy. What would he think of a young woman who knew nothing of her background and might even be a thief?

No, Roxanne was certain she was not a thief. She did not know why she had the ruby in her possession when she was found, but she would not have stolen it—would she?

Sighing, she gave up the attempt to remember. She remembered nothing but her life with the travelling players and Sofia. The vivid pictures that flitted through her mind at times were merely Sofia's stories—put there to fill the blankness that had been there when she woke from her illness and cried for days.

'Oh, Sofia,' she whispered as she sat down on the

bed and ran her hand over the silken covers. 'What am I to do? I like him so much—but I fear that I am headed for trouble. I should run away now, go to London and forget him…but I feel as if something binds me to him.'

*'He will break your heart.'*

The words were only in her head. Sofia was no longer there to guide and comfort her. She was alone and must use her wits to keep herself safe. Luke Clarendon was offering an arrangement that would make her independent for the rest of her life. All she had to do was to play a part—and keep a little distance between them.

A tiny voice in her head told her it was already too late, but she was no longer listening.

Roxanne smiled and lifted her face to the sun. She had been staying here for almost a week now. Life was comfortable and pleasant; Roxanne was beginning to feel at home, but she did not dare to let herself feel too settled. She was here under false pretences and that made her feel a little guilty. Once or twice she had considered hiring a cab to take her into the centre of London in search of work at a theatre.

'Roxanne…' Mrs Mill's voice calling to her made her glance over her shoulder. She looked at her basket. She had enough flowers for now. 'His lordship has arrived.'

'Thank you.' She saw that Luke had come out into the garden in search of her and her heart quickened as she went to meet him. 'I thought you would not be here until this evening.'

'I was able to get away sooner.' He looked at her approvingly. 'That gown suits you well, Roxanne.'

'I am glad you approve. You chose it.'

'So I did,' he said. 'Fetch your bonnet and a shawl if you wish for one. As I rode here I saw a fair on the Heath. It is an age since I visited a fair. Shall we go, Roxanne? I'll buy you a toffee apple.'

She laughed and shook her head. 'I do not think I should care for it, but there will be other treats I dare say. Yes, if you wish, we may as well spend a little time there for it is a lovely afternoon.'

'Then we shall go and if you do not wish for a toffee apple I will win you a fairing at the shooting range.'

Roxanne agreed and ran inside to fetch her bonnet. She did not know why, but the prospect of spending the afternoon at the fair with him was delightful. She had come to know him a little these past days and to like what she learned of him very much.

The fair had spread out over much of the Heath. There were stalls of all kinds and the smells of hot pies and toffee apples were mouth watering. A man on stilts was walking through the crowds, telling people to visit the bearded lady and the dog with two heads, as well as to watch the wrestling match and the bowling for a pig. Luke paid to try his hand at the shooting range, but his shots went astray and he made a sound of annoyance.

'I am sure the barrel is not straight. I will have one more attempt. Walk a little further and I shall catch you up in a moment.'

Roxanne smiled and left him, feeling amused that

he was so determined to win her a fairing. She would not go too far, but wander around the stalls, which sold all manner of pretty trifles. She would have liked to buy a small gift for Luke, but her few pennies would not stretch far and she was afraid to spend them in case she needed them.

She stood for a moment watching a man swallowing a sword and juggling with fire. Then, feeling a tingling at the nape of her neck, she glanced to her left where a group of men were standing haggling over horses and a shiver went down her spine. A man with black hair and a swarthy complexion was looking at her. She knew him at once and felt the fear sweep through her. How unfortunate that he should be at the fair! If he came to her and demanded she return with him, he might force her to go.

She had to return to Luke! Yet if she did so, she might bring trouble on him; his leg was better than when he fell, but she knew it still pained him. Perhaps she could lose Black Bob in the crowd. Turning away, she began to walk hastily back the way she had come, but almost immediately collided with a man. He put out his hands to steady her.

'Whoa,' he said and laughed as she gave a cry of alarm. 'Where are you going in such a hurry, Roxanne? Were you running away from me?'

'Not from you.' Roxanne breathed a sigh of relief as she looked up at Luke's teasing smile. 'I saw someone I did not wish to meet.'

'The man you ran away from after Sofia died?'

'Yes.' Roxanne drew a deep breath. She glanced

back and saw that Black Bob had followed her but now he was hesitating, looking uncertain. 'Please give me your arm. He is watching us. I was afraid he might try to grab me; but he did not expect to see you. If you seem to be a friend, he may think he was mistaken.'

Luke offered his arm and she took it, her hand trembling slightly. He glanced down, a frown on his face. 'You are afraid of him, aren't you?' She nodded. 'Damn the fellow. Shall I thrash him for you?'

'No, please do not try. He was stronger than all the other men—and you are injured.' She glanced down at his tight-fitting breeches and long, highly polished boots. 'Is your leg better?'

'Much. My doctor bound it and instructed me to rest, which I have as much as I could bear. I have an ache now, but the sharp pain has gone. It was a dislocation after all and not the break I feared—so it seems our rustic physician knew his trade. My own doctor had nothing but praise for his work.'

'I did not doubt it, but you were in such pain afterwards that I feared he might have done some damage.'

'My physician told me I was lucky. Had the fellow not acted as he did, I might have had an infection in the leg and been far worse. I might even have lost the use of it. However, I fear I made too much fuss of a slight thing.'

'I am sure you did not. Do you think Black Bob is following us?'

Luke glanced back. 'I believe he has gone. He will have realised he was mistaken or given up, I dare say.'

'Yes, perhaps.' Roxanne caught her bottom lip

between her teeth. Luke's timely appearance might have put him off for the moment, but it would not stop him if their paths crossed again. 'I do not think I can continue to stay here. If that man discovered where I was living, he might make trouble for you—and for Mrs Fox when she takes up residence.'

'Surely he would not?' He arched his fine brows as if to dismiss her fears.

'You do not know what he is like. He is a violent, brutal man who never considers the wishes of others.'

'I believe you, but surely it is not necessary to hide from him?'

'If he found me, he would try to force me to go with him.'

'Then what would you like to do?'

Roxanne looked at him hesitantly. 'To be honest I do not know. Now that he has seen me here, London may not be the best place for me to find work.'

'Then let me take you to stay with my grandfather. We can announce our engagement—and you can help me do something kind. Had my grandfather not set his mind on this I should simply have ignored his demands. My lawyer tells me that he could in law withhold the income from my trust, though he is not the only trustee and my godmother might take my side. Yet because of his illness I would make his last months happy if I can. To engage in bitter arguments and legal battles could only shorten his life.'

'Are you sure he would accept me?' Roxanne glanced down at herself. Inside she was trembling. The life he offered was a golden prize. Yet she was wary too, conscious that she might be laying up trouble for herself. 'I know the clothes you have given me have made me look the part—but are you sure he will not see through my disguise at once?'

'I do not think it. You are everything Grandfather asked me to provide in the woman that I intend to marry, Roxanne. Charming, good mannered and conscientious—what more could he want in a wife for me? Besides, if he does not approve that will end it. I shall bow to his judgement, take you to Bath and make sure you have all you need to live in comfort for the rest of your life.'

Roxanne gazed at him in silence for a moment. Sofia's voice was in her head, warning her to be careful. Was he merely trying to deceive her into an illicit entanglement? No, no, she believed he had a true concern for his grandfather.

'You are quite sure you wish to do this?'

'I have given the idea more thought since I left you with Mrs Mills. She has served my family all her life and her opinion of you has confirmed mine. You may have lived in the company of travelling players for a few years, but before that you were strictly reared. I had wondered if I should need to teach you how to behave in society, but you know instinctively. Do this for me, Roxanne. Please, help me to make Grandfather's last days more content. Afterwards, you will be free to live your own life.'

'Supposing he lives much longer than you expect?'

Luke gave her a thoughtful look. 'You may have to marry me. I know it isn't what you want—but it would be temporary, and in time you could live your own life. We could have the marriage annulled and you would still be young enough to marry again.'

It would be like an acting contract with a theatre manager. She would play a part for some months, perhaps longer, and then move on. Easy enough, perhaps, yet supposing her emotions became involved?

'An engagement is easily broken but…' Roxanne hesitated, then, 'Marriage is a last resort and only if it becomes impossible to prolong the engagement. It cannot be what you wish for?'

'I have no wish to marry, but it would be a business arrangement, nothing more. I enjoy my life the way it is—but for Grandfather's sake I am prepared to play a game of make believe.'

'It is really just a part I must play, but on a smaller stage and in private rather than public,' Roxanne said thoughtfully.

'Yes, mostly in private—though I dare say Grandfather will give an occasional dinner for us.'

'I can manage that,' Roxanne replied confidently. 'Besides, your grandfather may think me unsuitable and then I can simply go away and disappear.'

'Yes, exactly.' Luke stopped walking and looked into her eyes. 'Will you do me the honour of wearing my ring for a time, Miss Roxanne?'

For a moment it felt as if he were truly proposing and her heart jerked, but then she saw the mischief in his eyes and smiled.

'Yes, I shall do as you ask, sir. Just until you decide that you are ready to abandon the masquerade.'

'Do not think of it as a masquerade. It is a gentleman's agreement between friends—a small deception for the best of reasons, do you not agree?'

'I cannot disagree when you wish only to give an old man peace of mind—and to honour your commitments,' Roxanne said. For a moment she wondered where Mrs Fox came into his plans, but dismissed her doubts. 'You will be my employer and may dismiss me when it pleases you.'

'Please.' Luke made a rueful face. 'You must not think of me in that way or it will show. I am Luke—the man you intend to marry.'

'Yes, of course you are, dearest.' Her manner was light and teasing, exactly right for a woman who had just become engaged to the man she loves. Roxanne placed her hand playfully on his arm. 'Do not be anxious, Luke. I shall not forget my part and let you down. The earl will have nothing to complain of in my manner or deportment.'

'We must order you some more clothes and then we shall leave.' Luke smiled, his eyes thoughtful. 'I am certain Grandfather will like you, but you must look the part. Tomorrow I shall take you shopping. I intend to write to my grandfather and tell him that I shall be bringing a young lady to meet him in one week from now.'

# *Chapter Four*

'Your belongings are strapped to the back of the carriage. Is there anything more you require before we leave, Roxanne?'

She thought of the two trunks packed with pretty gowns for all occasions, silk undergarments, stockings, shoes, slippers and gloves, besides several pretty bonnets. She had taken her pick of the wardrobe when acting in plays on their travels, but never had she seen so many beautiful clothes as Luke had so recklessly purchased for her. Too many by half and expensive, far more stylish than anything she'd ever worn before.

'You have been most generous and I have all I need, thank you.'

'Then we should go.' Luke offered his arm and they strolled towards the carriage. 'I intend to ride most of the way, Roxanne. We shall stop one night on the road—and your new maid will meet us at the inn, where we stopped before.'

'My maid?'

'Yes, of course. A respectable young lady cannot travel without a maid. I sent word ahead and I am sure a maid will have been provided by the time we arrive. Grandfather would be shocked if we visited without one.'

'What would he think if he should learn how we met?'

'It will not happen. I met you at the house of a friend and we liked each other very well. You have consented to an engagement, but we are waiting for your father's permission to wed.'

Roxanne stifled her feelings of unease. 'I pray you will not invent too many lies, sir, for I may forget them.'

'We shall keep your story as simple as possible,' he promised. 'You must expect some questions, Roxanne. Grandfather is bound to wonder why I have given into his request so tamely.'

'You must endeavour to look as if you are in love, Luke,' she said and gave him a smile of positive wickedness. 'Liking will not serve or he will sense a mystery. If you have resisted his plea thus far, he must be convinced of your sincerity or you may do more harm than good.'

'You are very right,' Luke agreed and looked thoughtful. 'Let us hope that I can play my part as well as I expect of you.'

'Watch me often and look pleased or brooding,' she suggested and her mouth pouted at him. 'It should not be beyond you, Luke. I dare say you have wooed enough ladies to know how to court the love of your life.'

'You have a wicked tongue,' Luke remarked and grinned. 'Do not be afraid of Grandfather, Roxanne. I think his bark worse than his bite—besides, he should be happy to meet you. You are exactly what he has looked for.'

'Let us hope that is the case. If not, you can apologise to him and take me away.'

'He wants me married and an heir,' Luke said. 'Play your part well and he will soon be eating from your hand, my love.'

'Yes, that is better,' Roxanne approved. 'You had the tone just right then. I was almost convinced myself.' She took off her smart leather glove, looking at the huge square emerald-and-diamond ring on her left hand. It was proof that she was truly caught up in this masquerade, pretending to be Luke's betrothed. 'This is magnificent enough to convince anyone.'

'I could not do less. Had I given you something paltry Grandfather would not have been fooled for an instant.'

'Any jewels you lend me will of course be returned when we part,' Roxanne replied. 'All I shall ask is a small income so that I can live quietly but respectably.'

'Yes, well, as to that we shall see. That ring belongs to you, Roxanne, whatever may happen when we get to Hartingdon.' Luke helped her into the carriage and stepped back. 'I shall be close by. Should you need to stop, you may tap the roof and the driver will oblige you.'

Roxanne sat back against the squabs and looked

out of the window. She had butterflies in her stomach, for the role she was about to play was important, far more demanding than anything she had accomplished before. If she failed, she would be letting Luke down and perhaps hurting a vulnerable old man.

She would not fail. Roxanne did not think she had come from Luke's class, but she was certain that she had been reared as a gentlewoman. Why had she run away from her home—and what had frightened her so much that she'd lost her memory?

It could not matter. Her engagement was merely make believe and intended to be a temporary arrangement.

Would the earl be fooled by their little charade? Luke wondered as he rode just behind the carriage. It was perfectly possible that he would throw them both out and disown his grandson, as he had threatened. That would be a deuced nuisance and the ensuing row would be messy and unpleasant. He could not let Beth Fox and her son Harry down. He had promised to support her for the rest of her life in comfort and would keep his promise, which meant he must fight for his income if forced. He would also need to keep his promise to Roxanne if things went wrong.

Luke wanted to avoid a quarrel if at all possible. He had no desire to be the cause of the earl's death—nor did he particularly wish to inherit a large and cumbersome estate that would require a much larger commitment than his own did at present. It would suit him if the earl lived for some years longer, yet he needed his own income intact.

It was such a coil and so unnecessary. Why must the earl be such a pompous fool, making unreasonable demands on his grandson? Anger mixed with regret as he considered his childhood. Alone and grieving for his parents, he had looked for a sign of love or softness in the earl and found none. Because he was hurt, he had drawn into himself and rejected his grandfather. The estrangement between them had begun years ago and they had drifted apart. For a long time Luke had believed there was nothing between them, but now he was not so sure.

Had he been as indifferent to his grandfather as he had pretended to be since reaching his maturity, he would simply have walked away and left him to make Harte his heir. However, that particular rogue would rejoice at the earl's early demise and make short work of his fortune. He might behave as if butter would not melt in his mouth when in the earl's presence, but Luke knew him for what he was—and that was something that left an unpleasant taste in the mouth. Naturally, he would never mention Harte's true nature to his grandfather.

On the other hand, Hartingdon might embrace Roxanne with open arms and demand a marriage sooner rather than later. At the moment she was resisting the idea stoutly, but once she had become accustomed to her surroundings she might change her mind. Luke had dismissed the idea of a convenient marriage for years, but since coming up with the idea of this make-believe engagement, he had found that he did not dislike it as much as before—providing the young woman in question was Roxanne.

The calm and enterprising manner in which she had embarked on this whole adventure had made Luke admire her more than any other young woman of his acquaintance. Her circumstances would have broken a lesser spirit, but she seemed resilient and eager for life. She was courageous, honest, and, of late, he had found her both charming and amusing as a companion. It might be perfectly possible to have the kind of businesslike marriage they had spoken of with Roxanne—if she could be brought to agree.

Love was something he still felt belonged to the realms of myths and fairy tales. However, he did like the young woman riding in the carriage ahead of him, and if she were to agree, he would not entirely dislike the idea of marriage and children.

Yet there might come a time when he found someone he truly wished to wed. Luke shook his head. His father had strayed from the marriage bed, not just into the arms of a mistress, but with a woman he professed to want too much to give up. That day in the carriage when his parents had argued so disastrously, Luke's father had been talking of a separation or a divorce. When Luke's mother became hysterical he had begged her pardon, but she would not listen—and then it was too late for all of them.

Thrown clear of the wreckage that had taken their lives and changed his own so dramatically, he had vowed that he would never hurt anyone as his father had hurt his mother. A sham marriage built on lies was bound to end in bitterness and tears—but a business arrangement was another matter and perhaps a sensible young woman like Roxanne would be able to see its advantages.

As yet they hardly knew one another. Some time spent visiting the earl would rectify that and, if they continued to get along, Luke could suggest that they turn this make-believe engagement into a real marriage.

Naturally, she would still be free to lead her own life much of the time, as would he. Their children would be in the nursery, cared for by a nurse and— No! Suddenly, Luke recalled his own childhood after he was left to the mercy of his grandfather. He would wish to spend time with his own children and to help teach them what life was about. They should not be left to the sole care of servants.

Luke frowned, for the thought brought complications. It might not be as easy to partition his life into different compartments as he had imagined.

Perhaps for the time being it would be best to stay with his original idea and separate once his grandfather was dead. He was amazed at how disappointed that thought made him feel.

Roxanne's heart thudded as she glanced out of the window and saw the huge sprawl of Hartingdon. She had known it must be a large house, but this was so big, way beyond her expectation, some parts much older than others and an ancient tower at one corner. How did one ever find one's way about in such a place? She had thought she would find it easy to play the part of a respectable young lady, but suddenly the task seemed far more daunting than she had imagined. She would be unmasked immediately and the earl would have her thrown out on her ear.

Risking a glance at the girl sitting opposite her, she saw that Tilly was looking terrified. The girl had no previous experience of working in a house such as this, though she had sometimes helped ladies who stayed at her aunt and uncle's inn without their own maids.

'Do not be too anxious, Tilly.'

'It is a big house, miss.'

'Yes, it is. I dare say you will soon get used to it.'

Roxanne smiled reassuringly, though her stomach was tying itself in knots as the carriage slowed to a halt and then stopped. A groom opened the carriage door and immediately stood back, allowing a man in a black-and-gold uniform to assist her. She took the footman's hand and was helped down just as Luke gave the reins of his horse to a groom and came to her.

'Have courage,' he whispered. 'It looks daunting, I know, but it is just a house.'

Roxanne lifted her head proudly, but she could not quite control the trembling of her hand as she placed it on his arm. Briefly, Luke covered it with his own and smiled at her. They walked towards the door, where a small group of servants wearing the earl's colours of black and gold had assembled.

'This is Marshall, my grandfather's valet, and Mrs Arlet, the housekeeper.'

A tall thin woman dressed completely in black

dipped a curtsy. 'Welcome, Miss Peters. Please allow me to present the staff.'

Roxanne was led down a line of maids and footmen, ending with the scullery maid and the boot boy. She kept her head high and a smile on her lips, giving just the faintest nod to them all. It was the way a properly brought up young woman would act, she was sure, and brought her a look of respect from the housekeeper. However, she noticed that Luke chatted to one or two of the footmen and smiled at the pretty parlour maid. Such behaviour was acceptable from him, for he had known the staff all his life. She was a newcomer and should keep her distance, at least for the moment.

'Perhaps you would take my fiancée up to her chamber, Mrs Arlet?'

'Yes, my lord, of course. This way, Miss Peters.'

Roxanne glanced at Luke, but he was talking to the earl's valet. She steadied her nerves and followed the housekeeper up the wide magnificent staircase, her gaze moving to the high-vaulted ceiling of the entrance hall. The banisters were heavily carved mahogany, which had darkened with age and polish, the stone steps covered over with a rich blue Persian-style carpet. The entrance hall floor was tiled in black-and-white marble, but the hall upstairs was covered in the same carpet and looked a recent addition to the elsewhere-faded grandeur of the house.

'The earl ordered that you be given the best suite of guestrooms, miss,' Mrs Arlet said as she led the way along the hall and into the east wing. 'They have recently been refurbished. This is a large house and in constant need of repair or refurbishment. Some of the family rooms have not been used in an age, so nothing has been done to them. No doubt that will change when his lordship marries.'

'Yes, I would imagine so,' Roxanne said, her heart racing. Naturally everyone would expect a marriage to be forthcoming. A tiny pang of guilt pierced her, because the housekeeper looked pleased at the idea of change. 'I think—perhaps you would give me a little tour of the house one day, Mrs Arlet? Not just the main reception rooms—but the kitchen and anywhere else I ought to see.'

'Yes, miss. I should be pleased to, though Lord Clarendon will show you his own rooms, I dare say. The west wing is not often used, because the tower is in need of repair. Lord Clarendon's parents once occupied that wing but after the accident the earl closed the whole wing off, and no one bothers to go there.'

'The accident…'

'When the late Lord and Lady Clarendon were killed, miss.'

'Ah, yes,' Roxanne nodded. 'I was not sure of your meaning.'

'No, miss. I suppose there have been a few accidents in the family, what with the earl's only son dying of a fever when he was in his teen years—and then the earl's wife taking a chill after being caught in a rainstorm. I think it broke the master's heart when his daughter was killed so cruelly. He never quite got over it, for she was his favourite.' Mrs Arlet shook her head. 'They have not been a lucky family, but I am certain that is all about to change now, miss.'

'Yes, we must hope so,' Roxanne replied. It was amazing how much she had learned from the housekeeper in just a few minutes. Luke had told her his parents' story, but not the rest of it. She understood now why he was prepared to go through with this sham engagement in order to please his grandfather in his last months. She must not let him down, however hard it might be to carry off the part of a loving fiancée. 'That is up to me in part, is it not?'

'There's been a different atmosphere here since the letter came,' Mrs Arlet said. She unlocked a door and stood back for Roxanne to enter. 'The earl gave orders for most of the rooms to be opened up immediately. We'll be giving a ball to celebrate his lordship's engagement, miss. Everyone will want to meet you.'

'Oh...yes, of course,' Roxanne said and took a deep breath as she looked about her. 'This is beautiful, thank you. When will the ball be held? I am not sure I brought a gown suitable for a grand ball.'

'No doubt that can be rectified, miss. There are bales of silk in the sewing room waiting for just such a purpose. We'll fetch the seamstress from town and she will be pleased to serve you. You'll be the countess one day, after all.'

'Yes.' Roxanne looked round. 'I think perhaps I should tidy myself.'

'Yes, miss. The earl will be waiting for you in the main parlour downstairs. If you could be ready, I shall serve tea in twenty minutes.'

'I can be ready, but I'm not certain I know where to go.'

'Lord bless you, miss. Just go down the stairs to the main hall and someone will direct you. The footmen are here for that very purpose and we are all eager to make your stay at Hartingdon as pleasant as possible.'

Roxanne thanked her and she went away. She was left standing in a small but pretty sitting room and beyond that was a bedroom. The main colours were green, gold, cream and yellow, which gave the rooms a light bright appearance. Roxanne ran her fingers reverently over the surface of a delicate and very pretty desk suitable for a lady. An elbow chair was set ready for use; the sofa was covered in green-striped silk and there was a rolled cushion at each end. Small occasional tables were dotted about the room and a bookcase with leather-bound volumes and porcelain figures behind the glass doors occupied the length of one wall.

Going into the bedroom, which was equally well furnished with a dressing table, matching chests and a padded stool at the end of the bed, Roxanne took off her pelisse and let it fall on one of the pretty chairs. She sat down in front of the dressing table and studied her reflection in the shield-shaped mirror. The frame was fashioned of smooth mahogany and inlaid with satinwood, set on a stand so that it could be moved to give a better view. The table was set out with silver items, including brushes and combs and perfume pots. How much luxury there was in a house like this!

She had removed her bonnet earlier and now took the brush to smooth over her hair, pulling at the tendrils that framed her face. She was wearing a silver brooch in her lace, but otherwise had no jewellery other than her ring. Touching the brooch, she smiled because it reminded her of Sofia and she could almost hear her friend applauding.

'Now we shall see if I really am fit to be a lady,' she said softly. 'Wish me luck, dearest Sofia.'

*'You were born to the part, dearest.'*

For a moment it was as if her friend were with her and she felt her courage return. Her part here was not to deceive for advantage, but to bring comfort and joy to an old man's last days.

Roxanne's things had not yet been brought up so she did not have the opportunity to change her gown; deciding that she looked the best she could after her journey, she left the bedroom and retraced her steps to the landing.

At the bottom of the stairs two footmen were discussing something and she caught the words *'beauty and better than expected'*, before they became aware of her standing there.

'You were quick, miss,' one of them said, a faint colour in his cheeks. 'Mrs Arlet said to take you to the back parlour when you came down. It is the master's favourite room these days. He mostly uses it when he is alone, though we'll be using the drawing room for tea in future.'

'Shall you?' Roxanne said, controlling the urge to smile. Clearly the servants here considered themselves part of the family and that was somehow fitting. 'There is no need to stand on ceremony for my sake. Please take me to the earl—I believe Mrs Arlet said your name was Jarvis?'

'Yes, Miss Peters,' he replied, seeming surprised that she should remember. 'If you would like to come this way.'

'Thank you,' she said and inclined her head in her most regal manner.

Roxanne's heart was hammering against her ribs as she followed the footman through to the back of the house. He paused before a pair of impressive double doors and then threw them open with a little flourish.

'Miss Peters, my lord.'

Jarvis stood to one side so that Roxanne could enter; when she did so, he closed the doors behind her with a snap. Immediately, she saw the elderly man rise to his feet. He was tall, though a little stooped about his shoulders, thinner than she thought healthy, his hair dark pewter and his white brows bushy and slightly raised, intimidating. His eyes, though, were of a similar colour to Luke's and for some reason that made her smile. She was, she imagined, looking at Lord Clarendon as he would be one day in the distant future. The two gentlemen were very alike despite the years between them.

'Miss Peters? You are down sooner than that graceless scamp my grandson.'

'Since I could not change my gown to greet you, I thought it better to come sooner rather than later,' she replied and moved towards him, her hand outstretched. 'Luke has told me a little about you, sir—and you are very like him.'

'You are the first to say so in an age, though his mother often told me that he would be my image one day. Unfortunately, she did not live to see it. I have thought that a good thing, for she would have been disappointed in the young rogue—but now I am not so sure.'

'I know that Luke has not always behaved in a way that pleased you,' Roxanne said. 'But you must not disparage him to me, you know.'

'You are prepared to defend him if I do?'

'I should be a poor fiancée if I did not—do you not think so, sir?'

The earl glared at her for a few seconds, then gave a harsh laugh. 'I think he has done better than I imagined. I was prepared for you to be one of his doxies—but you ain't, are you?'

'Certainly not. I have been no man's plaything and have no intention of it.' Her eyes flashed a challenge at him. 'Do you really think so poorly of him, sir? It would be unkind to bring a lady of that nature into your home. From what I know of Luke, he would not be so discourteous to you.'

'You're an outspoken miss. I can see why he picked you, Miss Peters.'

'I fear I was taught to speak my mind and to be independent as much as possible. I should be happier if you were to call me Miss Roxanne—or simply by my given name.'

'You have an older sister?'

'No—but everyone always calls me Miss Roxanne. I prefer it.'

'Do you, now? I wonder why?' He stared at her a moment longer, then took her hand and bent over it, lifting it to his papery-dry lips to salute her with a kiss. 'Come and sit down and tell me something about yourself.'

'I am quite unremarkable, sir,' Roxanne replied. She sat in the chair at the opposite end of the imposing fireplace so that he too might sit. 'I have little family and, until she died, lived with the lady who cared for me after…I lost my home.'

'Clarendon's letter said that your father is in India and you do not wish to marry until he gives his permission?'

'Do you not think that the proper thing to do, sir?'

His bushy brows met in a frown. 'Humph. Clever with words, ain't you? No fortune, I suppose—are you after his money, girl?'

'I did not agree to this engagement for money.'

'It was a bit sudden. He told me nothing of you the last time he was down here, then announces he's engaged. Why would he do that—and why should you agree?'

'I should be a liar if I said that Luke's proposal was not appealing. I was in some difficulty and I am almost alone in the world, for I have not heard from my father in years. However, I have respect and liking for Luke and I believe he feels the same. I consented to the engagement—with the understanding that it would not continue if you should dislike it.'

Hartingdon's gaze narrowed. 'Willing to give him up for a consideration?'

'I said no such thing,' Roxanne replied, refusing to be ruffled by his pricking at her. 'I should not wish to cause trouble between you, for I know that he holds you in affection. You do not need to pay me to make me go away, sir. I shall leave at once if my presence here offends you.'

'Do not talk rubbish, girl. You look and behave like a lady. Might not be out of the top drawer, but I ain't fool enough to send you packing—at least until I discover the truth of the matter. If he really means to settle down and provide me with an heir, you will do well enough, I dare say.'

Roxanne was not called upon to reply for the doors opened and a footman announced Lord Clarendon. Luke advanced into the room, looking strangely apprehensive.

'Roxanne, I intended to be with you when you met Grandfather,' he said, his gaze going from one to the other. 'Everything all right, sir? How are you today? Better, I trust?'

'Well enough. Don't fuss, boy. I cannot abide people fussing over me. That fool of a doctor is bad enough without you.'

'I see your mood has not much improved, sir.' Luke's mouth firmed. 'I hope he has not bitten your head off, Roxanne? I assure you he is not always this ill tempered.'

Roxanne looked from one to the other and then laughed. 'Oh dear, you both look so cross—like two bulldogs who have been quarrelling over a bone, which has been suddenly snatched from under your noses by a mongrel pup.'

For a moment there was silence and then Luke grinned. 'You are perfectly right, dearest. It is ridiculous to argue over trivial things. Forgive me, Grandfather. I did not come down here to quarrel with you.'

'Why did you come?' The earl looked at him suspiciously. 'Am I supposed to believe that you truly intend to settle down and do your duty?'

'What is my duty, sir? I hope that you will continue to live for some years yet in the full enjoyment of your estate. If you need help or advice with business matters I should be pleased to give it—though whether you would wish to receive it is another matter.'

'I have agents and fellows enough to run the place,' the earl grunted, 'though you might take the trouble to ride the estate with Tonkins while you are here. Some of the cottages may need renovation. It was in my mind to do it some years back, but I let things slip, though I've no cause for complaint in Tonkins's management as far as I know.'

'I shall be pleased to do so, both with him and on my own, while we stay with you,' Luke told him. 'May I take it that Roxanne and I have your blessing?'

'You puzzle me, Clarendon. You have flouted my wishes since you reached your majority and became independent. Now, it seems you wish to please me—why? Afraid of losing your inheritance?'

'I find that it does not suit me to be at odds with you, sir. Is that so very strange?'

'I suppose it threw you into a blue fit because of

that little incident.' The old man glared at him. 'Well, I mustn't nag on at you or your fiancée will scold me. I am pleasantly surprised, Luke. When your letter came I scented a rat, thought you would try to play one of your tricks on me, but Miss Roxanne seems a decent gel. For the moment I shall reserve judgement.'

'I hope I shall not let you down,' Roxanne said. 'The marriage cannot happen until I have my father's permission, so there is plenty of time.'

'Indeed, I might argue with that,' the earl said. 'What makes you think your father will write if he has not done so for years?'

'I can only hope that he will do so, sir.'

'And if he does not?' Hartingdon's eyes gleamed suddenly. 'I shall give you three months to seek his permission. If after that there is no word, I shall insist on the banns being called.'

Roxanne looked at him and saw the challenge in his eyes. She sensed that he was testing her and smiled, but before she could answer Luke spoke.

'I am certain we could agree to that,' he said. 'After all, your father could not blame you for going ahead if he makes no attempt to contact you, Roxanne.'

'It is so long since I heard anything, he may be dead,' Roxanne said carefully. 'If in three months' time nothing has changed—and we are all content with the situation—I shall agree to the banns being called.'

'Then you have my blessing,' the earl said and looked smug, as if he had gained what he sought. 'However, there is one caveat—and that is that Miss Roxanne remains here with me so that I may get to know her. If you have business elsewhere, Luke, you may leave us for as long as it takes. Your fiancée will reside here.'

'I'm not sure…' Luke looked stunned. Clearly he had not expected anything of the kind. 'Roxanne—how do you feel about living here with Grandfather?'

Roxanne hesitated. She had expected a visit of two to three weeks at the longest. To live in this house for three months under the eye of the earl would be a huge challenge.

'I…' she began and then encountered a strange expression in the old man's eyes. The challenge was there, as she had expected, but there was something more—a vulnerability and frailty that seemed to be pleading with her rather than demanding. 'I think that would be an excellent idea. I have a great deal to learn if I am to be the mistress here, Luke. I hope you will stay with us as much as you can, dearest, but I shall be perfectly content to help Mrs Arlet. I believe she is quite keen to open up some of the family rooms that have been under covers for years.'

'Told you that, did she?' For the first time there was a glimmer of true respect in the earl's eyes. 'Jane Arlet knows quality when she sees it. If she approves of you, miss, I expect you will do. Don't worry that I mean to keep you a prisoner. We shall have guests to entertain and you can visit our neighbours, though I do not go out at night these days. Barely go further than the garden even in summer, but I'm not too decrepit to entertain the family and our neighbours. We shall have a ball in a couple of weeks. Mrs Arlet will give you a list and you can write the invitations, girl. You can write, I suppose?'

Roxanne laughed softly. 'Sofia said I had the most beautiful copperplate hand she had seen, sir.'

His brows met in a frown. 'And who, pray, is Sofia?'

'She was my dearest friend, almost a mother to me. Unfortunately, she died recently. I miss her very much.'

'Humph…' His gaze narrowed thoughtfully. 'Name seems familiar, though I can't think why. Well, why are you both still here? It is a beautiful morning. Get off out and leave me in peace. You should show Roxanne the gardens, Luke.'

'Yes, sir, delighted.' Luke held out his hand as Roxanne rose to her feet. She took it, smiling up at him when his fingers closed about hers. 'Would you like that, my love?'

'Yes, I should,' she agreed and bobbed respectfully to the earl. 'Thank you for receiving me, sir.'

'Come and see me again tomorrow in the morning and we'll talk. I may dine with you this evening, but we have no guests until the following day. I wasn't sure whether you would really come.'

'Or whether I should be presentable,' Roxanne said and gave him a look that was deceptively demure. He glared at her, but she thought there was a glimmer of appreciation in his eyes. 'Please dine with us if you feel able, sir.'

She took Luke's arm and they left the earl's room, going downstairs, through the hall and out of a side door into a small walled garden. It was square with rose beds on all sides and a sundial in the middle. Most of the roses were still in tight buds, though some had begun to show signs of opening.

'Was it too much of an ordeal?' Luke asked and looked down at her, a flicker of doubt in his face. 'He seemed to like you, though you might not have thought it—but believe me, he can be much worse.'

'Yes, I dare say he could. You told me not to be afraid of him and I thought it best to speak out from the start. I believe he prefers plain speaking.'

'He cannot abide mealy-mouthed women. I have a godmother, who was also a great friend of my mother's. Hartingdon was abominably rude to Lady Paula the last time she was here. She left in tears, vowing she would never visit again.'

'I dare say he can be intimidating if he chooses,' Roxanne said. 'Yet I think underneath the growling and the harshness, he is lonely and vulnerable.'

'Good grief.' Luke stared at her in astonishment. 'You saw that too? I thought I might have imagined it—he does his best to drive everyone away, you know. All the time I was growing up, he never showed me any sign of affection. He shut himself away from everyone after my mother died and often went for days without speaking to me. He was a harsh disciplinarian, though, when I look back, I believe he was fair. I dare say I was a rebellious lad and even more so as a youth.'

Roxanne laughed and hugged his arm. 'I can understand why you rebelled when you reached your majority. Sofia always said that if you tied a dog to a short lead it made him wild when let free—and I think it is much the same with us. The best discipline is that which we apply to ourselves, do you not agree?'

'You are amazing,' Luke said. 'You seem to have wisdom beyond your years, Roxanne. How old are you actually, do you know?'

She shook her head. 'I think I may be nineteen or perhaps twenty. Sofia was never certain, but I was with her for more than five years and must have been thirteen or fourteen when she took me in. If I seem wise, it is because I spent all my time listening to her. She was an intelligent woman with great experience of the world and its foibles.'

Luke nodded, his eyes intent on her face. 'You still recall nothing of your past?'

'Nothing.'

'Then what are you hiding from me? I have sensed something, but did not wish to pry lest it was painful for you.'

Roxanne hesitated, then made her decision. She must trust him with her secret. 'I have in my possession a ruby of great value. Sofia says I was clutching it in my hand when she found me. I held on to it fiercely and would not be parted from it for some days. When I finally did release it, she hid it and kept it for me. I had forgotten about the jewel until she reminded me just before she died. She says that when I was found, I was dressed in good plain clothes, but not silk, and I had no other ornament.'

'Are you thinking that you may have stolen it?'

'I do not know. Sofia told me that I should sell it and set myself up as a lady, but I should be reluctant to do so. It is the only clue I have to what happened before Sofia found me. Besides, it may not be mine to sell.'

'You think you took the ruby and ran away? Are you certain it is a real jewel and not simply glass?'

'Sofia thought it valuable. I will show it to you later. I do not know if there is any way to trace the rightful owner…'

'How do you know that you are not the rightful owner?'

Roxanne looked at him, wrinkling her brow in thought. 'Sofia told me that I kept saying it was mine, but after I relinquished it to her, I seemed to forget about it and did not ask for it again.'

'It must have held great importance to you at the time.' Luke looked thoughtful. 'You told me that India came to mind when you thought of your father. It is quite possible that a man who either served with the British army or for the trading company might acquire such a jewel. Perhaps it belonged to your father.'

'Why would I steal a jewel from my own father?'

'He might have given it to you.'

'The memory of India was just Sofia's game.' Roxanne sighed. 'I have tried so hard to remember, but I cannot.'

'Did you keep the jewel hidden in the secret pocket beneath your gown when you travelled?'

'Yes, in the place where I put your gold to keep it safe. It is not there now. I will show you this evening and then you can tell me your opinion of its worth.'

# *Chapter Five*

Roxanne took the jewel from the dressing case Luke had bought for her. She had placed it in the secret compartment for safekeeping. It was as large as a pheasant's egg, a strange oval shape with slightly pointed ends and a deep dark red in colour. When it caught the light from the candles on her dressing table it sparkled and glowed with fire. Something about it at that moment sent a shiver down her spine. She had not noticed before, but there seemed something mysterious, even sinister, about the jewel.

She tucked it into the bodice of her gown and went out of her room, her heart beating faster. It was a relief to share her secret with Luke, because it had lain heavy on her conscience ever since she'd rediscovered the ruby in Sofia's things. Making her way down to the smaller of the two dining parlours, Roxanne wondered if it would be possible to trace the origin of the jewel. She thought Luke was right. It had most likely been brought from India—but was it a gift to her from someone or stolen from its rightful owner?

The earl had decided that he would dine with them that evening. Dressed immaculately in evening clothes that belonged to an earlier age, he seemed more formidable than previously, a proud autocratic man with a strict manner. However, he was the soul of courtesy to Roxanne and did not once give her reason to blush or feel uncomfortable. With Luke he was sharper on one or two occasions, but, receiving only polite answers, he lapsed into silence and then glanced at Roxanne.

'Do you play chess, Miss Roxanne?'

'Yes, sir. Sofia taught me. We played in the evenings for there was little else to do…except sew, of course.'

'You did not have an instrument?'

'No, not for some years.'

'We have some excellent instruments here. You are welcome to use them whenever you wish. I enjoy music. I could employ a music master for you if you wish to be taught.'

'I shall attempt the pianoforte tomorrow,' she promised. 'If I have the aptitude, a music master might be useful to improve my skill. I am good with the needle.'

'Do you like to sketch or paint?'

'I think I have not had the opportunity.'

'Your guardian was remiss in your education. You may need some social skills, Miss Roxanne. Perhaps we should send for your godmother, Luke. She is a foolish woman, but might be of some use in giving our gel a little nudge. What do you think?'

'I believe I shall leave the decision to Roxanne, sir. I am not certain Lady Paula would come.'

'Nonsense. Write to her and ask her to come down for the ball. She will be here before you have time to turn round. Her curiosity will bring her, if nothing more.'

The earl waved the footman away as he offered more wine. 'Nothing more for me. I think I shall leave the pair of you to amuse yourselves. If I stay up this evening, I shall not be fit for guests tomorrow. No, no, do not get up. Finish your meal. Jarvis, give me your arm. Goodnight, Miss Roxanne. My suggestion was for your benefit, not an order.'

'I thank you for the thought, sir.'

'Well, he is certainly taking an interest,' Luke remarked as the door closed behind his grandfather. 'Shall we go through to the parlour, Roxanne? I thought we might use the front parlour when we are alone. It was my mother's favourite and the drawing room is far too large. Shall I ask Mrs Arlet for some tea and coffee?'

'Would you not rather have port or brandy? Tea will do very well for me.'

'If you do not mind, I shall have brandy.' He nodded to the remaining footman. 'In twenty minutes or so, Smith.'

Roxanne proceeded him into the front parlour. It was of a similar size to the one the earl preferred, but its décor was a little in need of refreshment, though comfortable and with a pleasant aspect out over steps leading down to a wide expanse of lawn in the sunken garden. At that moment the light was fading and she could not see beyond the windows, for the candles had been lit.

'Did you bring it?' Luke asked, having made certain the door was closed behind them. 'I must admit I am curious to see this jewel.'

Roxanne reached inside her bodice and took out the ruby. It was warm where it had lain nestled against her breasts. She held it out on the palm of her hand and it glowed in the candlelight.

'Good grief,' Luke exclaimed as he saw it. 'I have never seen its like. This must be worth a king's ransom, Roxanne. It looks as if it came from an Indian maharajah's crown.'

'Then it is valuable,' Roxanne said as he held it to the light between his thumb and forefinger. 'Sofia said as much, but I was not certain. How could I have come by it, do you imagine?'

'I believe it must have come from India. The secret of its origin must lie locked in your subconscious, Roxanne. Could your father have brought it home? Did something happen that made you take it and run away?'

'I truly wish I could answer that question.' She looked thoughtful. 'I have wondered if Black Bob guessed I had something valuable. He was determined I would be his woman—did he know that Sofia had hidden this for me? He would not have dared to steal it from her. The other players respected and revered her. Had he stolen from her or harmed her, I think they might have turned on him.'

'So he waited until she was dead.' Luke inclined

his head. 'It is possible that he might have suspected something. One of the others might have seen it in your hand when you refused to be parted from it.'

'Yes, perhaps. What do you think I should do about this? Would it be possible to trace the rightful owner?'

'I dare say a good few would claim it as theirs if they could whether or not they had the right,' Luke said. 'I suppose I might place a vague advert in *The Times* newspaper and see what happens. I should ask any respondent to contact a solicitor by letter and see what replies we get, but I think we must take great care of the jewel, Roxanne. If Sofia told you that you claimed it was yours, it may be—and this ruby is extremely valuable. If no one likely comes forward in response to the advert, I think you should accept that you own the jewel.'

'Would you have it placed somewhere safe for me? I was nervous enough of carrying it before, but now—I should hate to be accused of being careless if it was lost.'

'I shall have it stored in my grandfather's strong room until I return to London,' Luke said. 'We keep all the more valuable heirlooms there when they are not being worn. Hartingdon thinks them as safe here as in a bank and I think he is right. The strong room was once a dungeon and the locks have been made stronger.'

'Is it in the old wing—where the tower is?'

'Yes. We seldom use that wing, because parts of the tower are unsafe. Grandfather hasn't opened the strong room in years, but I shall ask him for the key. You will not mind if I show him the ruby?'

'Supposing he asks where it came from?'

'I shall tell him it is your inheritance from your friend, which in a way it is. Had Sofia been other than she was, she might have sold it long since.'

'She would rather give me all she had than take something of mine,' Roxanne replied with a smile. 'Yes, it should be safe in the strong room—though if it is claimed we shall need to explain.'

'I doubt it will be,' Luke said. 'The only person who might know of the ruby would be the owner, whoever that might be.'

'My father…' Roxanne sighed. 'I think it must have been his and that it came from India, just as we have surmised, but perhaps I wish to believe it. Perhaps I have invented the fairy tale?'

'Did Sofia never try to find out where you had come from?'

'We were always moving from one place to another. Besides, I think she was afraid someone would take me away from her. She says that I was very quiet and I cried in my sleep for months when she first took me in. It was in her mind that I had been harmed in some way. She would not have given me up to someone who might hurt me.'

'A jewel like that might cause many people to do things they would not otherwise do,' Luke said and frowned. 'I shall seek the advice of my lawyer before placing the advert, Roxanne. It may bring more than we would wish for and I must be certain it cannot be traced back to you.'

'You think I might be in danger?'

'I cannot know for certain—but there must have been something that frightened you or you would not have been in such distress when Sofia found you. If you were so determined not to give the ruby up, you must have had good reason to think it was yours.'

'Sofia has said much the same to me.' Roxanne looked up at him. 'I would willingly return it to its rightful owner if it is not mine.'

'Yes, well, we shall see what happens,' he said and his eyes were thoughtful, as if wondering how much he could believe of what she'd told him. 'Do not worry about it, Roxanne. I think Grandfather seemed pleased with life this evening, do you not agree?'

He had pocketed the ruby and Roxanne was glad to see it in his safekeeping. She did not wish to be responsible for such a jewel and felt she would not mind if she never saw it again—and yet, according to Sofia, as a young girl, she had been determined not to give it up.

'I hope he will be as pleased with me in a few weeks. I am doing my best, Luke, but he is bound to discover gaps in my education. Sofia taught me so much about the world, and I read plays and poetry, but I know little of the things most young ladies learn.'

'And your mind is all the better for it,' Luke said. 'You cannot imagine how boring some of them are, Roxanne. I would swear you could discuss Shakespeare in more depth than most.'

'Yes, at least the roles I have played,' she said and dimpled. 'I shall not mind if the earl employs tutors to rectify my lack. It will pass the time and give me something to strive for.'

'Have you thought about what happens in three months?'

'It is a long time,' Roxanne said. 'I dare say he will have discovered I am a fraud and declare me unsuitable to be the mistress of a house like this long before that, and if he does not...well, that is up to you, I think.'

'Would you go through with the wedding if I asked it?'

'On the terms you offered before?' He inclined his head and Roxanne was silent for a moment. 'If we are both of the same mind in three months, I think I might.'

Why on earth had she agreed to marry him in three months if he should ask her? Roxanne wondered what had got into her head. A sham engagement was as far as she had been prepared to go initially, but, oddly enough, she had begun to find the idea of marriage to Luke Clarendon more and more appealing.

What else could she do with her life that would bring her comfort and safety? A woman alone in her position would be prey to rogues and predators, men who would trick her and seduce her for their pleasure. As Luke's fiancée, and perhaps his make-believe wife, she would have respect and a settled income. Surely that was enough for any woman?

Yet there was something inside her that wanted more. How foolish she was! Luke had never intended more than a temporary arrangement, but now the earl was insisting on a marriage after three months. No doubt he wanted to know a grandchild was on its way before he died.

Luke's child. For a moment the thought sent a warm spiral curling through her and she smiled. How pleasant the picture was, though quite impossible, of course. They must try to please the earl in his last months, but a child would be too much. She frowned as she recalled her first meeting with the earl. He looked frail, but he did not look particularly unwell.

Could Luke have overreacted to the earl's illness? Was he truly as sick as his grandson believed?

What would she feel if Luke expected her to provide the heir?

The questions went round and round in her head as her maid helped her prepare for bed. When she was in her nightgown, Roxanne sent the girl away and curled up on the deep window seat to gaze down at the gardens. She was already beginning to feel more at home here and she could not help but think it might be nice to live in a house such as this, not just for a visit, but as the mistress.

'Foolish,' she murmured aloud as she twirled a strand of red hair over her finger. 'It is not poss…'

The words trailed away as she saw the shadow of a man reflected on the lawn in the moonlight. He appeared to be trying to hide in the shrubbery, but the moon was at his back and cast a shadow for a few seconds before he moved further back into the darkness and was lost to sight.

She did not think it had been Luke and it was certainly not the earl. Perhaps one of the servants? Yet it had seemed to her that there was something furtive about the man, as if he wanted to watch the house without being seen.

Could Black Bob have followed her here? For a brief moment the thought sent cold chills winging down her spine, but then she dismissed them. The leader of the travelling players was an opportunist. Given the chance that day at the fair he might have grabbed her and forced her to go with him, but she did not think he would spend days following her to this house, only to hide in the shrubbery and spy on her.

Now she was being very foolish. Why should the man in the shrubbery be spying on her? Luke had said something about having an enemy when they first met. It might be that someone had followed him, intending some harm.

It was too late to go in search of Luke now. She did not know where his rooms were. Besides, the servants would be shocked if she went looking for him at this hour. She would just have to wait until the morning. Slipping into bed, Roxanne tried to be sensible. The man in the shrubbery was probably only one of the servants.

'Someone hiding in the shrubbery watching the house?' Luke looked incredulous when she told him her fears at breakfast. 'I imagine it must have been one of the keepers. They probably take a walk round the house at night just to make sure everything is secure.'

'Yes, I expect you are right. Though, whoever it was seemed a little furtive, as if he wanted to watch the house without being seen, but perhaps that was my imagination.' She helped herself to a little scrambled egg and ham from the vast array of dishes under silver covers on the sideboard and carried her plate to the table. Luke was finishing his rare beef eaten with sauté potatoes and pickles.

'I dare say he was being discreet rather than furtive. Grandfather would not want the keepers to be patrolling in full view of the house, but I think that is what you saw, Roxanne.' He pushed his plate aside and poured more coffee into a delicate porcelain bowl.

'I am relieved to hear it. I wondered if Black Bob had followed us here, and then I thought that perhaps—you spoke of an enemy when we first met?'

'An enemy?' Luke looked puzzled, then smiled ruefully. 'In truth, I do not have an enemy, Roxanne. Are you anxious about this fellow who threatened you before?'

'No. He would grab me if he saw me by chance, but I do not think he would take the trouble to follow us here. I am sure you are right. The man in the garden was merely a keeper on patrol. I shall not give it another thought.'

'You are safe now, dearest,' Luke said and smiled across the table. 'You have me to look after you—to say nothing of the earl's household.'

'Yes, of course. I am not anxious for myself, but I thought I should tell you what I saw.'

'I am glad you did. What are your plans for this morning, Roxanne?'

'I have been invited to visit the earl at eleven o'clock.

Until then I think I shall try to make myself familiar with the house.'

Luke got to his feet, tossing his napkin on the table. 'I would love to stay and show you round, but I have an appointment with Grandfather's agent and bailiff. Perhaps we can spend the afternoon together? Do not let Grandfather bully you, Roxanne.'

'I have no intention of it. He is a peppery gentleman, but I rather like him.'

'You do?' Luke arched his brow, a smile quirking at the corner of his mouth. 'Well, I wish you luck. He is seldom at his best in the morning. Excuse me, I must go or I shall be late—finish your breakfast at your leisure. Had you wished, I am sure you could have had a tray in your room.'

'I like to rise early. Please do not let me keep you from your appointment.'

After Luke had gone, Roxanne drank her coffee and then pushed back her chair. She examined the contents of the silver dishes and saw that most had not been touched. Leaving the room, she glanced at the maid hovering outside the door.

'You may clear now, Maisie—it is Maisie, isn't it?'

'Yes, Miss Peters.'

'Please call me Miss Roxanne. Everyone does and I prefer it, as I have told Mrs Arlet.'

'Yes, Miss Roxanne. Mrs Arlet said she was at your service if you should care for a tour of the house.'

'I think I should like that very much.'

'I'll tell her you're ready, miss, before I clear.'

'How kind of you, Maisie, but I think I know where

her sitting room is; she told me where to find her yesterday.'

Maisie bobbed a curtsy and went into the breakfast room. Roxanne wandered through the hall to the back stairs and then went down to the area that was used exclusively by the servants. The housekeeper's sitting room was on a small landing just above a short flight of stairs, which led to the servants' hall and the kitchen. Pleased that she had remembered correctly, Roxanne knocked and was invited to enter.

'Miss Roxanne,' the housekeeper said and looked surprised. 'I would have come to you if you'd sent for me.'

'I wanted to see if I could find my way here,' Roxanne said. 'I should like to begin with the kitchen, if you please. I have no intention of interfering with the way you do things, Mrs Arlet, but I think I should know the layout and the way everyone works. It is a long trek for the servants to carry the food to the dining room. I find it hardly surprising that things get a little cool sometimes.'

'Yes, miss, that is a fault. Cook has been asking if we couldn't have a serving hatch somewhere. It would save Mr Marshall going up and down those stairs so much—and the food would keep hotter.'

'Would you like me to speak to the earl for you?'

'If you think he is up to it, miss. When he was down a year or so back, his lordship did mention having a modern range put in and a tap in the scullery to save us fetching water from the well, but nothing happened.'

'I dare say he might have forgotten,' Roxanne said.

'Gentlemen have such a lot to think of, do they not? They tend to leave the house to us.'

'Well, Miss Roxanne, it is a treat to have a sensible young woman in the house. We've servants enough, it's true, but life could be a bit easier for us all and there's no mistake. A house like this needs constant attention to keep it right.'

'I am certain it does,' Roxanne said. 'We shall begin with a tour of the house this morning, then, when I know my way about, we shall discuss menus. Cook is providing a huge choice of food in the morning. That is as it should be when we have guests, but we hardly need so much for the family.'

'The master eats like a bird, miss. I think Cook likes to show what she can do when his lordship is down.'

'Yes, of course. Well, we are to have guests very soon now and she will have plenty of chance to show off her skills.'

Roxanne noticed a glimmer of respect in the house-keeper's face. She suspected that too much waste had gone on for years with no one to keep a check on things and Cook probably sent leftovers to the village or the servants took it home with them. Since there was no need for strict economy, Roxanne would not interfere—providing the neglect was not actually abuse of the earl's laxity. She felt it did no harm to let the servants see she intended to keep an eye on such things.

Where had she learned about these things? Roxanne frowned. She did not know why, but her instincts were guiding her.

'Did you say something, miss?' the housekeeper asked, looking at her curiously.

'No, nothing at all,' Roxanne said and smiled. The memory had been so clear for a moment but she did not wish to think of it now. 'Shall we go down to the kitchen?'

'So, Miss Roxanne, you have been inspecting the kitchens,' the earl said when she bent to kiss his cheek. 'Discovered they are cheating me, have you?'

'I think too much waste has been going on,' Roxanne said. 'I am not sure you have been cheated, sir. Waste food is usually passed on to the poor or beggars, is it not?'

'I can't be bothered with that business,' he said. 'It will be your place to see we are not being abused now—and to sort out any problems. Do not bring them to me. There is an allowance for repairs and maintenance below stairs. Ask Clarendon if you must, but, otherwise, deal with it.'

'In that case, I shall authorise a serving hatch, a new sink in the kitchen and taps, also a larger, more modern cooking range—but I shall not trouble you other than to ask who has charge of the allowance for repairs.'

'Tonkins, of course. Clarendon is with him this morning.'

'Your agent, I imagine. Very well, sir, this is the last you shall hear of it.'

'Good.' He glared at her. 'What do you make of the rest of it—think it an old wreck of a place? Clarendon does. He'll tear it down and build new when I'm gone, I dare say.'

'Oh, I do not think it, sir. I have no idea what it costs to run a house like this, but I imagine it is a great deal. Perhaps if you were to pull down the tower and the wing you never use, you might build a more modern section there—and keep the rest of this lovely house as it is.'

'Humph. Think you're the first to come up with the idea? Clarendon's mother wanted me to do it years ago. She always hated the tower—said it was haunted.'

'Is it?'

'Don't believe in that rubbish, do you? The roof has gone in parts and rooks nest there. The sounds people hear are wind and birds or rats in the eaves.'

'Yes, I expect you are right,' Roxanne said. 'At night it is easy to imagine all kinds of things.'

'You are a woman of sense,' the earl said, his gaze narrowing. 'Is it all an act, Miss Roxanne? The ruby Clarendon showed me—it doesn't fit with the rest. What are you keeping from me, miss—and does Clarendon know it all?'

'The ruby is my inheritance. I wasn't sure it was valuable, but Luke says it is and I believe him.'

'He told me he has to return to London tomorrow. He will be gone for a few days and then he intends to stay until after the ball. What do you think of that, miss?'

'I expect he has some business in town. There is little he can do here, really. I am sure he will have sorted any estate business this morning.'

'Don't mind him running out on you, then? What if

he decides not to bother about coming back until the day before the ball?'

'I should miss him, but I believe he will keep his word.'

'You have a deal more faith than I, Miss Roxanne. He usually stays two days at the most and then I don't see him for months.'

'Things are different now, sir.'

'Are they?' The earl's eyes seemed to pierce her with their intensity. 'I thought this was just a masquerade to keep me sweet—are you telling me that you are really going to marry him?'

Roxanne looked at him in silence for a long moment, then smiled. 'We have to wait for three months—but if you give your blessing and Luke still wants to marry me, yes, I shall.'

'I haven't made up my mind about you yet, miss. There's something you're both hiding—but I'll get it out of you or him. Wait and see if I don't.'

Roxanne hesitated, then, 'Tell me, sir—what is it that you want most in the world?'

'To see my great-grandson and know there will be someone to carry on here when I've gone. Clarendon will never settle here—but you might. Is that the idea? You'll give me what I want and he gets to live in town as he pleases? You won't like that much, girl, and you're a fool if you settle for it.'

'Please, do not think so ill of him, sir,' Roxanne pleaded. 'I know things have not always been right between you—but will you not give Luke a chance to make this work? He is genuine in his desire to mend fences.'

The earl's gaze narrowed, his mouth pursed. 'Hmmm, we shall see.'

'I hope Grandfather did not bully you too much?' Luke said when they met for nuncheon later. Roxanne shook her head and he nodded in satisfaction, looking so much like his grandfather that she had to hide her laughter. 'Well, what would you like to do this afternoon? I know you can manage a horse—have you done much riding? Proper riding, I mean, not as part of a circus show.'

'All kinds,' Roxanne replied. 'Barebacked, astride, but I have not much experience of riding sidesaddle. I can drive a caravan. I dare say I could learn to ride like a lady easily enough.'

'I am sure you could and I will arrange a suitable mount for you when I return from town. For this afternoon I think perhaps we should drive round the estate, just to give you an idea of its size and where it is pleasant to walk when you are alone. When I was out with Tonkins this morning everyone was asking about you. Since it is a pleasant afternoon we can use the curricle and allow the curious to see my fiancée. It is only necessary to wave and smile at this juncture.'

'I think that would be very pleasant. Did you have a good morning with your grandfather's agent?'

'Yes. Why do you ask?'

'I understand the monies for minor repairs to the kitchens are lodged with him. Mrs Arlet has spoken to me about various needs and your grandfather has told me it is up to me to sort out domestic problems in future.'

'Has he, indeed? Clearly he trusts you more than me, Roxanne. I spoke to him about a serving hatch some months back and he sent me about my business, told me he didn't need help with arranging his household.'

'Well, perhaps things have changed. I have been told not to bother him with trivial domestic affairs and I shan't—but the hatch would improve the quality of the food for us and make less work for others. I think it would repay the cost many times over.'

'I can see the future of this place is in safe hands, at least for the moment.' Luke frowned and stood up. 'I shall arrange for the curricle to be brought round. It is warm, but there may be a breeze so you will want your bonnet and a pelisse.'

'I shall fetch them,' Roxanne said.

She was thoughtful as she walked upstairs. Luke had not seemed particularly pleased with the news that the earl had placed domestic affairs in her hands. Perhaps he was beginning to regret bringing her here? His idea of a temporary engagement seemed to be getting out of hand.

Had Roxanne been able to read Luke's mind she would have discovered that he had mixed feelings and was in something of a turmoil regarding the situation between them. It was surely a good thing that the earl should feel able to place his domestic affairs in Roxanne's hands. He was uncertain of her true feelings regarding the situation. She had been quite adamant that there would be no wedding, just a fake engagement for a few months, but she seemed to have changed her mind since their arrival at Hartingdon.

She had been running from a man who was determined to make her his mistress when they met, her future dubious to say the least. It would be tempting for any woman in such difficulty to be seduced by the house and the obvious wealth here. Yet if the ruby truly belonged to Roxanne she had money of her own. Luke did not know exactly how much it would fetch, but he was sure it would be more than a few hundred—perhaps as much as two thousand pounds or more to the right person? With such a sum she could set up her own establishment and live comfortably for the rest of her life or until she found work or married. She did not need to live here at the mercy of a cantankerous old man—or to marry a man she did not love.

So why had she changed her mind? She was unsure if the ruby was legally hers, but she might have sold it and risked the consequences had she been less than the honest woman he believed her.

Having placed the ruby in his safe keeping, she had surrendered her independence and shown great trust in him. Luke could not recall anyone else placing that amount of faith in him and his reactions were a mixture of gratification and panic. At the start he had thought the sham engagement might eventually lead to a physical arrangement between them. Luke would have been very ready to become her protector had she chosen a life in the theatre. He had been aroused by Roxanne's vibrant beauty from the beginning, but did he really wish for marriage? Luke had avoided being caught in what he thought of as a trap for so long, he could not help wondering just what he had got himself into.

It was to be merely a sham marriage, of course. That was the reason Roxanne had agreed to it when the earl insisted on the three-month engagement. She knew that he would keep his word to let her go once the earl had died.

Roxanne would give him his freedom once the earl was in his grave. He was certain that she would keep any bargain he made with her, but by the time he was able to ask for his freedom, would he still wish for it?

Damn the earl for interfering in his life! Hartingdon had no right to dictate terms to him and his threat to restrict his income could be overcome in a court. How could he think of destroying the man who was his only close family? Such a breach would surely kill the old man. Despite the anger and frustration inside him, Luke knew he would never deliberately harm his grandfather. It might be that he would have to make more than a sham marriage and actually give the earl his heir.

Roxanne would never agree to it—would she? He could not expect her to provide an heir and then simply disappear when the marriage ended. Yet need it necessarily end so finally? There was always the alternative of a marriage of convenience.

No, he had vowed he would never go down that road. His parents had been so desperately unhappy. He had witnessed his mother's tears too many times. His father had been a heartless brute who cared only for his own pleasure and Luke suspected he might be the same. To marry under false pretences might cause too much pain in the future.

The Roxanne who had bound his leg and threatened an intruder at the inn was exciting and amazing, but if she settled into a life of domesticity to please the earl Luke might become bored and begin to stray.

He knew his own faults only too well and he liked Roxanne too much to want to hurt her. It might be as well to remind her that this relationship was a temporary affair. It would be best to stick to the business arrangement they had made at the start.

The earl's estate was vast, much larger than Roxanne had imagined. She had no experience of land husbandry, but from what she could see as Luke drove her about the estate it was in good heart. The people looked prosperous and they smiled and waved, the labourers and farmers doffing their hats to her. Some children ran out of one of the farms and stood waving and giggling as Luke brought the curricle to a halt.

'Mam said to wish you happy, sir,' one of the boys said. 'She wants to know if there's to be a bit of a do for the tenants and all.'

'Yes, I am sure we shall arrange something when the wedding happens, but it is not to be just yet.' Luke thrust his hand in his pocket and brought out some silver coins, which he tossed to the children before driving away.

'Your tenants seem pleased to see you, Luke.'

'They will be disappointed if there is no wedding,'

Luke remarked. 'Perhaps we should hold some sort of fête in the park this summer. Grandfather always had a late summer party in the gardens for the tenants and labourers. I suppose an engagement is as good an excuse as any other. I'll speak to him later.'

'Your grandfather suspects you of trying to fool him, did you know that?' Roxanne said, keeping her gaze to the front. 'If we were to break the engagement too soon, he would be certain that he had been right all along.'

'We shall see whether his health improves. We might have to marry to satisfy him, but do not worry, Roxanne. I should give you your freedom afterwards. He can push us into marriage, but even he cannot hurry the arrival of an heir. It should content him to know that I am married—if you are still prepared to go so far?'

'Yes, of course. I know that the last thing you want is a life of domesticity, Luke. You need not fear that I shall cling to you and beg you not to leave me. I will not ask for more than we agreed.'

'No...' A little pulse flicked at his temple. 'Well, we shall see how things go, but you must tell me if the situation becomes too difficult for you here. I know Hartingdon is a past master at inflicting wounds.'

'I think he is a lonely, unhappy man. He shut you out when you were younger, perhaps because he was grieving for your mother—but then, when he might have reached out to you, it was too late. You are very like him, you know.'

'Like Hartingdon?' Luke turned his head to look at her in astonishment. 'What on earth makes you say that? I do not think I have given you cause to fear me?'

'No, you have not—but neither has the earl. He may be grumpy and harsh at times, but I do not fear him. Indeed, I rather like him. I should not wish to be the source of pain to him.'

Luke made a face of disbelief. 'If he appears to reciprocate, beware. He is probably trying to get beneath your guard to discover your secrets.'

'You are unfair,' Roxanne replied and gave him a look of reproach. 'Why does neither of you trust the other? You say you wish to make his last months happy—yet you will not allow him to have a heart or a conscience.'

'If he has a softer side, he has given no sign of it in my presence.'

'You are so used to quarrelling with each other that neither of you can see how foolish it is. If you let down your guard, Luke, you might actually enjoy a pleasant relationship with him—become friends or at least respect one another.'

'If I offered affection, he would throw it in my face. My advice to you is to be careful, Roxanne. Allow him to get inside your head and he will hurt you. Do not imagine that anything he has said of late means he is happy to accept you into the family. I have no doubt that from the moment I told him I was engaged, he instructed agents to discover who you are and where you came from.'

'He is unlikely to do so.' Roxanne kept her face turned from him as she said, 'Since I am well aware that this is all a masquerade I am not likely to be hurt, whatever happens.'

'That is as well,' Luke said. 'Neither of us is to be completely trusted, Roxanne, but you have my word that you will never want for money for the rest of your life. I intend to have the ruby valued when I am in town; I shall try to discover if it has a history—but regardless of what I discover, my promise to you holds true. When this is all over I shall set you up with a house and an income that will be more than adequate.'

Roxanne made no answer. He was merely reminding her of their arrangement. Luke Clarendon had never pretended to care for her. She ought not to feel disappointed or upset. Indeed, she would not allow herself to feel anything. She would simply make the most of her time here—and when it was over she would know what to do.

# *Chapter Six*

After Luke left for London the next day, Roxanne set her mind to the tasks she had taken on in the house. A list of guests for the ball was drawn up and the invitations written carefully in her best copperplate hand. She spent an hour with Tonkins and set the work in hand for the improvements to the kitchen, and, after speaking to the head gardener, arranged for fresh flowers to be brought to the house each day.

When she carried a bowl of yellow roses into the earl's sitting room that evening he stared at her as if she had run mad.

'What is that for, miss?'

'To brighten your room and bring some sunshine indoors to you. The weather is so delightful, sir, and the gardens are glorious. We have so many lovely blooms it would be a shame not to enjoy some of them indoors.'

'Like flowers, do you?' His thick brows knit as he stared at the offering.

'Yes, I love them. I think I should like to improve some parts of the garden—if I stay here for long enough, of course.'

'What would you do?'

'There are some unused areas at the back of the house that are merely grass. I would like to make a wild garden, with your permission, sir. I have spoken to the gardener and he says there were plans to make a garden of box hedges and herbs there once, but it never happened. I thought something similar, but less formal. I should like plants that invite butterflies and birds to visit often, and perhaps some running water—a fountain of some kind.'

'The herb garden was my wife's intention, but she died.' The earl glared at her, seeming angry or at the mercy of some deep emotion. 'I suppose you can do as you please—if you stay long enough.'

'Luke says you will have instructed agents to discover who I am and where I come from, sir.'

'And what if I have? Worried about what they will find, miss?'

'I believe I have done nothing of which I ought to be ashamed, sir.'

'There's something, though. I've sensed it since the beginning. You are a mystery, Miss Roxanne—but I don't dislike having you visit me, and the roses can stay.'

Roxanne smiled. Impulsively she bent and kissed his cheek. 'Perhaps there is a mystery, sir—perhaps even

I do not know its answer, but believe me when I say I would not harm you or Luke. Indeed, I would rather go away, disappear altogether, than bring shame on either of you.'

The earl grunted, making no other reply, but his eyes looked very bright as she glanced back from the doorway. Walking down to the hall, Roxanne felt at a loss. She had become acquainted with all parts of the house, including the disused wing. The tower was out of bounds so she had not attempted it, but, walking up to the stairway to look at the curving stone steps, she'd heard a screech and some fluttering that she took to be the rooks the earl had spoken of once.

The tower had no appeal for her and she decided to walk in the garden for a while. Perhaps she would have a talk to the gardener or the bailiff about the new wilderness. It could not hurt to make plans for her wild-flower plot, even if her stay here was only temporary. Walking round past the tower to the back of the house, something made her glance up. For one moment she saw something at a window about halfway up, but in an instant it had gone. She frowned, because it had looked like a face—a man's face, dark-complexioned and strange—and yet she was sure that the earl had given orders no one was to go up the tower because it was unstable.

It must surely have been a trick of the light? Why would anyone be in the tower? The earl's servants were all aware of his orders—and yet there might be good reason for someone to visit surreptitiously. When he spoke of putting the ruby somewhere safe, Luke had told Roxanne that the earl's strong room was somewhere either in the tower or beneath it.

Would a thief try to find the entrance and break in? Roxanne did not know what to think, because it seemed so unlikely. If no one had ever attempted it before, why should it happen now?

Had Luke been at home, she would have told him immediately, but the earl was not to be made anxious or worried about something of this nature. It might be nothing more than imagination, but rather than simply leave it, she decided to speak to someone. Knowing that Tonkins had gone into town that day, she thought of the bailiff. She'd seen Higgins going into his office earlier and turned in the direction he'd been heading, which was towards the stable block.

Higgins was in conversation outside his office with a stout man who looked as if he might be one of the earl's tenant farmers. He lifted his battered brown hat to Roxanne as she approached, nodded to Higgins and went off.

'Forgive me for interrupting you, Mr Higgins,' Roxanne said. 'It is a small matter—but, since Lord Clarendon is away and Mr Tonkins has gone to the market, one I thought should be brought to your attention, sir.'

'Nothing is too much trouble for you, miss. Was it about the plants for the wild garden?'

'I was hoping to speak to Minty about that later,' Roxanne agreed. 'It may have been a trick of the light, Mr Higgins—but as I passed the tower just now I thought I saw a face at the window—not at the top, but at that little round window halfway up.'

'You didn't investigate yourself, miss?'

'I know it isn't safe, which is why I thought it curious that anyone should be there.'

'Everyone knows it isn't safe, miss. None of our people would dream of going there—unless ordered to by the earl and then we should send a party armed with ropes for safety's sake.'

'No one who knows that it is unsafe would go up the tower—but a stranger might. A stranger intent on robbery or some such thing.'

'Lord Clarendon told you about the strong room,' Higgins said and nodded. 'Only a handful of us know the secret, miss. I've never known anyone to attempt a break in, but I suppose there is always a first time. His lordship may have been seen when he visited it recently—though I cannot think any of our people would consider doing such a thing. The door is solid iron. It would be impossible to break it down—but I'll make sure the lock has not been tampered with. I'll go there myself now, miss.'

'Do you think someone should accompany you?'

'I'll take a pistol with me, but I doubt there's much to worry about, miss. As you said, it will be a trick of the light.'

'May I come with you?'

'Now that I can't allow, miss. I couldn't live with myself if you were to fall and have an accident. You'll find Minty in the hothouses. Go and have a talk with him, discover what he has to say about your wild garden, miss. I'll let you know if I discover anything.'

Roxanne agreed and left him. She was almost sure

that it must have been a trick of the light and half-wished that she had not put Mr Higgins to the trouble of investigating.

Returning to the house after a long and pleasant talk with the head gardener, Roxanne washed her hands and changed into a fresh gown for lunch. She had instructed Mrs Arlet that she would have just a little bread and butter and cold chicken in the small parlour. Her meal was finished and she was about to leave when the housekeeper came in.

'I am sorry to disturb you, Miss Roxanne, but Mr Higgins has asked if you will visit him at home.'

'At home?' Roxanne was puzzled. 'Is he not in his office?'

'It appears he had an accident, miss. Johnson will take you in the governess's cart—if you wouldn't mind travelling in such a way?'

'Of course not. I shall get ready at once. Is it far?'

'Not far, miss, but Johnson says he was instructed you wasn't to walk there alone. He's to take you and wait to bring you back.'

'I shall fetch my pelisse at once.'

'I took the liberty of sending for it. Tilly is waiting in the hall to help you with it, miss.'

Roxanne thanked her. Going into the hall, she put on her pelisse and bonnet and then went out to the courtyard at the back of the house, where the groom was waiting with the governess's cart.

'Is Mr Higgins badly hurt, Johnson?' Roxanne asked as she was helped up into the little seat at the back.

'He's got some nasty cuts and bruises,' the groom replied. 'His wife made him lie on the sofa in the parlour and the doctor told him he should go to bed and rest for a few days, but he won't until he's seen you, miss.'

'Please take me to him at once,' Roxanne said. 'I know this must be important or he would not otherwise have sent for me.'

She twisted her gloves in her hands, feeling a heavy weight of responsibility. Higgins had gone to the tower on her behalf and it was her fault if he had taken a tumble down the stairs. She was distressed because he was hurt and blamed herself.

The bailiff's cottage was through the park, at the edge of the road that led to Harte Village. It would have taken her a good half an hour to walk here, but the drive was accomplished in a fraction of the time. The groom helped her down and, as she walked up the path of the neat garden, the front door opened and a plump, pleasant-looking woman opened the door to her.

'I've been watching out for you, Miss Roxanne,' she cried. 'I am that grateful you've come. Higgins won't go to bed until he has spoken to you—and the foolish man has refused to take his medicine for fear it sends him to sleep.'

'I came as soon as I heard,' Roxanne said. 'I am so sorry, Mrs Higgins. I fear I am to blame for this.'

'You, miss? I should say not—but come through to the parlour and let my man tell you himself.'

Roxanne followed her into a pleasant parlour with

a sunny aspect at the back of the house. Mr Higgins was lying on a large comfortable sofa with his head on a pile of pillows and his eyes shut. He opened them as she approached and sat up, looking anxious.

'Please do not disturb yourself, sir.' Roxanne drew a parlour chair and sat close to him. 'Did one of the steps give way beneath you? I am so sorry for sending you there. I do hope you are not badly hurt?'

'It was not the steps, miss, though one or two are crumbling, but I didn't go up the tower. The place we spoke of is below it. I went to look at the lock and found some signs that someone had tried unsuccessfully to open the door. I was about to leave and report it to Mr Tonkins when something hit me from behind. I went down like a light and it must have been some minutes before I came to myself enough to get up and stagger out. One of the gardeners saw me fall as I left and called for help.'

'You were hit on the back of the head? That is terrible.' Roxanne felt shivery all over. 'So I was right—there was someone in the tower. I am so sorry you were hurt, Mr Higgins.'

'Serves me right for going there alone, miss. I thought you had imagined the face and took a risk. In future I'll be more careful and respectful of what you say. I gave instructions that a search should be made. Six of the men went to take a look in the tower after they brought me home—and I've since heard that someone has been camping out in the tower.'

'Good gracious! How long has this been going on?'

'A day or two at most the men think. It might have

been a tramp, miss—or it might have been a thief, as you suggested. Whoever it was, he didn't want to get caught.'

'No, indeed, but this is serious, Mr Higgins. You must take great care and rest, as your doctor told you.'

'I shall for a day or so, if only to appease Mrs Higgins—but you must promise me you will not attempt to visit that wing or the tower again, miss. His lordship would never forgive me if anything were to happen to you. One of us should have noticed something before you did, and that can't be denied.'

'I shall certainly not attempt to enter the tower,' Roxanne assured him. 'I have been wishing that I had not told you. I am so sorry you were hurt.'

'It was my own fault for not taking anyone to guard my back. I didn't give you credit, miss, and I should have known you're not the sort to imagine things. I've given instructions that the grounds are to be patrolled at all times. If there are dangerous intruders about, we cannot be too careful.'

'I thought I saw a man hiding in the shrubbery outside my room the first night I came here,' Roxanne told him. 'Lord Clarendon thought it must have been one of the keepers, but now... Why would anyone watch the house and then hide in the tower?'

'There's something he's after,' Higgins said and looked grave. 'I don't know what it is, Miss Roxanne. We've never had anything like it before—so why now?'

'I do not know,' she replied. 'I promise I shall take great care when walking in the gardens—and you must rest, sir.'

'I shall for a day or so, miss. It seems I've a tough skull for the blow did no more than knock me unconscious. I may have a headache for a while, but I'll be as right as rain soon.'

'I am relieved to hear it.'

'Shall you tell the earl, miss?'

'No, not unless he has heard something,' Roxanne said. 'As you know, his health is not good. I do not wish him to worry. I dare say the intruder has gone. With the increased security he is unlikely to return.'

'I doubt he will risk it again—unless there is something he desperately wants to get his hands on. You cannot think what that might be, miss?' The bailiff looked at her hard. 'No idea what he's after?'

'No,' Roxanne said. 'I cannot tell you, for I do not know.'

Yet as she was driven back to the house some minutes later, Roxanne was thoughtful. Had the intruder been after her ruby? It would explain why the attempt on the strong room had happened now—but was the jewel valuable enough to bring whoever it was here? It had been in the strong room only one night, because Luke had taken it to London with him to be valued.

Besides, no one knew she had it. How could they? Sofia had kept it hidden for years and no one had tried to take it from them. Roxanne had wondered if Black Bob suspected she had something of value, but would he attempt to break into the earl's strong room? It did not fit with what she knew of him. Petty thieving or cheating a traveller of his purse was the gypsy's style, but not robbery on the scale that had been planned here. To break into an earl's treasury would be a serious matter.

Yet if it was the Hartingdon heirlooms that were wanted, why had it happened now and not at some time in the past?

What was so special about the ruby that it had provoked an attempt to break into the earl's strong room and an attack on his bailiff?

Why had it been in her hand when Sofia found her? She had been so determined to keep it, so adamant that it belonged to her. The earl was right when he said something did not fit with the rest. How could a girl of modest family come to own a jewel like that one?

Roxanne thought about the game they had played when she was recovering from her illness. Sofia was an intelligent lady. Had she suspected that the ruby had come from India? She might have invented the game to try to jog the memories in Roxanne's mind. It was possible that as she lay delirious she had said something that made Sofia believe she had once lived there. Rather than try to force her to remember, Sofia had invented the game.

The face at the tower window had been dark and not English. Roxanne strained for a memory, anything that would make sense of what was happening, but nothing came to her. Yet there was something that warned her she might be in danger, some instinct that told her Mr Higgins had been set upon by someone who wanted that ruby.

The thoughts went round and round in her head

like a trapped animal trying to escape from its cage. If she could remember what had occurred to frighten her when she ran from her home, she might be able to understand what was happening now.

'What is this I hear about Higgins?' the earl asked when Roxanne visited him that evening before going down to supper. 'What on earth was the fool doing in the tower in the first place? He knows it is dangerous.'

She hesitated, then, 'Do you truly wish to know the answer, sir? You might find it concerning.'

'Damn it, I ain't on me last legs yet. Tell me the truth, girl. All of it, for I shall know if you lie.'

'I saw a face at the round window halfway up the tower earlier today. I told Higgins, because I knew the strong room was there somewhere. He went to investigate, found an unsuccessful attempt had been made to open the iron door—and someone knocked him unconscious. The tower has since been searched by some of the men and no one is there now.'

'So the rogue has escaped. Is Higgins badly hurt?'

'No. I think he has a sore head and is shocked—but the doctor said the blow was not severe enough to kill him. Perhaps whoever it was did not wish to murder him, merely to stun him while he made his escape.'

'Humph. Got it all worked out, have you? Answer me this—why now? That strong room has been there for a hundred and fifty years and no one has ever tried to break in before this—couldn't if they tried. It would take a team of men to break that door down—and then they couldn't open it unless they knew the trick. It's a secret puzzle lock known only to me and now Luke.'

'I do not know why now, sir. Why do you think it happened?'

'I knew there was something suspicious about that ruby. Who did you steal it from?'

'I did not steal it.'

'Where did it come from then? It ain't the kind of thing a girl like you ought to have—unless you got it from a lover. Have you been the mistress of a rich man, girl? Did you steal it from him in a fit of pique?'

'No, I have not been a rich man's lover, sir.' Roxanne hesitated, then, 'I am not sure of its history. Luke is trying to find out what he can for me. I had it in my hand when—Sofia found me. I was about fourteen, very ill, alone and frightened—and I had lost my memory. I did not know my own name then and to this day I do not recall it. She says I would not let go of the ruby and claimed it was mine. When at last I did let her take it from me, she hid it and I forgot about it for years, until she reminded me as she was dying.'

The old man's eyes gleamed. 'I knew there was something. You were too good to be true, miss. I suspected something was wrong from the start.'

'Well, now you know it all. Do you wish me to leave?'

The earl was silent for a moment, then, 'You had best tell me all of it, girl. How did you meet my grandson—and why did he bring you here as his fiancée?'

'After Sofia died I was not safe amongst the people we travelled with. One of them wanted me as his mistress so I ran away when he was making arrangements to give a performance at a theatre in the town nearby.'

'You are an actress?'

'Yes, I have been an actress—but Sofia was certain I had been properly reared, though I have no memory of my past.'

'So it was a lie about your father being in India?'

'It was just something that came into my mind. I believe there may be a connection between the ruby and India. I do not know who my father was—or if he is still alive.'

'You think it has a connection with India, but you do not know?'

'I am not certain, but recently the idea has become stronger.'

'So how did you meet Clarendon?'

'He had a tumble from his horse. His ankle was painful and we thought it might be broken, though it was actually a displaced bone. I helped him and then recaptured his horse. We went to an inn to stay for the night and a doctor was called. The landlord sent someone to break into the chamber and rob Clarendon when he was sleeping, because he was unwell and vulnerable—but I had stayed to care for him lest he took a fever. I was awake and I had a poker. When the intruder saw that I was ready to fight him, the rogue ran off. The next day, your grandson begged me to stay with him until he was safe in London—and he took me to stay with someone called Mrs Mills.'

'Saved his backside for a second time, did you?'

'He insisted I had saved his life, but I dare say it was

no such thing. The lady I visited was very respectable. I might have been in London still, but at a fair on the Heath I saw Black Bob and told Luke I must leave. He asked me to enter into an engagement and—you know the rest.'

'I knew it.' The earl glared at her. 'It was all a masquerade from start to finish.'

'No…not quite. Luke wanted to make you happy. At first I agreed reluctantly, but then I came here—and I wanted to stay. If this had not happened I might have married Luke, if he wished it—and you agreed. I think we might have given you an heir and then, if he wished, parted. Now I think perhaps I should leave before he returns.'

'Leave the sinking ship, eh? Is that all you're good for—running away? I thought you had more spunk than that, girl?'

Roxanne's cheeks flamed. 'No, that is not fair. I would have married Luke if he wished…but you cannot want me to stay now you know the truth. You cannot wish him to marry a girl who does not know her own family.'

'Know my mind better than I do, do you?' The earl stared at her hard. 'You've told me the truth as you know it?'

'Yes, sir.'

'Held nothing back?'

'Nothing, I swear.'

'I ought to send the pair of you packing—but I want that heir. Clarendon isn't going to oblige me in a hurry if I send you away, so you can stay. You will marry him in a month or so. No reason to wait for three months if a letter isn't coming.'

'You want me to marry Luke?'

'Nothing the matter with your hearing, is there? I don't know who your father was or whether he gave you that damned ruby, but I can see quality in you. Tell you the truth, our family goes back to a privateer who came from yeoman stock and rose to be an earl through pleasing Good Queen Bess. Since then we've married into good and bad blood. It may be time we had some fresh blood in the family. If you've lied to me, we may both be sorry, but I'm going to trust you—on one condition.'

'That is?'

'Luke is not informed that I know the truth.'

'You wish me to lie to him?'

'You have been lying to me.'

'No—at least I didn't actually lie. I merely allowed you to think what you would, sir.'

'I said you were clever with words. I suppose that comes from being an actress. Is it all an act or do you actually care for the fellow?'

'I believe you know the answer, sir.'

'Humph. He's bitten off more than he can chew, hasn't he?'

'I shall not demand more than he is willing to give.'

'My grandson chose to play a little trick on me—now I've turned the tables, but it may all be for the best. So—what do you say?'

'I can only say yes—and thank you.'

'Nothing to thank me for, girl. I'll still throw you

both out on your ear if I discover you've spun me a tissue of lies.'

'I promise you I have not—though in truth I do not know who owns the ruby. Perhaps I did steal it. I cannot know for certain.'

'Damn the thing. If the owner wants it back, he can have it. You won't want for jewels as my grandson's wife—there's a strong room full of the damned things if you've a mind to wear them.'

'If there were some pearls I could wear to the ball, I should be glad to borrow them, but I have no great desire either for jewels or huge wealth. However, a beautiful home where I feel safe and might do some good is a precious thing I should value.'

His eyes glittered. 'You are either a treasure or a consummate liar. We shall just have to see whether you fall flat on your face, Miss Roxanne.'

'I still do not know why someone should attempt to break into your strong room. How could anyone know I had the ruby or that I had given it to Luke?'

'Whoever it was may have tried to enter the strong room on the chance it was there. If he followed you here in the first place, the rogue must have discovered you have the ruby. Perhaps he has only just discovered that it is in your possession?'

'Yes, perhaps.'

Roxanne was thoughtful as she left the earl's apartments. It did seem as though the intruder might have been after her ruby—if she was the rightful owner. How could she have come by it unless someone had given it to her?

Why was it so important and why could she not remember her past life? What had happened to make her forget so completely?

She tried to recall more of the game she had played with Sofia. Fragments of Sofia's story came into her mind, but she had forgotten it as the years passed and she had become a woman.

*'Who was the prince, Roxanne? What did he look like?'*

Had Sofia actually asked her that question or was it merely a part of the game?

Roxanne wished she could lift the curtain that hid her previous life, but it remained as firmly down as ever. Yet she was growing ever more certain that the ruby was part of a mystery that she must solve before she brought danger to the people she had come to care for.

'That is a remarkable jewel, my lord,' Mr Brandon remarked. 'What exactly is that you wish me to do for you?'

'My fiancée believes she was given this by her father as a child,' Luke replied. 'However, she wishes to be certain that she is the rightful owner. She has not heard from her father in years; he may be dead. We were thinking of placing an advert asking for information about the ruby and offering a small reward—say a hundred guineas.'

'You want me to place the advertisement for you so that it cannot be traced to you?'

'If you are willing, I feel that it may be for the best.

We are not sure where the jewel came from and should there be a dispute would wish to hear the claimant's story. However, an advertisement of this kind may bring unscrupulous rogues who would lie to gain something that was not theirs.'

'Your wording is vague.' Mr Brandon read the words Luke had written, *'A ruby of good colour and size. Lost five years ago. Anyone with any information concerning this jewel should apply in writing to Mr Brandon of W. R. Brandon and Associates.'*

'I kept the wording vague on purpose,' Luke agreed. 'Nothing may come of it. If we do not hear within a few weeks, I think we may assume that my fiancée's recollection is correct. We shall at least have tried and may then use or dispose of it with a clear conscience.'

'I dare say most would simply have sold it,' the lawyer said. He frowned as he looked at the jewel. 'If I were you, I should place that in the bank for safekeeping. I do not think I have ever seen such a magnificent ruby—and yet there is something about it that makes me feel it may be dangerous.'

'A ruby is simply a ruby,' Luke said and laughed. 'I shall not ask you to keep it here, sir. If no one comes forward to claim it as theirs, I may have it set as a pendant for my wife.'

'The shape of it is unusual,' Mr Brandon said. 'It could almost be a large eye…'

'It is an unusual shape,' Luke agreed and slipped it back into his breast pocket. 'I think perhaps I shall lodge it at my bank, Brandon. You will let me know if you hear anything of interest?'

'Yes, of course, sir. As for the other little matter, I shall set that in hand at once.'

'If you could bring the papers down, sir? You might like to attend the ball at Hartingdon next week.'

Mr Brandon looked pleased. A short stay at the country house of a wealthy client was a break from the routine of life in London.

'I should enjoy that very much, my lord. I am certain we can have the papers ready for your signature by the fourteenth—and I should be delighted to attend your engagement ball.'

'We shall look forward to seeing you,' Luke said and shook his hand. 'I have ordered a gift for my fiancée. My bank is near the jeweller's, so I may as well kill two birds with one stone.'

Luke left the lawyer's office and crossed the road. He was lost in thought and did not notice the man following a short distance behind as he walked the length of two streets and entered his bank, before making his way, some minutes later, to a large jeweller's establishment at the opposite side of the road.

He did notice the man who entered a few moments after him and asked to look at a tray of diamond rings, because he was young, attractive and spoke in a soft voice that sounded foreign and his skin was deeply tanned. An Indian of a high caste, perhaps, Luke thought as the man took his time examining the expensive rings, perhaps the son of a wealthy maharajah. His English was perfect and he was dressed in Western clothes, but his accent was definitely not English.

'Your pearls, sir,' the jeweller said and opened the

black velvet box to show Luke the single strand of large creamy pearls. 'I hope they are to your liking?'

'Yes, they are perfect. My bank will settle your account as usual.'

'Thank you, sir. Do you wish them wrapped?'

'No, the box will fit into my pocket,' Luke said. He noticed that the shop's other customer had agreed to purchase one of the rings as he slipped the box into his pocket and left the shop.

Outside, he hailed a hackney cab and asked the driver to take him to his club.

A few moments later, the dark-skinned gentleman came out of the shop and stood on the pavement in thought for a few minutes before turning away.

'Luke, you are back!' Roxanne cried as she saw him leave the house by way of the French windows and enter the rose garden. She moved swiftly towards him, her hands outstretched and a smile of welcome on her lips. 'Your grandfather thought you would not arrive until the day before the ball.'

'I told you I should not delay,' he replied and took her hands. 'How are you? I hope the old scoundrel has not been too grouchy?'

'Luke! You really must not.' She laughed and shook her head reproachfully. 'He has been very kind to me. I must tell you that time goes very quickly here. The curate has been giving me piano lessons. He comes twice a week in the morning—and the earl actually left his apartments so that he could listen. They are both of the opinion that I have been taught to play, but need to practise often to become proficient.'

'And do you enjoy your lessons?'

'Yes, I do,' she said. 'No, do not look so dubious. I find playing very worthwhile and relaxing. I may never be as good as your mama was, but if I play well enough for my own amusement and the enjoyment of others it will be sufficient. I tried my hand at sketching, but I do not think it will suit me. I have no talent for it, I fear.'

'You have talents enough, Roxanne. Do not be bullied into doing anything you do not wish to do.'

'No, I shall not. There is more than sufficient to keep me occupied here. I have with the earl's permission begun to plan a wild garden at the back of the house and the kitchen renovations have already started. The invitations for the ball took two days to complete, but since they went out we have been inundated with kind letters—and also some generous gifts. I have written thank-you notes, which the earl was good enough to frank for me.'

'And so he should since he insisted that we hold a ball.'

Roxanne looked up at him, caught by an inflection in his tone. He sounded annoyed, almost bitter. 'Did you not wish for a ball?'

'It makes no difference to me one way or the other—I thought it might be difficult for you, since you do not know any of our friends and relatives.'

'We have had several morning visits since the news got out,' Roxanne said. 'Just a few of the earl's neighbours. They were all very pleasant and friendly. I do not think the ball will make me uncomfortable.'

'I am relieved to hear it.'

The look on his face struck her as brooding and she felt her stomach twist with nerves. He was regretting the ball—and perhaps his impulsive suggestion that they should become engaged. Had he visited Mrs Fox in London? Was that why he seemed moody and disgruntled? If she was the woman he truly loved and could not wed, this arrangement must irk him. A sharp pain struck her to the heart, but she ignored her doubts and lifted her head to meet his gaze.

'Yet the sooner it is all over the better.'

'Is something wrong, Luke? It is not too late. If you wish to change your mind, I can leave. You could cancel the ball and tell everyone I jilted you—or was not suitable.'

'Do not be foolish. Nothing has changed. Why should it? Grandfather seems to have accepted you and I see no reason to disappoint him. If you were agreeable, I might persuade him to have the wedding sooner than later—what do you say?'

'If we are to be married, I see no reason to wait,' Roxanne replied, though she could not meet his eyes. 'I made a bargain with you, Luke—and I shall keep it to the last letter, if you wish.'

'You mean you are willing to give Grandfather an heir?' His gaze narrowed, intent and seeming to penetrate her mind, his look almost an accusation, though of what she did not know.

Roxanne's cheeks were burning, but she did not look

at him as she replied, 'Yes, I think we should not disappoint him if it is possible to oblige.'

'Supposing an heir comes along—and then the old devil dies on us? What terms will you demand of me then?'

'I have never demanded anything of you,' Roxanne replied a trifle haughtily. Her head went up, her manner proud. 'I should want to be a mother to my son, either here or somewhere else. Naturally, you would visit him, or, as he grew older, have him to stay with you wherever you wish.'

'I do not much care for this place, but my son will inherit it one day. You could continue as its mistress, Roxanne. Unless you wish for your freedom, divorce is hardly necessary. I do not believe I should wish to remarry. I think I am not the domestic type.'

'No, perhaps not,' Roxanne admitted, her throat tight. Each word he spoke was like a blow to her pride and her heart, but she managed to conceal her feelings. She held herself stiffly, speaking carefully. 'I believe you are telling me not to expect love or attention. You will continue to live in London and visit us occasionally—is that your wish?'

'Yes. I have come round to the idea you suggested, Roxanne. I do prefer you to almost any other lady I have met. You do not bore or irritate me and I think we should suit—but I want your promise that you will not weep and reproach me if I take a mistress or stay in London for months on end. I cannot give you love and you must not expect it.'

Roxanne hesitated. Could she keep such a promise? Her feelings for him had gradually become deeper since they had first met and she was very much afraid that her heart was already engaged. She ought never to have agreed to accompany him to London in the first place, or to entertain what was meant to have been a sham engagement. Somehow they had been drawn into something far deeper and for her more meaningful. It hurt to realise that for him nothing had changed. Yet Roxanne knew that she could not bear to walk away from him now. She must just bring all her arts as an actress into play and allow him to believe her feelings were not affected.

'You know my situation, Luke. Here at Hartingdon I am safe from Black Bob—and I enjoy living here. I believe I should be happy as its mistress and as the mother of your children. If you truly feel there is no need for a divorce, then we may continue the marriage after the earl dies. However, I must tell you that he seems much stronger of late. He has come downstairs for the last three evenings and says he means to walk in the gardens with me tomorrow if it is fine.'

Luke inclined his head, the tiny flicker of a pulse at his temple. 'I am glad to hear it. However, I have it from his own doctor that he could have a fatal attack at any time, so we must take care not to upset him over small things.' He hesitated for a moment, then, 'We are of one mind that there is no point in delaying the wedding—if Grandfather agrees?'

'None whatsoever,' Roxanne said, though her heart raced and for one second her knees felt weak.

'Then it is settled.' He smiled and her breath fled. 'I

see no reason why it should not be a pleasant arrangement for us both, Roxanne. I may not believe in the fairy tale of romantic love, but I know how to please in bed, and I believe we should suit well enough. Now tell me—has anything much happened since I left?'

Roxanne flinched, but managed to show no emotion. 'Yes. I shall tell you in a moment—but first, pray tell me what happened in London. Is your lawyer to place the advert?'

'We have worded something vague, but enough to arouse curiosity if someone feels they lost a similar jewel.' Luke frowned. 'You have remembered nothing?'

'I remembered that Sofia once asked me what the prince looked like. At the time it was a part of the game we played, but I have wondered if Sofia had reason to connect the ruby with India and if her game was meant to jog my memory.'

'How could she?'

'When I was ill I may have rambled in my mind, said something that made her wonder.'

'Would she not have asked you outright?'

'Sofia cared for me as if I were her own. She would have done nothing that might hurt me—and perhaps she feared what might happen if my memory did return.'

'Yes, perhaps. It seems odd she made no effort to find your family.'

'She had no money to hire agents. Besides, I had bruises on my arms and legs, and she wanted to protect me. I think if anyone had asked after me, she would have lied to keep me safe.'

'My lawyer was of the opinion that the ruby came from India. He thought it sinister and found the shape odd, which I suppose it is in a way. Had you noticed that if you turn it on its side it has the shape of an eye?'

'I cannot say I had thought of it that way, but I suppose it does—an elongated eye with pointed ends, but, yes, I can see what he means. Did you have it valued?'

'No. I placed it in the bank in London. I hope you do not mind?'

'It may be as well,' Roxanne said. She took a deep breath, 'There was an attempt to break into your grandfather's strong room when you were in London and Mr Higgins was struck over the head when he went to investigate a face at the window of the tower room.'

'Good grief!' Luke looked at her in horror. 'Was he badly hurt?'

'Fortunately not. I visited him at home afterwards and he said it was his own fault. I told him that I had seen someone at the window about halfway up the tower. Mr Higgins was not impolite enough to say so, but he thought it my imagination. The tower has since been searched and there were signs that someone had been there, but has now gone.'

'Frightened by what he had done, I dare say.' Luke frowned. 'Did the rogue manage to get inside the strong room?'

'No, I believe not,' Roxanne said. 'Do you think it was because of the ruby? It does seem a little odd that it should happen now, do you not think so?'

'The ruby?' Luke considered for a moment. 'How could anyone know you had given it to me for safekeeping? I placed it there for one night, no more. Only the three of us knew. Unless you told someone, it was impossible for them to know. Besides, there are more valuable jewels in the strong room. It is mere coincidence that it has happened now.'

'Of course you are right.' Roxanne drew a breath of relief. 'It was just that the face I saw was not English—the man had dusky skin and I thought he might be Indian, which was why I wondered if he was searching for the ruby.' It had all seemed to fit in her mind, but now she felt a little foolish. Of course her ruby was not that important.

'Did anyone ever come looking for either you or the ruby when you were with the travelling players?'

'Not to my knowledge. However, Sofia was respected and loved. If she asked the others to keep the secret, no one would have given us away while she lived.'

'So the only man who might look for you is the one you ran from that day at the Heath—might it have been he?'

'No, I do not believe it was, though he would have hit poor Mr Higgins and he might have attempted to break into a door that looked intriguing enough to hide valuables. However, I am almost certain that his was not the face at the window.'

'Then it must have been an itinerant, an opportunist who found himself a place to sleep and attempted to break open a locked door. I am sure the incident had nothing to do with you or the ruby.'

'I am glad of your good sense. I had been feeling

guilty,' Roxanne admitted. 'Now I can forget it and concentrate on other things.'

'You should certainly not let it bother you. Shall we go in and have some tea?'

Roxanne took the arm he offered and walked into the house with him. She was glad to have him back, even though there was pain mixed with the pleasure.

# *Chapter Seven*

Luke paused in the act of tying his cravat before dinner that evening. His talk with Higgins had elicited no more information than Roxanne had given him earlier—apart from one thing.

'There was a strong smell,' Higgins said. 'Just before I was hit I smelled perfume—not the kind Miss Roxanne uses, but something heavy and exotic. Nothing I've ever smelled before. I forgot when I was telling her about it, but then it came back to me. One of my men found a length of cloth in the tower and it had the same smell about it.'

'Might the cloth have been used for a turban, do you think?'

'Yes, sir. As you know, my son is an army sergeant and he sent me a tinted drawing of an Indian soldier he served with when he was in India. The cloth that was found could easily be from a turban.' Higgins seemed puzzled. 'What do you think a person like that would be doing in the tower, sir?'

Luke was thoughtful. 'I think it best we keep this to ourselves, Higgins. At the moment we cannot be sure of anything.'

'Yes, sir. I understand. The men will keep a sharp eye out for any strangers. Do you think there is something odd going on, my lord?'

'At the moment I am not certain,' Luke replied. 'It may just have been a vagrant who saw an opportunity and then panicked when you arrived. Or it may be more sinister. We shall employ more men and patrol the grounds day and night.'

'Right you are, sir. May I say how happy everyone is that you are spending more time here, sir. Mr Tonkins is a good man and I've done my best, but there are times the earl just does not want to listen.'

'He has always been stubborn, but he is frailer than I like, Higgins. Any problems regarding this business should come to me, not my grandfather.'

'You'll be staying here now then, sir?'

'At least until after the wedding. What happened may be just an isolated incident. Unfortunate for you, but over. However, if anything else happens I may have to rethink my plans.'

Now, as he tied his snowy white cravat into intricate folds, Luke was remembering the dusky-skinned gentleman who had followed him into the London jeweller's. He had noticed a rather exotic perfume that day, though of course it could all be a coincidence. Yet

Brandon had disliked the ruby, implying that there was something dangerous or sinister about it.

It could be that there was something significant about that ruby, something that made it worth sending people to England to search for it—but why now?

Luke had told Roxanne not to worry, dismissing her fears that her ruby might have brought the intruder here, but he could not help wondering if he had been too hasty. The ruby might have more worth to someone than the amount it would fetch in a jeweller's shop. Luke had not considered it important at first, but now several threads were running through his mind.

Damn the thing! He had more to concern him than the blasted ruby. Having spoken to his grandfather that afternoon about bringing the wedding forwards, Luke knew that he had committed himself to marriage. While doubts remained, he could not deny a feeling of satisfaction. It was as if he had been resisting subconsciously, but now that had fallen away and he found he was looking forward to the wedding—but first there was the engagement ball.

While in town he had given Roxanne's measurements to a French seamstress and she had promised to deliver the gown he had ordered in time. She was coming herself to fit it and make any last-minute adjustments. He knew that Roxanne had some idea of making a gown herself, but the magnificent creation he had bought for her would be a surprise—as would the pearls he had purchased in the London jeweller's.

Once again he considered whether the attack on Higgins and the man he had seen purchasing a ring in

London were connected. Had he been followed to the jeweller's that day? Had the man he'd noticed hoped to discover the ruby's whereabouts?

'Imagination,' he murmured aloud, fastened a magnificent diamond pin in his cravat and went down to dinner.

After Luke's return the days seemed to fly past so quickly that Roxanne hardly had time to think or worry about what she was doing. The incident in the tower had been dismissed from her mind completely and she was thoroughly enjoying each day.

Luke had purchased a beautiful mare for her. Rhoda, as he informed her the horse was named, was a chestnut and a perfect mount for her, being spirited and yet good natured, even playful. The mare had responded to Roxanne's touch and voice immediately and, if Roxanne did not watch her, would give her new mistress a sharp nudge in the back with her nose.

'She is lovely,' Roxanne cried as she thanked him. 'I am so grateful for your kindness.'

'You must have a horse of your own. The saddle belonged to my mother. It takes time to make one to suit an individual and we shall commission a new one once you have got used to this, which has been worn in and should be comfortable both for you and the mare.'

'It is perfect,' Roxanne said and ran her hand over the soft leather, which, though not new, had a pleasant feel. 'I do not think I need another just yet.'

'My mother was an excellent horsewoman, Roxanne.

I am certain you can do as well if you are willing to learn.'

Roxanne assured him that she was and allowed him to help her into the saddle and to explain how she should hold her reins. Although she had been used to riding astride when with the players, she immediately settled to the new position and needed telling only once how to sit and hold her reins.

Luke watched her walk the mare about the paddock, making only an occasional remark about posture or commands to the mare. After some minutes had passed, he nodded his head and walked up to her as she halted the mare.

'Are you sure you have not ridden this way before?'

'I may have done years ago…'

'When you were a child in India?'

'If I was ever there. Sometimes in my mind I seem to see a beautiful pink palace with cool rooms and fountains in the gardens—but it may just be one of Sofia's stories.'

'Are there people in your dream?'

She shook her head. 'No, I have no real memories, Luke. I think the palace was where Sofia lived with her prince.'

'You are sure she never mentioned anything you told her when you were ill?'

'No, I am not sure of anything.'

Luke's eyes were very intent. 'You have not been lying to me, Roxanne? I would rather hear the truth from your lips now than discover it is all lies later.'

'Are you accusing me of trying to deceive you?'

She raised her head proudly. 'Why should I do such a thing? I have no wish to be other than I am.'

'Forgive me, that remark was uncalled for. It is just odd that you should have this feeling about India—and now it seems as if there may be a connection. Does that not sound strange to you? In my place would you not wonder?'

'Yes, perhaps,' she agreed. 'May we speak of something else now? Your grandfather spoke of dancing lessons, but it may have slipped his memory. The curate is coming this afternoon. If he played for us, would you teach me some steps, please?'

'Yes, of course. I should be delighted. I will call the groom. You have done enough riding for today. You should learn at least one or two dances before the ball.'

'Count in your head, Roxanne…one two three, one two three—and follow me. Trust me and you cannot fail.'

'Thank you, I shall try.'

Roxanne stood as he placed his right hand at the small of her back and let herself relax, feeling the warmth that flowed through her. The curate's playing was pleasant and she felt as if she floated on air as they waltzed the length of the gallery, where the ball was to be held.

'Yes, that is exactly right,' Luke told her. 'You were born to dance, Roxanne. It is a natural talent that may be learned, but you feel the music and you are like thistledown in my arms.'

Roxanne closed her eyes. In her head she seemed

to hear strange music and for a moment she felt light-headed, as if she were not quite herself. Luke's voice came from a distance. The dreamlike state still held her and she stumbled, falling into his arms.

Luke caught her and carried her to a sofa, sitting her against the soft cushions as she stirred. She opened her eyes, looking at him in a puzzled way.

'What happened?'

'You were faint for a moment. Are you ill?'

'No, I do not think so. How foolish of me.'

Luke placed a hand to her forehead. 'You do not seem to have a temperature, but you said something just before your faint.'

'Did I?' She looked up, feeling bewildered. 'For a moment I thought I was somewhere else.'

'You said a word I did not recognise. I think it may have been another language—perhaps Hindu or some such thing.'

'How could I know an Indian word?'

'Easily, if you were truly brought up there.' He frowned. 'This business of the ruby has been playing on your mind. It might be that the face you saw at the window was Indian. A turban cloth was found at the tower when the search was made.'

Roxanne shivered. 'That is a little worrying, Luke. What is so important about the ruby that someone would follow us here and attempt to break into your grandfather's strong room?'

'If we knew that, I think the mystery might be solved.' Luke offered her his hand as she attempted to rise, catapulting her into his arms. It surprised them both and Luke's kiss was completely without intention. He kissed her lightly at first, but it deepened to intensity before he let her go. 'It was the look in your eyes,' he excused himself. 'There is no need to fear, Roxanne. I shall protect you.'

'Yes…' Roxanne spoke in a faint voice unlike herself. 'I am not afraid, just curious as to why the ruby is so important.'

'Yes, it is curious,' Luke replied. 'I think enough dancing for today. We shall send for some tea—and I think our kind pianist should stay and enjoy it with us.'

'Yes, of course, Luke,' Roxanne said and went off to speak to the curate.

Luke's eyes narrowed as he watched her. She looked every inch a lady—but supposing she had lied in an attempt to ensnare him? Supposing she'd stolen the ruby? She might be Black Bob's accomplice; they could have stolen it together. Perhaps she'd wanted the jewel for herself and run off with it. That might be the reason she was frightened of being found and dragged back to her former life. He knew a moment of intense pain at the thought. If she had played him for a fool, he would feel betrayed.

Luke was aware of a sense of unease. He knew that he was being drawn into something beyond his control. What exactly did Roxanne want of him? She had refused to enter a sham marriage at first, but now she seemed prepared to become his wife and to give him an heir.

Could he trust her? More importantly, perhaps, could he trust himself? The feelings he'd had for Roxanne from the beginning had grown stronger, but surely a night in her bed would satisfy his hunger. It had always been that the chase was more important to him and he soon tired once the game was won. Perhaps he was a shallow fellow, incapable of feeling more than a fleeting affection—if that were so, why was he beginning to feel obsessed by Roxanne and a need to know the truth about her past?

He was a fool to let down his guard. Until he was certain this was not all an elaborate plot to ensnare him he refused to feel more than liking for her. He had met many beautiful women, but none had touched his heart—why should it be different now?

Roxanne glanced at herself in the mirror as she prepared for dinner that evening. Why had Luke kissed her that way earlier? She could not convince herself that he cared for her, so why had he suddenly kissed her with such intensity? Was it merely a passing impulse—or lust?

He'd told her that he did not believe in romantic love, yet he knew how to please a woman in bed. Her mouth felt dry and her stomach cramped with nerves. Luke felt physical desire for her and he would be a passionate lover.

She supposed men often felt desire for a beautiful woman. Roxanne had seen lust in the eyes of men many times, but she had never been kissed like that because she'd always avoided any involvement. Sofia had warned her to be careful, telling her that men were not to be trusted—especially the aristocracy.

Was she a fool to let herself be used both by the earl and his grandson? They both wanted something from her, but were either of them prepared to give her anything of value in return? Luke had offered an income, but money was not important to Roxanne. She wanted to be respected, liked, even loved for what she was—especially by Luke.

How foolish she was to have let down her guard even for an instant. Luke had made it plain from the start that he did not wish for a true marriage. It was a business arrangement and she must accept it—or walk away.

To walk away would cause too much pain. She had become fond of the earl and must do nothing that would bring on his illness. Luke might come to admire her qualities in time and it should be possible to have mutual respect.

Was that enough in a marriage? It had to be, because Roxanne knew that she could not expect more from a man who refused to give his heart.

'Would you like to wear your hair up this evening, miss?'

Roxanne's thoughts were recalled to the present. She looked at the face of her young maid and smiled.

'Yes, thank you, Tilly. I shall have it dressed with a ringlet for the ball, but tonight I would prefer it to be quite plain.'

'Yes, miss.' The girl took up the brush and began to stroke it through her hair, leaving Roxanne free to continue her thoughts.

* * *

That evening they dined with friends of the earl and Roxanne began to understand what her life would be like here. Although curious, the earl's neighbours were friendly and prepared to accept her, because Hartingdon had made his wishes clear.

'This young woman has done wonders for the house already,' he remarked to a gentleman of similar years. 'I never expected to see such a day and I am truly grateful to her. Clarendon is fortunate to have found her.'

'I'm sure he knows it,' General Forster said and nodded approvingly. 'Luke, you must bring Miss Roxanne to dinner soon—and I should be delighted to take you fishing in our lake one day, should you care for it.'

'Very kind of you, sir,' Luke said and sent a brooding glance at Roxanne. She thought that he was learning to play his part very well. 'It is a while since I went fishing.'

'Do you enjoy music, Miss Roxanne?'

She turned to the young man sitting beside her. 'Yes, Sir James, very much. I fear I am an indifferent pianist, though I am attempting to improve.'

'Do you sing at all?'

'Yes, I do,' Roxanne said, recalling some of the performances she'd given when with the players. 'I enjoy listening to others play and sing. I also enjoy the performance of a play.'

'Ah yes, I'm fond of the theatre myself.' He beamed at her. 'You put me in mind of something, Miss Roxanne. I mean no insult when I say that you remind me of an actress I once saw. She was very talented, but just a provincial actress, not famous at all—however, the likeness is superficial.'

'I am glad to hear it,' Roxanne said and laughed, hiding the fact that his remark had made her heart beat fast. 'Tell me, where was she performing?'

'I hardly remember—an open-air performance, as I recall, at an inn or somewhere like. Do not be offended by the comparison, for I meant none.'

'I am not offended.' Roxanne smiled as the moment of panic receded. He did not remember her. 'If the lady was talented there is no reason.'

She had been apprehensive for a moment but she saw there was no need. Even though the young man had undoubtedly seen her performing, he did not dream that Roxanne was the actress he'd watched. He thought the likeness superficial, which indeed it was for she had changed considerably since those days. That girl had been left far behind as she became more confident and sure of her place here.

'Oh, very talented. I thought she belonged on the London stage. I would have spoken to her about it, but I could not stay until the end of the play.'

'Roxanne, may I speak with you?'

She stood up as Luke came up to her, nodding her head to her companion and moving aside to the window.

'You looked slightly disturbed. James was not annoying you?'

'He wished me not to be offended, but saw a vague likeness in me to an actress he'd once watched performing somewhere.'

'Ah, I see…' Luke nodded, his gaze intent on her face. 'You are not distressed?'

'No, certainly not.' Roxanne lifted her head proudly, every inch the great lady. 'You wished to speak with me?'

'I forgot to mention it earlier, but a seamstress is coming down in a couple of days. She has made a gown for the ball for you and will fit it and make any adjustments needed while she is here. I thought you might like her to make a wedding dress for you? We shall buy most of your trousseau in Paris after the wedding—if that suits you?'

'Of course, if you think it necessary.' Roxanne's heart thudded in her breast, her throat tight suddenly and for no good reason. 'Your grandfather looks a little tired. If there is nothing more, I shall see if he wishes to retire.'

'No, nothing more,' Luke replied with a little frown.

'Then please excuse me for the moment.'

Luke watched as she walked to the earl. The old man listened to what she said to him and then inclined his head. Roxanne gave him her arm and they left the room together. For a moment the earl's face was unguarded and his grandson saw real affection in his eyes as he responded to her caring.

It was evident that a bond had formed between them while he was absent. Luke wasn't sure how he felt about the situation. Roxanne seemed fond of the earl and sure of her place here. For a moment he was irked by the affection between them. Roxanne had found a way past the prickly outer skin the earl had used to shut out everyone else, including his grandson. Why was he prepared to accept her when he had shown little but indifference towards his own flesh and blood?

Luke ought to be delighted that his plan to make his grandfather's last days happy was working so well and yet once again he had a sense of unease—almost fear. It was ridiculous to feel trapped. He could walk away, go back to London whenever he chose, and yet something was holding him here. It was as if invisible chains bound his limbs and he did not understand his own feelings.

It was not as if the marriage was to be a true one. He felt passion for Roxanne and knew that he would find great pleasure in teaching her the delights of the bedroom—but he was not sure that she felt anything for him.

She was always welcoming, pleasant and amenable to his wishes, but was that what he wanted from her? Was this show of affection and content merely a consummate actress at work? He had made a bargain with her and Roxanne was playing her part all too well.

Luke wasn't sure what he wanted or expected of her—or what he hoped the future might bring. His uncertainty had not improved his mood and he was on edge, moody, anger simmering beneath the surface—but he did not know why he was angry.

Roxanne was surprised at how many people had come to wish them well. She had written the invitations to whole families and it seemed that uncles, aunts and cousins had turned out in force. They had been arriving for the past two days and the house was already overflowing. The arrival of neighbours and friends later that night would ensure that the ball was a success.

'That's a beautiful gown, Miss Roxanne,' the housekeeper observed when she brought up a posy of fragrant lilies the gardener had sent. 'I think you will be the centre of attention this evening—as you deserve to be, miss.'

'Thank you, Mrs Arlet,' Roxanne said. 'Lord Clarendon ordered the gown in London, as you know. He has excellent taste. Those flowers are lovely—did they come from his lordship?'

'I think it was Minty's idea, miss—though I dare say his lordship asked for flowers suitable for the occasion.'

'Well, they are delightful,' Roxanne said and the housekeeper left. She glanced at her reflection, thinking that the gown called for an ornament of some kind. Her request to the earl for the loan of some pearls had not been met and she regretted her lack. She was just considering whether she could pin a single flower to her gown when someone knocked. Opening the door, she was surprised to see Luke. 'Oh…I am nearly ready.'

'You look beautiful, Roxanne,' he said, staring at her in such a way that her heart fluttered and her mouth was suddenly dry. 'I brought you a little gift to wear this evening—if it pleases you.'

Luke offered her a black velvet box, which Roxanne took and opened. Her breath caught in her throat as she saw the single string of beautiful creamy pearls fastened with a clasp of emeralds and diamonds.

'Oh, these are beautiful. My maid has gone—would you fasten them for me, please?'

'Yes, of course.' Luke followed her into the bedchamber. Roxanne lifted her hair and he placed the pearls around her throat, his fingers lingering against the sensitive skin at her nape. 'The clasp is meant to be at the front.' He turned the necklet, his hand just brushing against her dipping décolletage for an instance.

The dizzying sensation that shot through her at that moment almost took her breath. Roxanne's lips parted on a sigh and she felt a spasm of desire and need so strong that it required all her willpower not to melt into his arms. Just for a moment she wished there was no ball, nothing but Luke and a soft bed where they could lie together.

The sensation was sweet and overpowering, but Roxanne forced herself to remain aloof. To beg for kisses and more would shame her and she had no intention of allowing her feelings to become plain. Luke wanted a business arrangement and that was what she must accept because anything else would end in pain. The last thing Luke wanted or needed was a clinging wife who would love him and make him feel guilty for neglecting her when he returned to the life he enjoyed.

She would be a poor actress if she could not hide her feelings for him, but she must remain outwardly in control. He would hate her to fall in love with him. He had no wish for a clinging wife.

Glancing in the mirror, Roxanne was satisfied that apart from a faint flush in her cheeks she had given no sign of the intensity of her feelings. She touched the emerald clasp and smiled.

'How did you know that I longed for such a necklace?' she asked, for all the world without a care as she met his brooding look. 'The pearls are wonderful, Luke, and the clasp goes so well with my ring.'

'That was my intention,' he said, a faint smile in his eyes. 'Grandfather asked me to find something for you in the strong room, but I told him I had my own gift for you.'

'I see.' Roxanne nodded, because that explained why the earl had not kept his promise. 'I must thank you so much for my gifts, Luke.' She looked up at him, seeing a blaze of passion that made her tremble. 'Luke—what are you thinking?'

'I think we should go down before I am tempted to lock the door and stay here with you instead of entertaining our guests.'

Roxanne's heart pounded. Her stomach clenched with something she instinctively recognised as desire. The look in his eyes was so hot that she could not doubt he felt desire for her, but she was certain that his feelings were no more than that; he wanted her, but love was not something Luke was prepared to give. His touch would make her flesh sing, but love was the forbidden fruit she must not taste.

'Yes, we must not keep our guests waiting or the earl,' Roxanne said, painting a smile in place as she lifted her head. 'Our audience awaits, Luke.'

'A performance? Is that all this is to you, Roxanne?'

'Of course. What else?' she said. 'That is what you required of me, as I recall.'

She moved past him into the hall, then turned and waited expectantly. Her composure was perfect, she was ready for the stage.

'You're a clever actress, Roxanne. I dare say you will have our friends eating out of your hand, just as you have Grandfather. He prides himself on his judgement, but you have him purring like a kitten.'

She felt as if he had pricked at her with long thorns, but kept her smile in place. 'If I have the ability to make people like me, that is a good thing, is it not?'

'I think they will love you. Grandfather certainly does.'

*Loved by all, but not by you.* The words were in her head, but not spoken aloud.

Lifting her head, she looked into his eyes. 'His happiness is your main concern, is it not? That is the reason you brought me here?'

'Yes…' Luke's gaze narrowed. 'I would not wish to see him hurt, Roxanne.'

'Then we are of one mind,' she said and took his arm. 'Come, Luke, need you look so sober? This is meant to be an evening of pleasure for us as well as our guests. You must try to look as if you are enjoying yourself or your friends will wonder.'

'You are right.' He smiled suddenly and her heart skipped a beat. 'I have no right to expect more than you wish to give. We shall dance and enjoy ourselves this evening. More serious matters can wait for another day.'

Now what did he mean by that? Roxanne wondered,

but she put the little puzzle from her mind. Tonight she was playing the part of a girl very much in love who was announcing her engagement to the man she loved. It was not a difficult part to play, as long as she did not remember that Luke did not love her.

# *Chapter Eight*

As Roxanne had imagined, the evening was a huge success. The ballroom was decorated with banks of fragrant flowers from the hothouses and reels of white-silk tulle hung in drapes above the dais where the musicians were seated. Sparkling chandeliers threw out showers of light, which were picked up by the glittering jewels worn by both ladies and gentlemen. They had come dressed in their best finery, prepared to enjoy the celebrations, and laughter reverberated through the rooms, the sound of chattering voices almost deafening.

Roxanne soon discovered that she was the centre of attention.

'To tell the truth I never expected to see this day,' Luke's Uncle Frederick on his father's side told her as he claimed one of the first dances of the evening. 'I believe Hartingdon had given up all hope of Clarendon ever doing his duty.'

'Surely not?' Roxanne gave him an amused smile. 'Luke is not in his dotage, I think?'

'Good lord, no, he's a young man, but he seemed set in his ways. I always knew it would take an exceptional young woman to catch my nephew and it seems I was right.'

'Thank you for the compliment,' Roxanne replied mischievously. 'I shall do my best to live up to what is expected of me.'

'You'll do very well,' the talkative gentleman said. 'Beauty and brains, to say nothing of charm. Now that is a combination not often found, Miss Roxanne. Luke is a lucky fellow.'

Since that seemed the consensus of the guests, Roxanne did not find herself left without an admirer at her side all evening. She danced every dance, sipped at, but did not finish, several glasses of champagne brought to her by a string of helpful gentlemen and ate sparingly of the delicious supper that had been provided for them.

'Where did you meet Clarendon?'

The question had been asked again and again by curious aunts and cousins throughout the evening. Roxanne gave the same reply to all of them.

'I was staying with a friend and we met by chance when Luke was out riding,' she told them, embroidering the truth only as necessary. 'We were mutually attracted and liked each other immediately.'

Surely that much was true. Roxanne *had* felt an instant liking for the man she'd helped in the woods, despite his hostility. He'd been angry and in pain at first, but later he'd been grateful for her help. That meeting seemed so far away now, her life revolving round the earl and his grandson these days. Sometimes she almost forgot that she had ever known another life.

The Roxanne who had lived with a band of travelling players was someone different. *She* was Miss Peters and her father lived and worked in India… The story she'd invented for herself was now so real that she believed it must be the truth.

As far as she understood, Luke's lawyer had heard nothing from the advertisement. Roxanne might never discover whether the ruby was truly hers or the property of another person. Perhaps it was not important. She had become a part of Luke's family, welcomed and accepted amongst them. It did not matter that she could not remember her own family—at least she must try not to let it matter.

She had danced three times with Luke during the evening. Each time it had been a waltz and Roxanne felt as if she had been floating on air, his nearness giving her such pleasure that she felt she could melt into his body. The feeling was so perfect that she knew she could become his lover easily. There would be no hesitation on her part, because already she felt as if she belonged to him, in his bed, in his arms. He had called her a clever actress, but he gave such a convincing display of affection towards his fiancée that Roxanne might have been deceived herself had she not caught a hint of mockery in his smile once or twice. It was as if he were showing her that he, too, could play his part.

What was in his mind? What did that look mean?

Sometimes she thought he was like a cat playing with a bird it had caught in its claws.

'Have you enjoyed this evening?' Luke whispered as the hour grew late. 'I believe you have charmed all my uncles and my cousins have fallen in love with you. Cousin Horatio is quite eaten up with jealousy, though I am not certain whether he envies me you—or my grandfather's estate, of which he had hopes before you arrived.'

'Luke…' Roxanne tapped his arm with her fan '…that was not well said of you. Mr Harte was charming to me and told me how pleased he was that you'd decided to marry.'

'Horatio is charming when he wishes to be, Roxanne, but do not be fooled by him. I dare say he is spitting venom in private.'

Roxanne shook her head at him. She had noticed a certain underlying tension between the cousins, but there was often rivalry between gentlemen and she took little notice. Cousin Horatio was one of those staying overnight and she noticed that he was absent for a while towards the end of the ball, reappearing just as the guests that lived locally were leaving.

The earl had gone to his apartments soon after supper, and when there were only a handful of gentlemen left, all of them related and preparing for a last nightcap before seeking their rooms, Roxanne said her farewells.

She went upstairs to her own bedchamber and entered. She'd instructed her maid that she was not to wait up, because she could manage to unhook herself and would not need assistance. However, when she opened the door and walked in a feeling of shock ran through her. It was immediately obvious that the room had been searched.

The drawers had been pulled out of the chest and the contents scattered on the floor, her underclothes, scarves and gloves scattered in little heaps. The armoire had been opened and dresses pulled from the shelves, as if whoever had been searching had been in a hurry. Yet there was more, a kind of venom, almost as if the mess had been intended to punish and hurt.

Since the only things she had of personal value were her ring and the pearls Luke had given her, which she was wearing, there was nothing much for a thief to steal. The silver pots on the dressing table, which were the earl's property, were still there, though lids had been removed and the contents examined.

Who had been here and caused such upheaval? It did not seem to Roxanne that anything had been taken, but it was obvious that someone had been searching for something in particular. Who would dare to do such a thing when the house was full of guests?

Roxanne trembled, a slither of ice sliding down her spine. It was a most unpleasant feeling to discover that her room had been ransacked in this way. What had the intruder been looking for—was it the ruby?

She hesitated for a moment, wondering what to do for the best. It was too unsettling to sleep in her room like this, but she was unwilling to rouse the servants at this late hour.

Luke ought to be told. Roxanne knew that she must speak to him at once about what had happened here. There might still be an intruder in the house. He would know what to do, because the house ought to be checked. If an outsider had broken in while they were all at the ball, he might be dangerous. Perhaps other guests had had their rooms searched.

Still fully dressed, Roxanne made her way through the halls and up a short flight of stairs to the wing where Luke had his rooms. Would he have come up yet or was he still downstairs, taking a last drink with his cousins?

She tapped at his door and after a short pause, during which Roxanne wondered what to do if he were not there, Luke opened his door. He was still dressed in his breeches and shirt, but he'd taken off his coat and neckcloth and his feet were bare.

'Roxanne—what are you doing here at this hour?'

'May I speak to you, please?'

'Of course, come in,' Luke said, then took her arm and drew her inside his sitting room. It was furnished with two leather elbow chairs, a bookcase and a writing table and chair; there was also a collection of paintings of horses, also two bronze figures holding torches aloft, which held lighted candles.

'I am sorry to disturb you, but I did not know what else to do—my rooms have been ransacked.'

'What?' Luke looked startled. 'Your rooms—was anything valuable taken?'

'I was wearing the only items of jewellery I possess,

but the silver pots on the dressing table are all there and they have been opened.'

'Someone was searching for something they did not find.' Luke's brow creased. 'Do you suppose it was the ruby?'

'Yes, perhaps it was,' Roxanne said. 'Whoever it was must have taken the opportunity to search while we were all dancing. I suppose there were so many people about that he was able to slip in without being noticed.'

'Yes, I imagine it must have seemed a good opportunity.' His gaze narrowed. 'You saw no one—you are not harmed?'

'I saw no one and I am not harmed—but I felt uneasy and wondered whether to call my maid to tidy the room or sleep elsewhere this evening.'

'You must stay here for now,' Luke said. 'I shall put on my boots and check your rooms and the downstairs rooms also, Roxanne. I want to make sure the windows and doors are locked, though I prefer not to rouse the guests or Grandfather. I do not wish to disturb him.'

'No, of course you must not,' Roxanne agreed. 'I was not certain what to do, but I hope no one else need know about this unfortunate incident.'

'Mrs Arlet must be told and the servants will know, but it is best if the guests do not learn of this—unless any of them have suffered something similar.'

'Had they done so, I'm sure someone would have told you,' Roxanne said. 'I think it was just my room, Luke—and I believe it must be because of that ruby.'

Luke had sat down to pull his boots on. He looked at her thoughtfully for a moment, then inclined his head.

'It seems the most likely explanation. Unless Horatio wanted to see what he could find to discredit you. He knows what he has lost because we are to wed and he was absent for a time this evening.' He saw her look. 'You don't believe it was him. Well, you may be right. Stay here, Roxanne, and lock the door behind me. I shall take a look at your room and make a tour of the house. When I return we'll talk about this again.'

'Yes, of course. Please take care, Luke. I would not have you come to harm for the sake of that wretched jewel.'

'I shall be perfectly safe. Whoever wants that ruby seems not to mean harm to either of us. There has been plenty of time for him to attack me had he wished it. No, it is the jewel he wants for some reason best known to himself.'

Roxanne went to the door with him and he locked it after he went out. She chose one of the elbow chairs and sat down, but could not rest. As she paced about the room, the minutes dragged by and, when Luke did not return after more than half an hour, Roxanne went into his bedchamber. Luke was not particularly tidy and she noticed discarded neckcloths and a dressing gown lying abandoned over a chair. She sat on the edge of the bed, then laid down, resting her head on a pillow that smelled faintly of the cologne he sometimes wore. Lying with her knees pulled up to her chest, she closed her eyes.

* * *

Movement close by woke Roxanne and she opened her eyes and then sat up as she saw Luke standing there looking at her.

'Is all safe?' she asked, her heart pounding.

'I discovered a window catch in the library that was loose and I believe that may have been how our intruder got in. There was a smear of earth on the window-sill and what may have been a footmark. I think our intruder was bare-footed.'

'He wore no shoes?' Roxanne frowned. 'I remember that Sofia told me shoes are not worn in the house in India. The face at the window in the tower might have been Indian—it all seems to point to the ruby, do you not think so?'

'Yes, it would seem the jewel is important to someone,' Luke agreed. 'I wish whoever it is would just ask for the damned thing. My concern is for your sake, Roxanne. If he becomes frustrated, he may attack you…'

Roxanne got to her feet. She shivered, feeling chilled and uneasy.

'I'm sorry to have caused you so much trouble. I wish I could remember what happened…why I had the ruby…' A tear spilled from the corner of her eye. 'Who am I, Luke? Am I a thief? Why did I have that ruby? I wish I could remember.'

'Don't cry, dearest,' Luke said softly. He reached out and wiped away the tear with his fingertips. 'You mustn't be upset over this. I'm here. I shall protect you, Roxanne.'

'But why is all this hap—' She got no further for Luke's arms were about her. He drew her close to his body, his head bent towards hers, his mouth covering hers in a kiss so hungry and intense that all else fled from her mind. Roxanne's arms folded about his neck, her fingers reaching into his hair at the nape as the kiss deepened between them. Then Luke was lifting her in his arms, carrying her back to the bed. He placed her amongst the covers and lay down beside her, gazing into her eyes.

'I want you so much,' he whispered passionately against her ear. 'I've wanted you from the moment I first saw you, Roxanne. You are so beautiful and you're mine. I swear that no one shall harm you. I will protect you with my life. You must never be afraid while I am with you.'

'Luke…' she whispered hoarsely. 'Luke, hold me, love me. I want you, too. I love you…'

As soon as the words left her lips Roxanne regretted them. She had not meant to say the one thing she knew he would not want to hear, but her feelings had rushed to the forefront because of her distress and the words had slipped out. She thought that for a moment he stilled, as if he would withdraw from her, but then he was kissing her again, hungrily, passionately, as if his need was as great as her own.

Giving herself up to desire, Roxanne responded to Luke's loving with an equal passion of her own. She had never known that such feelings lay within her, waiting to burst forth in a torrent of need and hunger. All the years of not knowing who or what she was, all the pain, uncertainty and fear, the need to be loved came out of her in a frenzy of wanting and loving. His hands were gentle but firm as they explored her body, seeking out the secret places of her femininity, touching her where no one else had touched her, bringing her sweet pleasure. Her hands moved over his arms, his back, following the firmness of his shoulders and the honed muscles, moving over skin that was now naked and slicked with sweat as their bodies came together in sweet ecstasy. His throbbing manhood sought entry and she felt pain, but then the pain was forgotten in the sweet pleasure of his kisses.

'Yes…' Roxanne moaned as he moved within her, deep and firm, bringing her to such exquisite delight that she writhed and arched beneath him. She moaned and clung to him, her breath soft and sweet as she sighed. 'So good…so very good.'

'My sweet, beautiful Roxanne,' Luke murmured against her ear. 'Such passion and heat. No one has ever made me feel as you do, my darling. You are exquisite, perfect. I want to hold you and make love to you always.'

His words were so tender and loving that Roxanne felt tears of joy on her cheeks as they lay together, entwined, satiated and at peace before they slept. During the night, they woke, loved again, as sweetly and as urgently as before. Roxanne slept deeply, curled into his body, her legs captured and held as he clasped her against him. Her long red hair was spread over the pillows and had entangled itself about him as they loved.

* * *

When in the morning Luke moved her hair from his face, carefully disentangling himself from her limbs that curled about him, Roxanne did not wake. She was caught up in a dream so sweet that her lips curved in a smile of content.

'Love you,' she murmured. 'Always love you...'

Luke knew that she was still sleeping and that she did not know she had spoken. He frowned as he moved carefully about the room, collecting the clothes he needed for riding. He watched Roxanne sleep while he dressed, a look of gravity on his face, then went out, leaving her to rest.

He needed to ride and to think about the future. Roxanne's distress the previous evening had led him into something he had not planned and he was not sure what it meant for the future. In her dreaming state she had spoken of love, but was it real or part of the story she'd invented for herself—and did he want his marriage to be more of a real marriage than he'd intended?

He suddenly felt trapped again. He was being drawn into something that threatened to overturn all he had believed and he could not handle the feelings churning inside him.

He must think about what had happened the previous night and what it meant—and he must question the men he'd had patrolling the grounds. Why had they not seen the intruder and who had been so desperate to find Roxanne's ruby that they had risked breaking into her room when there was a house filled with guests?

* * *

Roxanne stirred and stretched, a feeling of well being stealing over her as she opened her eyes. What had happened the previous night to make her feel so good? Letting her gaze move about the room, she realised that she was not in her own bed and then the memories came flooding back. Suffused with warmth, she felt herself blush as she recalled how gladly she had surrendered to Luke's loving the previous night. She had gone to his arms like a wanton instead of the gentlewoman she was supposed to be, giving no thought to propriety or the future.

What did that say about her? What kind of a woman was she truly?

Sitting up in bed, she saw her clothes strewn over the floor and recalled the way they had come off with such abandon. Indeed, she'd behaved like a harlot. No well-bred young woman would behave in such a way—and yet she did not regret it. Roxanne knew that she would do it again, because one night of love like that was something she would never forget. Even if Luke did not love her in his heart, he'd made her feel loved and needed, and something deep inside her had responded, had been waiting for him. She'd felt as if her whole life had been waiting for that moment—the moment she became one with him.

Rising, Roxanne picked up her clothes and dressed. It was time she returned to her own room. She was about to do so when the door of Luke's bedchamber opened and a maid entered. She did not seem surprised to find Roxanne there and bobbed a curtsy.

'Lord Clarendon said to tidy your chamber, Miss Roxanne, and then inform you that you could return. He told us he gave up his room for you last night because of what happened, miss. It must have been such a shock to find it that way.'

'Yes, it was,' Roxanne replied and glanced towards the bed. The sheets were open, as she'd left them, and she could see some small bloodstains. Her cheeks felt warm as she left the room. Luke had told the servants that she'd slept alone, but the maid would see the evidence of what had taken place here and she could hardly be expected to keep such knowledge to herself. The servants would smile to themselves and whisper that Lord Clarendon had anticipated his wedding night.

It was an embarrassing thought, but there was nothing she could do to change things. She could not go back and act differently, nor did she wish to in her heart. The dice was cast now. She had given herself to Luke body and soul. Roxanne had no intention of drawing back. If Luke did not wish for a loving wife, he would make his feelings known. She loved him, but she was strong enough to let him go when he needed to be free. She would not cling and weep as his mother had to her husband. Perhaps next time Luke came to her bed she would be more prepared and be able to control her feelings, giving herself with less abandon.

Making her way back to her own room, Roxanne wondered where Luke was. At what time had he left her and where had he gone?

Her bedchamber had been put to rights, everything back in its place and the scent of fresh lavender polish making it seem welcoming and normal. A frown touched her forehead as she remembered her distress the previous evening; it was that distress that had prompted Luke to kiss her and carried them both on a tide of passion.

What must he be thinking of her now? Roxanne knew that she had been abandoned, almost wanton in her passion, and wondered what Luke thought of the bargain he'd made. Was he regretting it? Was that why he'd left without waking her, because her passion had disgusted him—or did he simply want to ride in the early morning, as she knew he often did?

Roxanne washed in the warm water she found waiting for her and dressed in a fresh morning gown. She had brushed her hair into a knot at the back of her head and was about to leave when the door opened and her maid entered.

'I did not ring, Tilly,' she said. 'I was able to manage for myself—but if you will take away my soiled things and see to them, please.'

'Yes, Miss Roxanne.' The girl bobbed a little curtsy. 'I've washed all the things that were on the floor, miss, because I knew you would wish it. I came to tell you that you're needed in the earl's chambers. Marshall said to tell you that Lord Hartingdon is a little out of sorts this morning. It may have been all the excitement of last night, miss.'

'Yes, perhaps.' Roxanne looked at her in dismay. 'Is he just a little tired or unwell?'

'I'm not sure, miss. Marshall said to ask if you would come at once—and I think the doctor's been sent for.'

'I see…thank you,' Roxanne said and went hurriedly from the room. If the doctor had been sent for, it was more than just a little tiredness.

Her heart was thudding as she walked along the hall to the earl's chambers. She had become more than a little fond of the elderly gentleman and it would distress her if he were seriously ill. Luke had known that his grandfather was frail; it was for this reason that she had been brought here as Luke's fiancée, but somehow she hadn't expected anything to happen. Indeed, she'd hoped, expected that Hartingdon would go on for some years yet. If he died now…Roxanne shut out the unwelcome thought. She did not wish to think about such a prospect.

Reaching the earl's room, she knocked softly and then entered. His manservant was in the small sitting room, but there was no sign of the earl.

'How is he?' she asked, her throat catching with emotion. 'I was told he wished to see me?'

'His lordship had a bit of a do first thing, miss,' Marshall said. 'I've persuaded him he should stay in bed and called the doctor just in case. His lordship wanted to see you, miss. He's very fond of you—if you don't mind my saying it.'

'Not at all.' Roxanne smiled at him. 'The feeling is mutual. I was most concerned to hear he was unwell. May I see him, please?'

'Go right in, miss. He might be dozing, but if you sit in the chair I've put ready he'll see you when he wakes.'

'Yes, of course. Thank you, that was so thoughtful, Marshall.'

'We're all pleased to have you here, miss. The family and servants both. We've taken you to our hearts, Miss Roxanne.'

She thanked him, her cheeks a little warm. Marshall would never show by gesture or innuendo that he knew she'd spent the night with Luke, but she doubted it was a secret. If her first child was not long in coming, the servants would count the months after the wedding back to the previous night.

The earl was resting as she walked softly into his bedchamber. He was lying back against a pile of pillows, his eyes closed, but as she bent over him to kiss his cheek he opened them and looked up at her.

'Ah,' he said in a satisfied tone. 'There you are, girl. You did me proud last night, Roxanne. I was complimented on Luke's happy choice many times. Most of them seem to think I must've arranged the whole business. I didn't contradict 'em. You're either a truly great actress or you were born to be a lady.'

'Does it matter now, sir?' Roxanne asked. She sat down on the edge of the bed and took his hand. 'It was a tiring evening for you. I hope you mean to be sensible and keep to your bed for a few days?'

'You're right, it don't matter where you came from,' he said and sighed. 'You'll make a good mother for my boy's children and that's what counts. I'm not sure he'll make you a good husband, but you took him on and I think you'll see it through. You won't let me down?'

'Do I look like a bolter?'

He gave a harsh laugh. 'It's a while since I heard that expression. Luke's godmother used it when she was younger. She didn't come to the ball. I was disappointed that she stayed away. Her influence on Luke was always for the good—but I suppose I scared her off with my harsh tongue. I must make it up to her before the wedding. I've mellowed a bit. In the old days I was sharper than a razor.'

'I'm glad you've mellowed, sir.'

There was a hint of laughter in her voice and his brow lowered. 'Are you mocking me, miss?'

'Just a very little, sir. Do you not think it is time that someone did? Perhaps you have taken yourself a little too seriously at times—would you not say so?'

He glared at her, then made a sound between a snort and a guffaw. 'You're a minx, Roxanne. Think you've got me eating out of your hand, do you? I'm not to be fooled by a few smiles, miss.'

'Why would I wish to fool you, sir? All I wish for is that we should live together happily as a family. I want to make you happy.'

'Want to make Luke happy too?' He raised his bushy brows at her. 'Planning on getting him to settle down to married life—is that it?'

'I am not sure that would be possible,' Roxanne replied honestly. 'However, it seems to me that you are very alike, sir. If what you both want is an heir for the family, I shall do my best to oblige.'

'And what do you get out of it?' The earl's eyes were very bright. He was intent as he waited for her answer.

'A home and perhaps affection,' Roxanne said. 'I shall make no demands on you or your grandson, sir—but if things go well I shall have children and perhaps they will give the unconditional love both you and Luke seem incapable of giving.'

'Will that satisfy you, girl?'

'I think it may have to,' Roxanne replied. She saw his eyelids flicker and moved to the chair beside the bed. 'You should try to rest for a little before the doctor comes, sir.'

'You're a fine girl, a decent girl,' the earl said. 'I'm not sure we've been fair to you. This is a selfish family, Roxanne. I think you deserve better.'

He closed his eyes and she saw that he was drifting into sleep. It had been a huge effort for him to attend the ball and he was very tired. She hoped that he was not actually any worse than before. Perhaps all he needed was a little rest.

Luke was greeted by the news that the doctor had been called when he returned from riding. He threw his crop and gloves on the sideboard in the hall and took the stairs two at a time. When he entered his grandfather's sitting room, Marshall was just tidying the grate with a small brush. He put a finger to his lips.

'He's sleeping at the moment, sir. Miss Roxanne has been with him for the past two hours. The doctor came and said he was exhausted. He's not to be upset and he must rest for at least a couple of weeks. Miss Roxanne was reading to him just now, but I think he may have gone off again for a while, because she stopped. Now she's started again. She has a fine reading voice, sir. Your grandfather was chuckling away for a while there.

Reading Shakespeare she was, but in a way I've not heard before.'

'Thank you.' Luke said. 'Perhaps you have something you need to do elsewhere? I shall sit with my grandfather for a little now.'

'Yes, sir. I'll fetch up some brandy and warm water. It helps his lodship to sleep sometimes and the doctor said anything that made him rest was good.'

'Yes, you do that,' Luke said. He walked to the door of his grandfather's bedchamber and then listened. Roxanne was reading *The Taming of the Shrew* and acting out the parts. He heard his grandfather chuckle and hesitated, hardly liking to intrude on what was clearly an enjoyable companionship.

'You are a wicked minx, as I said before,' the earl said and laughed. 'I think you have missed your calling, Roxanne. You are wasted here. You should be on the London stage.'

'I would much prefer to be here with you and Luke.'

'I think you mean that,' the earl said. 'It isn't just an act with you, is it, Roxanne?'

'No, sir. I am very fond of you and…'

Luke walked in before she could finish. Roxanne was standing at the foot of the bed, a book of Shakespeare's plays in her hand. She was smiling, but when she saw him, her cheeks turned pink and she glanced away from his searching gaze.

'How are you, sir?' Luke asked and went to his grandfather's side. 'I hear the doctor has been to visit you. I think you found the ball too much, sir. Perhaps we should postpone the wedding for a month or two?'

'You will do no such thing on my account,' the earl said. 'It will take place as planned in three weeks from now or I'll want to know the reason why.'

'Please do not distress yourself, sir,' Luke said quickly. 'I was merely concerned for your health.'

'My health is neither here nor there. I did not summon the family here for you to change your mind the next day, Clarendon.'

'Please do not get upset, sir,' Roxanne said and bent to touch his cheek. 'I shall leave you with your grandson—Luke, you should not tire him. The doctor told me it is important that your grandfather rests as much as possible.'

'Of course.' Luke inclined his head stiffly. 'I shall speak to you later, Roxanne.'

'Of course, Luke. Whenever you wish.'

'You'll come to visit me again later, girl?'

Roxanne looked at the earl and smiled. 'Of course. You must have a sleep when Luke leaves you, but I shall come back before dinner.'

Roxanne was sitting in the back parlour she favoured when Luke entered later that day. He frowned to find her alone and asked why she was not in the drawing room with their guests.

'I wanted a period of quiet reflection,' she said and stood up. 'I shall join your Aunt Jane and Uncle Frederick for tea. Most of the others left an hour or so ago. Your Cousin Horatio asked for you, but I was forced to say that I did not know where you were, since I was told you were not with Grandfather.'

'The earl asked to be left alone. He seems weaker than before. I fear that he may not live much longer. The doctor told me that if he takes a turn for the worse it could be his last illness.'

'I know he seems very tired, but the ball took a great deal of his energy. I pray that he will recover. He so longs for an heir. It would be wonderful if he could at least know that a child was on the way.'

'After last night that may already be the case.' Luke frowned, turning to gaze out of the window. 'I should apologise for what happened, Roxanne. I did not behave, as a gentleman ought. If I could change things, I would, but unfortunately we cannot turn back the clock.'

His words stung like the lash of a whip. If the previous night had been as wonderful for Luke as it had for her, he would not need to apologise.

'I think no harm was done since we intended to marry as soon as the banns are called,' she said. 'It need only be a small affair. I see no reason why Grandfather should be forced to attend. He will be satisfied if all is done as it should be.'

'You seem to be on excellent terms. I must bow to your superior judgement in this matter.'

She glanced at him. His lips were white and set in a thin line.

'Are you angry with me for caring about his welfare?' Roxanne asked in a carefully flat tone. His manner was so rigid, his anger barely under control. 'The earl requested that I call him Grandfather. If it annoys you, I can be more formal.'

'Why should you? He clearly likes it and you.' Luke frowned as he turned to look at her. 'Forgive me. I was anxious and when I'm anxious I become angry. I had no right to interfere.'

'You have every right. I have not forgotten the reason you brought me here, Luke—but I find that my affections are engaged. Grandfather has been generous to me with his own affection and I genuinely wish to make him happy. I hope he will rally again, but I know that he could take a turn for the worse.'

'If he should die, you would not need to keep your bargain.'

'Should I not? That would be your decision, naturally.' Roxanne got to her feet. 'Excuse me, I should go and take tea with your family. If you wish to disappoint everyone, you must take the necessary steps, Luke. I gave my word to the earl and I shall not break it. However, I shall not hold you to a bargain you dislike so much. Please inform me of your wishes when you are ready. Now, if you will excuse me.'

She walked out of the room with her head high. Luke cursed himself for a fool. She had been on the verge of tears, but hiding it as best she could. He had hurt her and it was the last thing he wanted to do and yet he was hurting too, so badly that he was striking out blindly. He was so confused at this moment that he did not know what he wanted.

Waking to find Roxanne sleeping so sweetly in his bed had thrown his senses into disorder. She was beautiful, generous and passionate—what more could any man want in a wife? He knew that he had discovered a treasure beyond price and it frightened him. How could he ever deserve such a woman?

One day he would break her heart and she would leave him—she might be killed in an accident because he'd broken her heart. To know that he was guilty of bringing her to such misery would destroy him. If he loved her, he would lose her. Far better not to love than to love too much.

# *Chapter Nine*

Roxanne saw the last of the guests leave and then went upstairs. She knocked at the earl's door and was invited to enter by his manservant.

'How is he now, Marshall?'

'Not so clever, miss. I was just about to send for you to ask what you thought. He doesn't want a fuss, but I wondered if we should have the doctor again?'

'I think he would prefer just to rest. There is very little the doctor can do for his condition, you know. I'll sit with him for a while now. He seems easier when I'm with him, I think.'

'Yes, he does, Miss Roxanne. I've not seen him take to anyone as he has to you, miss, not for years. He's laughed more these past few weeks than he has since his wife died. He became almost a recluse after his daughter died young. If it had not been for Master Luke he might have given up altogether. Yet he found it hard to show his feelings—just as Master Luke does. I know the earl better than most and I can tell you that his heart has been broken more than once.'

'I dare say he missed both his wife and his daughter a great deal.'

'Not that he let on. He just became more buttoned up, if you'll excuse the phrase—but I think you're right, miss. Shut himself off, he did, but he's come back to us since you arrived. I don't know what he'd do without you now, miss.'

'Yes, I think he is happier than when I first came,' Roxanne said and went into the bedchamber. The earl was lying with his eyes shut, but when she sat down close to his side, he opened them and looked at her.

'You've come, then,' he said. 'I hoped you might when they'd all gone. Has that grandson of mine gone too?'

'No, I do not think he plans to leave us just yet,' Roxanne said. 'He cares for you more than you might think, sir.'

'He never showed it before you came. Mind you, I haven't exactly been loving towards him. I was grieving and so was he. We lost touch and when a breach opens up it's hard to cross it. We're both too damned proud for our own good and that's the truth. We can't say sorry—and neither of us knows how to love.'

'I would not say that, sir. Perhaps you find it hard to show your love. I imagine it must be difficult, particularly for two very prickly and stubborn gentlemen.'

'You've worked us out, haven't you?' The earl nodded as she merely smiled. 'I underestimated you when you first came. I wonder if Luke has too. He doesn't wear his heart on his sleeve, girl. I was just the same as a young man. It took my Emily to make me realise what love should be and when she died she took my heart with her.'

'Yet you do love Luke and he loves you. Do you not think you should tell him before it is too late?'

'Perhaps you're right,' he agreed. 'I've held back all my life—afraid of making a fool of myself or being hurt again, I suppose.'

'It is hard for everyone to trust once they've been hurt. Now, would you like me to read to you for a while or would you prefer to sleep?'

'I've all night for sleeping. Tell me about yourself, Roxanne. Tell me about Sofia—and the life you led with her and the travelling players. I knew a young woman by that name once. She was very beautiful, but she never looked at me. Who knows, had she given me encouragement everything might have been different.'

'While Sofia lived I was happy with her,' Roxanne said. 'She was like a mother to me and she took away the dark emptiness inside me. I wish I might tell you who I am, sir, but apart from a vague feeling about India, which may be merely a game we once played, I remember nothing.'

'I can tell you that you're a lady born,' Hartingdon said. 'I've watched to see if you would let the act slip and you never have. If it were an act, Roxanne, you would make a mistake. No, you're a lady—and you love my grandson, whether he deserves it or not.'

'Yes,' Roxanne said softly. 'I do, but please do not tell him that for he may not wish to hear it. Sofia was a lady, too, though she did not care for society. She found the social drawing rooms shallow and too insipid. For her drama and life lived to the full was more exciting than a life of domestic cares. She led an exciting life, but in the end I think she regretted that she had not known a true and lasting love.'

'And you—are you like her, Roxanne?'

'No, I do not think so. I believe I should enjoy a life in the country, devoted to family and friends and the service of others. I do not wish to be a courtesan and have princes fight over me, as she did.'

'You're like my Emily,' he said and closed his eyes. 'Tell me some more…about your acting and…' His voice trailed away and she knew he was sleeping.

Roxanne sat quietly by his side. He woke after a little while and smiled at her, then drifted off to sleep again, reassured that she was there. She held his hand for a while and gave him a drink when he asked.

It was almost midnight when the door of his bedchamber opened and Luke entered, wearing a long silk striped robe, his feet bare.

'Are you still here?' he said softly. 'You should go to bed now, Roxanne. I shall sit with Grandfather for a while.'

'I will return in a few hours,' Roxanne said. 'I do not want him to be left alone, Luke. It is important that he feels loved and wanted, because then he will have the strength to go on.'

'You really do care for him, don't you?'

Roxanne inclined her head. She wanted to tell him

that the earl was not the only one she cared for, but the words remained unspoken. She'd said too much the previous night and Luke's anger had shown that he did not wish for her love. He had offered her a business arrangement, not a loving relationship. Unless she wished to end it, she must let him think that her emotions were not truly involved. Luke had been deeply scarred; he was afraid of loving, afraid of commitment.

'Yes, I have become very fond of him,' she said. 'I shall sleep because I must, but call me if you need me.'

'Yes, of course. If he wakes and asks, I shall send for you, Roxanne. Goodnight, sleep well.'

Roxanne made no reply as she walked from the room. Her thoughts were with the earl, but as she opened the door of her bedchamber, for a moment she was apprehensive as she recalled the events of the previous night. However, her room was just as it ought to be.

She refrained from summoning a maid and managed to unfasten her gown without help. In bed she lay for a moment, her eyes stinging with tears she would not allow herself to shed. It was her fault for allowing herself to fall in love. Luke had never promised her love, only comfort and a home. She told herself it was enough and then at last she slept.

Roxanne was not summoned to the earl's side that night but at half past six the next morning she went to his room and found that Luke was still there, his long legs stretched out before him as he dozed in the armchair. He woke as she entered and looked at her sheepishly.

'I must have dozed off,' he apologised. 'I do not think he called out or I should have heard.'

Roxanne looked down at the earl. His eyes were closed, but as she bent over him, he opened them and then deliberately winked at her.

'Good morning, Grandfather,' she said and bent to kiss his cheek. 'How are you this morning?'

'Better,' he grunted. 'What on earth that grandson of mine wanted to sit there all night for I've no idea.'

Luke had risen to his feet and was stretching his shoulders, clearly feeling the effects of an uncomfortable night. 'Roxanne would have insisted on sitting with you had I not taken a turn,' he said. 'I'm glad to see you better, sir. I will call and see you later. Please excuse me.'

'Much good he would have been,' the earl said as the door closed behind him, but there was no malice in his words, just a hint of amusement. 'His snoring would waken the dead.'

'I'm sorry Luke's snoring disturbed you. How long had you been awake?'

'An hour or so, perhaps. I hadn't the heart to wake him, but I need Marshall's assistance. Fetch him to me, girl, and then take yourself off for a few hours. You must have something you need to do?'

'I believe I shall speak to Minty about flowers for the wedding,' Roxanne said and smiled. 'You're a sly old fox, sir. If I didn't know better, I would think you had a plan to bring us all to heel.'

'Do that graceless scamp good to think of someone else for a change. He's like me, too selfish and careless of others—but you were right, girl, I do care for him and I shall tell him so next time he comes. No good leaving it until it's too late.'

'I shall see you later,' Roxanne said and went off to summon his manservant before going in search of the head gardener.

After an hour spent in delightful discussions about the various flowers needed for the church and the reception, Roxanne returned to the house. Entering the hall, she discovered Luke reading a letter. He turned to look at her with a frown.

'This is from my solicitor. He writes to tell me that he has had no replies to his advertisement as such—but his office was ransacked by persons unknown the night he stayed here for the ball.'

Roxanne went cold all over. 'You think someone was searching for that ruby? What is so important about it? I know it is valuable, but it is not priceless—or is it? Is there something special that draws others to it?'

'I think we can be certain that someone is desperate to recover the ruby. I should be prepared to give it back to whoever is the rightful owner—if that is your wish?'

'Yes, of course.' She shivered. 'It is a dangerous thing, Luke. I wish I'd never seen it.'

'When Grandfather is well again I shall place another advertisement and offer to return the damned thing to the person who has been searching for it. We shall all sleep sounder in our beds once this business is over.'

'Yes, I believe so,' Roxanne agreed. 'I think Grandfather is better this morning. His health is clearly still fragile, but I believe he was just exhausted after the ball. We should keep the wedding list to a minimum so as not to tire him too much.'

'If I know Grandfather, he will insist on having a grand affair, even if he goes to bed for a week afterwards. This wedding means a great deal to him.'

'Yes, but if we told him we wished for a quiet ceremony I believe he would agree.'

'I'll have a word later,' Luke said. 'You look very well, Roxanne. Have you been for a walk?'

'Only to the hothouses. Minty has been showing me his pride and joy, which are some very rare plants. We were discussing flowers for the wedding.' She looked at him uncertainly. 'You do wish to continue with this?'

'Yes, of course. If I have given you reason to think otherwise, I apologise, Roxanne. I will admit to having a temper and I am sometimes rash when anger gets the better of me.'

She swallowed hard, her heart thumping. He was not saying that he loved her, merely that he wished to continue with the make-believe wedding they had planned.

'Then I shall begin to write out the cards. I will send the family invitations first and you must tell me if there are friends you wish to ask, Luke.'

'You have none you would wish to ask yourself?'

'Perhaps Mrs Mills if it would not be too far for her to travel? I have no other friends or family, Luke, or none that I know of—but I shall content myself with yours. Your Uncle Frederick is a very pleasant man and I like his wife. Some of your neighbours are very companionable and I am sure I shall make friends here.'

'You are quite settled here,' Luke said with a rather odd look. 'I think you would be happy to make it your home, even after Grandfather dies?'

'It is such a lovely house and the estate is thriving, the people honest and hard working—and I should enjoy helping to keep it in good heart. To live as the steward of such a house and care for its people is a good life. Do you not think so?'

'I like London,' Luke said. 'When a man is tired of London he is tired of life.'

'A profound sentiment, Luke. Is it your own?'

'No. I believe it was once a favourite saying of Dr Johnson.'

'Ah, yes. Grandfather spoke to me of Dr Johnson's dictionary, something he would like to add to his library, I believe.'

'I must see if a copy can be subscribed,' Luke said. 'I will enquire when I go up to town—which puts me in mind of your wedding gift. Is there any particular jewel you like, Roxanne? I gave you pearls and emeralds, but you might prefer something different.'

'Oh, no, I am very happy with what I have,' she denied, her cheeks warm. 'I do prefer simple things—a gold brooch for wearing in the mornings might be nice, but I have no particular need.'

'People will expect you to have jewels to match your status, Roxanne. If I did not give them to you, they would imagine I neglected you and my duty. I am very sure Grandfather would have given you something for the ball had I not had my own gift to give you that night.'

'We have been given several gifts for our engagement,' Roxanne said. 'Mrs Arlet told me that a silver tea service arrived from your godmother this morning. Your uncles and aunts have also been generous, and Cousin Horatio gave us a particularly beautiful silver inkstand. Shall I write to thank them all or would you prefer to do it yourself?'

'If you have time, I shall leave you to do the honours,' Luke said. 'There are estate matters enough to occupy me while I stay here.'

'Are you thinking of leaving for London soon?'

'I may go up in a day or so. I should probably get this business of the ruby over as soon as possible, Roxanne. I will arrange for an agent in London to handle the affair. We do not need to be involved ourselves.'

'Yes, of course,' she said, conscious of a feeling of disappointment. No longer angry, Luke was being considerate and generous once more, but he had given her no reason to think that the feelings that had boiled over on the night of the ball had been anything more than an impulse he had since regretted. 'It must be just as you wish.'

'Must it?' Luke's gaze narrowed, becoming brooding and thoughtful. 'I wonder what you would say if I told you what I wish for, Roxanne?' She raised her brows and he shook his head, laughing ruefully. 'If only I knew, my dear. I fear I am an impossible fellow and I dare say you are wishing you had never come to my aid that day in the woods.'

'No,' Roxanne said. 'I have never wished that, nor shall I. You may have regrets, Luke, but I regret nothing.'

With that she walked away, leaving him to stare after her and wonder what was in her mind.

'Ah, you look better, sir,' Luke said as he saw his grandfather sitting propped up in bed reading the latest newssheet from London. 'I wanted to see how you were. I have some business to attend in London, but did not wish to leave until you were over the worst.'

'Running off before the wedding?' The earl looked at him over the small round glasses that he wore perched on the end of his nose for reading. 'Do you think that entirely fair on Roxanne?'

'Roxanne will not mind. She does not expect me to dance attendance on her all the time, sir.'

'No, of course not. She made a bargain with you and she'll stick to it, because she is honest and decent—but there's no cause for you to treat her as if she were a doormat.'

'I cannot think I have done so,' Luke replied, stung by the accusation. 'Roxanne has not complained to me—has she said something to you?'

'She would not complain, but I've had the truth out of her. She told me after that fellow attacked Mr Higgins. The gel doesn't know who she is or where she came from before Sofia found her. She's afraid she stole that wretched ruby, but I don't believe she's a thief.'

'Roxanne told you all this?' Luke frowned, his mouth thinning. 'Did she tell you everything?'

'About the bargain you made to give me something to please me in my last days?' The earl's gaze narrowed. 'I'd guessed some of it and I made her tell me the rest. Did you imagine I should be fooled, Luke? You haven't been behaving like a man who has fallen head over heels. She's a better actress than you—though I'm not so sure she's acting now. She's a tender-hearted woman, Luke—and I don't want to see her hurt.'

'What do you mean?'

'If you're doing this for my sake, perhaps you shouldn't,' the earl said. 'I know I've pushed you towards marriage, but that girl means something to me. If you don't love her, let her go and stop this masquerade before it's too late. I'll do something for her myself. Indeed, she is welcome to stay with me for the rest of my days if she chooses. You can go back to the life you enjoy. I know now that I was wrong to demand so much of you, Luke. It isn't right to force you into marriage for my sake. I don't want either of you to ruin your life for me. That gel cares about us both and I won't see her hurt. If you marry her, make it a proper marriage and forget this foolish bargain.'

'I think marriage to Roxanne would suit me well enough. It is no different to many marriages made for position or money. I doubt I shall ever fall in love or want to settle for domesticity. I'm a loner like my father. It wouldn't be fair to make any woman love me, because I should hurt her.'

'Your father may not have been what you think him,'

the earl said and sighed heavily. 'This marriage and an heir before I die would make me happy, Luke—but I've been selfish too often in the past. I want both of you to be happy and I'm releasing you from your promise. If you marry her, let it be because it's what you want.'

'Thank you, sir.' Luke inclined his head stiffly. 'I shall leave you to rest. You may be certain that I shall give this some thought.'

Luke left his grandfather's bedchamber, striding along the hall and down the stairs. He could feel the anger building inside him. Why hadn't Roxanne told him that the earl knew everything? Why had she allowed him to think that she was still going through the motions of a make-believe marriage?

She was in a plot with his grandfather to trap him into making this a proper marriage. Once his ring was on her finger there would be no going back. Luke could divorce her, but the scandal would be horrendous and he would never be able to face it. Hurting Roxanne would be like inflicting pain on himself. He'd meant it to be a simple arrangement with no ties on either side, but Roxanne had broken the terms of their agreement.

He felt resentful and bitter, because she had taken his grandfather's side against him. He could imagine them smiling over their plot, reeling him in like a fish on a line. How dare she talk about him behind his back?

Luke knew that he was the one who had swept her off on a tide of passion on the night of the ball, but he was struggling to keep his head above water and only by transferring the blame could he justify his own reactions. He'd meant it to be the way it was when he took a mistress, passion and pleasure but no emotional entanglement. Roxanne had declared her love in the heat of desire and it had sent him running in a panic.

He couldn't handle love. Luke's mouth was dry and his stomach was tying itself in knots. Love hurt too much. It was a black choking sensation that made small boys weep in the darkness and cry out for the mother they had lost. He wasn't in love with Roxanne. He couldn't love anyone. He was like his father. She had lied to him by keeping it secret that the earl knew of their bargain.

Roxanne was in her favourite parlour. She was matching silks against a piece of embroidery she'd found somewhere, a look of such perfect content on her face that his fury broke loose in a torrent of bitter words.

'How dare you lie to me?' he demanded without preamble, ignoring the look of shock on her face. 'Have you been plotting together—you and Grandfather? Did you laugh at how easy I was to fool?'

'I have no idea what you mean? Why should I wish to lie to you—or to make a fool of you?'

She rose slowly to her feet, looking as if he'd struck her. It was the way his mother had looked at his father so many times and it made Luke feel guilty. He struck out blindly, because he could not stand to feel her pain.

'You did not tell me that you had confessed everything to him.'

Roxanne's cheeks burned. 'Grandfather made me promise I would not tell you he knew. I could not keep it from him because he guessed a part of the whole and was angry. I thought he would send me away and I did not wish to leave.'

'It suits you to live here as a grand lady, I suppose,' Luke thundered, his expression one of fury and disgust. 'You've been fooling us both, haven't you? Laughing at us all the time. Who are you really? An adventuress out for what you can get? I fell right into your little trap, didn't I? You played me so well, pretending to be reluctant and making me persuade you into marriage and giving me an heir. You must have been laughing at my gullibility all the time.'

Roxanne was deadly white. He saw her hands shaking and knew that she was fighting her desire to weep, but his anger was so intense that he could not control it.

'Have you nothing to say to me?'

'I believe you have said it all,' Roxanne murmured between stiff lips. 'Excuse me. I think I must leave.'

'I'll save you the bother. I'm going to London.'

Luke strode from the room. His temper carried him as far as the stables and then he suddenly felt all his energy seep away. Leaning against the wall, he discovered that tears were streaming down his cheeks and he could not stop them. A choking sob broke from him as he mumbled, 'Roxanne, forgive me. Such a fool. I'm so sorry. So very sorry.'

What had he done? He'd said such dreadful things to her. Terrible, cruel, wicked things that she did not deserve. He knew that she was not an adventuress, nor had she planned this for material gain. Yes, she was glad of a settled home, but she was prepared to give so much in return—all the things that he had lost when his mother died. All the things his soul craved and he feared. He was a craven coward and deserved a horsewhipping for the way he'd spoken to her.

Roxanne would hate him. He had destroyed any feeling she had for him.

She'd said she must leave. In his rage he hadn't listened. Did she mean leave the room—or leave him? Go away for ever?

He might never see her again. The thought sent such a wave of agony lashing through him that Luke groaned. He had not realised what he had and he'd cast it away without a second thought.

Perhaps it wasn't too late. If he went back now and begged her pardon on his knees, perhaps she would stay—if not for his sake, for his grandfather's. She loved the earl. Surely she would not desert him?

Luke strode towards the house. Please let him be in time. If she'd already gone, he would find her. He would find her and bring her back for the earl's sake.

Even now he was in denial. Even now he could not quite admit that he needed her, needed her more than he had ever believed possible.

He had no right to care. He was not worthy of her love. He did not know how to love. She had the right to walk away if she chose, now that she knew him for what he was. His damnable temper and the way he hurt people—how could Roxanne ever love him?

Roxanne had left the sealed note on the silver salver in the hall. Mrs Arlet would find it and deliver it to the earl later. It would hurt him, though she'd promised that she would return to see him if she could one day—one day when Luke was back in London and she would not have to see him or the lashing scorn in his eyes.

How could Luke have said such things to her? Roxanne felt her throat tighten with pain. It hurt so much to know what he truly thought of her. How could he believe that she was pretending to care for the earl? He must know that she loved him. He must know that she loved them both so much that this was tearing her into shreds.

She was carrying one small bundle, very similar in content to that she had taken when she left the camp of the travelling players. She'd had no choice but to take the gown she was wearing, some underclothes and a spare skirt and bodice, but the ring and necklace Luke had given her were left on the dressing table in her room.

She had less money than when she'd fled from Black Bob. She'd had no need of money in the earl's house and none had been offered to her. Instead, Luke or the earl had met all the bills for her clothes and anything else she needed was provided.

She would need to find employment quite soon. Roxanne had packed her things, written her note and left in haste. She had not given a thought to what she would do in the future. Now she realised that she must begin working almost immediately. The ruby had gone and she was without friends. Her dream of becoming an actress must be put to one side for the moment. To eat and have a roof over her head, she must take any work that was offered.

She could not look for a position too close to the estate. People might know her and gossip and she did not wish to cause a scandal for Luke and the earl. There would naturally be some scandal when it was discovered that the engagement was over, but Luke could explain to his family that he'd been mistaken in her; they would sympathise with him and it would blow over after a few months.

Roxanne recalled that they had passed a staging inn on the way here. That meant that the mail coach would call there on its way to and from London. She might just have enough coins to travel a part of the way to London. She could find an inn or perhaps a farmhouse where they were looking for a girl to help with the chores. It was not the life she would choose for herself, but she must make the best of it until she could earn enough to set up for herself. Perhaps she could become a seamstress. She had some talent for sewing and she would prefer that kind of work.

She had left by a side door in order to avoid being seen and made her escape through the walled garden and out into a lane that led through the earl's estate to the village. Once there she could find her way to the staging inn and then... Roxanne choked back her tears and looked about her.

The lane had come to an end. She must either cross over a stile and a meadow, which appeared to be filled with cows and what she thought might be a bull, or go through the wood. She'd imagined the way across the field would lead her to the village, but now she knew she was lost. Hesitating, she avoided the meadow and the bull, which was eyeing her in a way that she preferred not to challenge. If she kept walking, the wood must lead somewhere and eventually she would find a main road or a village where she could ask the way.

She had been walking in the cool shadow of the wood for some twenty minutes or so when she heard something rustling in the undergrowth and then a stick snapped. Someone was close by. She turned her head, eager to find whoever it was and enquire the way, and then something struck her on the side of the head and everything went black.

'Fool,' the voice said as a pair of strong arms caught her as she fell. 'His Highness will be angry if you've harmed her. He gave orders that she was to be taken, but not harmed. May the goddess protect her and keep her from harm.'

Roxanne heard nothing of the argument that ensued, nor was she aware of being carried through the wood to where a closed carriage and four horses awaited. Although she was treated with respect after the first crashing blow, she had no knowledge of what was happening to her, her eyes closed and her face pale as the darkness held her mind.

'What does she say?' Luke asked as he watched the earl open his letter and read its contents. Discovering that no one had seen Roxanne, he had found the letter on the salver in the hall and taken it at once to his grandfather. 'Has she gone away? Has she left me? I think she left nothing for me.'

'What on earth did you say to her?' Hartingdon handed him the letter after skimming its contents. 'You have a careless tongue, but this was more than a harsh word, Luke. She begs my pardon for breaking her promise and regrets she must leave—though she promises to let me know how she is and to visit often if I wish it. Damn it, why does she need to ask? I did not wish her to leave me.'

'It is my fault. My fault entirely,' Luke said. 'Forgive me for hurting you like this, sir. I know you care for Roxanne. I was abominably rude to her and I said things I did not mean in temper.'

'She said we were very alike,' the earl grunted. 'I can imagine what you said, what you thought. You're a damned fool, Luke. You've thrown away your chance of happiness, boy. Couldn't you see that she was perfect for you? She loved you.'

'I know, at least I thought…' Luke caught his breath as the pain knifed through him. 'It was fear of her love that made me cruel, sir. I didn't want to do to her what my father did to my mother. I was afraid of hurting her, of breaking her fine spirit—and I've done just that, haven't I?'

'Your mother should never have married,' the earl said. 'I loved her, but she was a foolish silly girl and your father needed a woman with passion in her bones to help him forget. I should never have pushed them into marriage.'

Luke's brows knit in a frown. 'Help him forget—what? I do not understand you, sir.'

'Your father married on the rebound, Luke. As a young man he was very much in love. Your mother liked him when they first met at a society ball, but he didn't look at her that night. He was in love with Helene Digby, the woman he planned to wed, but she died of a sudden and terrible fever. I believe your father was with her, held her in his arms as she died. He never truly recovered from her death. A love like that comes but once in a lifetime.'

'My father was in love like that—really, deeply in love? I thought him a shallow fellow given to affairs and not capable of love.' Luke stared in disbelief, his memories in disarray.

'He loved too deeply, that was his trouble,' the earl said. 'When I coerced him into marrying my daughter he told me that he couldn't love her. I thought it an ideal marriage for my silly girl. She would live here with me, give me an heir for the estate, and her husband would go his own way. My silly Sarah couldn't let him go. She didn't truly enjoy the physical side of marriage, but she wanted a romantic husband to fuss over her and bring her presents. Clarendon wasn't that kind of man. If she'd had passion in her, she might have held him, but she didn't and so he broke her heart with his affairs. She should have let him go, been content with what she had, but she demanded too much of him.'

'Good grief.' Luke sat down heavily, his legs going weak as the shock went through him. 'I had no idea. All these years I've thought…'

'You thought you were shallow and worthless and I let you believe it. Instead of appreciating your qualities, I drove you away, blaming you for what your father did to my silly girl. It wasn't his fault and it certainly wasn't yours, Luke. I don't believe you take after either of them. You're like me—Roxanne knew it instinctively and she loved us both.'

It was like a light breaking over him, the realisation that he loved Roxanne with all his heart. Tortured by his memories that were false and seen through the eyes of a child, who did not understand what was happening between his parents, he had fought against his love for her. When he realised there was no longer a reason to hold her to her promise, he had lashed out in fear and despair, driving her away.

What had he done? All he had ever secretly longed for and needed had been within his grasp and he had thrown it away.

'I am a crass fool and I have to pray that she will forgive me.'

'She might if you can find her,' the earl said and frowned. 'You rode to the village and enquired, but no one had seen her?'

'One of the gardeners thought he saw her in the lane that leads to the meadow where the cows are. If she'd crossed that, she would have come out on the high road and followed the signs to the east, but there is also the wood and if she took that route she might end up on the road north.'

'Where would she go?'

Luke moved his shoulders negatively. 'She was heading for London when I first met her...'

'You must find her,' the earl said urgently. 'Don't blame yourself for the whole, Luke. I made her promise not to tell you that I knew the truth. I am as much to blame as you are in this.'

'No, sir. Roxanne certainly didn't run away from *you*. I'm the one that hurt her. I intend to find her, however long it takes me, and when I do I shall beg her to return, but it may be too late. Some things are unforgivable and, in truth, I do not deserve her forgiveness.'

'I think she may give it,' the earl said and smiled at him. 'You haven't yet realised how lucky you are, Luke. Roxanne is a wonderful and very loving person. You must find her because if you do not you'll regret it for the rest of your life.'

'Yes, I know,' Luke said. 'I think I must travel to London. Will you forgive me for leaving you at such a time?'

'I'm not going to die just yet, boy,' the earl said. 'Find Roxanne and bring her back for all our sakes.'

Luke smiled oddly. 'I promise I shall leave no stone unturned, sir, but for the moment it seems that she has disappeared into thin air.'

'That isn't possible, Luke. Roxanne was on foot. It would have taken her hours to walk anywhere.'

'Unless...' Luke shook his head. He would not distress the earl yet by suggesting that she might have been kidnapped. Somehow Roxanne had avoided detection, but he would find her if it took him the rest of his life.

# *Chapter Ten*

Roxanne stirred and moaned, turning her head on the soft pillow. She was dreaming and tears were on her cheeks as she cried out, 'Mama, please don't leave us. Papa, why must she die? I want Mama, I want my mother…'

*'Your mother is dying of a fever. Her heart is not strong enough to fight it. You should blame me, child. I should never have brought you both out here to this dreadful climate. It is my fault, but you shall not fall victim to this accursed place, as she did. I shall take you home to your aunt.'*

'Mama…please don't leave us. Mama…'

'Hush, memsahib,' a soft voice said and gentle hands stroked her brow. 'You are ill, but you will be better soon.'

'Mama is dying…' Roxanne's eyes flicked opened and she saw a face, the face of her nurse. The Indian woman was kind and loving and she was comforted. 'Mama is so ill.'

'That was long ago, little one. Rest now and when you wake you will be well again.'

Roxanne closed her eyes as the soft hands stroked her forehead and she smelled the exotic perfume of flowers and spices.

The dream was changing. She was in a different place and someone was saying she must die. Now she was lost…running from something…someone. Her uncle wanted her father's ruby, the precious jewel Papa had asked her to keep for him until he returned from India. Her uncle had demanded that she give it to him, telling her that she could not look after it properly.

'No…' she cried out. 'Please help me. He will kill me…he wants Papa's ruby.'

A cool dark hand touched her brow and a woman's beautiful, dusky-skinned face appeared through the mist for a moment.

'Do not fret, little mistress,' the woman's soft musical voice soothed her. 'You are safe now. My lord is angry they hurt you so. He will not let more harm come to you. Rest now and sleep.'

'My uncle…he wants the ruby,' Roxanne moaned, her eyelids fluttering as the words came tumbling out. She clutched at the bedclothes with restless hands. 'My aunt said she would steal it while I slept, but he said it would be best if I were dead. He says they will tell my father I died of a fever and the ruby was lost. I must get away…I must get away…'

'Hush, little one. You are safe now.'

'No…Luke, I want Luke…' Roxanne's cheeks were wet with tears as the fever raged through her. 'Please, ask him to come to me. I need him so…' She was sobbing, tossing restlessly on the pillow, her long hair damp and clinging to her forehead.

'The memsahib is very ill,' another voice said. 'Those fools hit her too hard. If she dies, the lord will be angry and he will punish them harshly. She must drink this medicine; it may ease her. She must live or all will be lost. Without her to help us, the ruby may never be recovered and our people will continue to suffer.'

'Give me the cup,' the woman's soft voice said. 'I will get her to swallow your potion, honourable doctor, but she is wandering in her mind and she may not remember where the ruby is or even her own name.'

'It is in the hands of the gods,' the doctor said. 'I shall pray for her life, for if she gives back what was stolen our people may prosper again.'

'Help me…' Roxanne cried. 'Sofia…help me. Papa, why do you not come back to me? I need you…I need you so.'

'Drink this and it will ease you.' The woman's soft voice was close to her ear and gentle hands stroked her face.

Roxanne gave a cry of fear. 'They are searching for me. I'm so hungry and thirsty. I want Papa…if they find me they will kill me.'

'No one will kill you. You are going to get well and strong again.'

'Sofia, please don't leave me, don't die. I shall be so

alone…' Roxanne sat up, her eyes wide open. 'Luke! Please don't hate me. I love you. I love you.'

'Hush then, the medicine will work soon.'

The soothing hands were stroking her brow, helping her to relax. Roxanne knew there was something she must do or say, but she was sinking back into the darkness and a strange lassitude was binding her limbs and her mind. She fell back against the pillows, her eyes closed.

'She will sleep now,' the doctor said. 'We must pray that the fever will leave her and when she wakes she will tell us what we need to know.'

Roxanne felt that she was dying and feared she would never see Luke again. The words she wanted to say were in her mind, but would not come. She was slipping away, away into a deep dark place. For a moment everything had been so clear, but the drug claimed her senses and she slept.

'She has not been seen in the village and she did not board the stage for London. The coachman and ostlers were quite adamant that they had not seen her. I do not know where to look next.' Luke ran his fingers through his thick hair in frustration. There was a shadow of beard on his chin and his clothes were less than immaculate. 'Where could she have gone?'

'She must either have been picked up by a carter or she has walked in another direction,' the earl said, looking at Luke in concern. He'd hardly slept for the past week, spending every daylight hour out riding or walking in the hope of discovering Roxanne's whereabouts. 'She cannot have gone very far on foot, Luke. Perhaps she has found work somewhere, in an inn or a farmhouse.'

'She would not?' Luke stared at him in horror. 'I think she had very little money. I gave her jewels, but she left them behind. She is proud and independent and would take nothing we had given her.' He sank down onto a chair, a look of despair on his face. 'What can I do, Grandfather?'

'You cannot give up yet,' his grandfather said. 'She must be somewhere, either hiding or working.'

'Unless…' Luke held back the fears that haunted him night and day.

'What?' The earl's brows met in a frown. 'You are hiding something from me, Luke. Tell me the truth or I shall worry more.'

'Someone has been searching for that damned ruby. I don't know why, but it is important and these people might do anything to recover it.'

'But she no longer has it. You placed it in a bank in London.'

'The men who want it may not know that—they may think Roxanne has it or that, if they hold her captive, we shall give it back to them.'

The earl looked at him in horror. 'You think she might have been kidnapped?'

'I don't know,' Luke said honestly. 'No one has seen her, but one man did tell me that a closed carriage was seen in the lane near the woods on the day Roxanne disappeared. It is possible that she might have been abducted.'

'Surely we should have been sent a ransom note? They must know she does not have the ruby by now.'

'Perhaps.' Luke shook his head. 'I think I shall search again in that direction. I will ask at the inns and farms, too, anywhere that she might have enquired for work. She must be somewhere and I intend to find her.'

'Yes, you must.' The earl looked anxious. 'If she was kidnapped her life may be in danger, Luke. We shall offer a reward for her return.'

'Yes, I'll arrange it before I leave. I may be gone for a while—you will be all right here alone?'

'I have Marshall and a house full of servants,' the earl grunted. 'I'm not about to die on you, Luke. Get out there and find our girl or neither of us will know a moment's peace again.'

Roxanne's eyelids fluttered and her eyes opened. She looked up at the woman bending over her. Her perfume was deep and sensual and it had become familiar as Roxanne lay in her fever, because the woman had tended her day and night, caring for her when she was raving and out of her mind.

She had thought when she was ill that she was her ayah and that she was a child again, growing up in India with her tall strong father and her sickly mother, but now she knew the woman was a stranger.

'Who are you?' she asked, her voice cracked and hoarse. 'Where am I?'

'My name is Shulie,' the woman smiled down at her

as she eased herself up against the pillows. 'You are at the house of my husband, Prince Ranjit.'

'Prince Ranjit...' Roxanne wrinkled her brow in thought, trying to remember. 'I think...I believe I used to know a Prince Ranjit. We played together in the gardens of the palace in India. My father...my father was the prince's tutor.'

Suddenly, it was as if a curtain had been pulled aside and she remembered everything: her life as a child in India and what had happened when her father had taken her to his sister's home and left her in her aunt's charge while he returned to his work.

'My lord has told me that you were his friend,' Shulie said and smiled at her. 'I am my lord's first bride and he trusts me. He gave me the honour of caring for you when you were ill.'

'I was ill? What happened to me?' Roxanne frowned and then gave a little cry. 'I was in the woods and someone hit me on the back of the head.'

'The prince was very angry that you were harmed,' Shulie told her. 'You must not think that he wanted you to be hurt, memsahib. He remembers his playmate Rose Marie very well and he did not believe that you would withhold the ruby if you knew its importance to our people.'

'That will do, Shulie.'

The man's voice made both women glance towards the door. A man of perhaps five and twenty, dressed in rich clothes and wearing a purple-silk turban with a magnificent diamond in its folds, was standing there, watching them. Shulie fell to her knees, bowing her head.

'Forgive me, my lord. I only wished to reassure the memsahib that she was with friends.'

'So, you have returned to us,' the man said and moved towards the bed. His dark eyes went over her. 'You look better, but I see that you are still not truly well. Shulie will continue to care for you and we shall talk when you are better.'

'Is it the ruby you seek?' Roxanne asked, holding the sheets against her defensively as she looked at him. This man was very different to the thin and gangly young prince she'd known and admired as a child. 'How is your family, sir?'

'My father is sick and we fear his death. Before he dies he wishes to see the eye returned to its rightful place.'

'The eye?' Roxanne was puzzled. 'I fear I do not understand, sir.'

'You may think of it as merely a ruby, but to others it is a sacred thing—but I shall tell you the whole story when you are able to leave your bed.' He turned to Shulie. 'Bring Miss Rose Marie clean clothes and food. She is to be told nothing more until she is able to hear the story from me.'

'Yes, my lord.'

Shulie approached the bed as the prince left the room. 'My lord has spoken. Please do not ask questions, for I may not answer them. I shall bring food, water for you to wash and clothes. You will feel much better when you have eaten.'

'Please, one thing,' Roxanne said. 'How long have I been here?'

'You lay in a fever for ten days,' Shulie said. 'We feared you might die, but the honourable doctor has saved you. It was the will of the gods.'

'Yes, perhaps,' Roxanne said. She lay back against the pillows, closing her eyes as the woman left the room. Ten days. She'd been here ten days—but what had happened just before she was brought here? Someone had hit her on the head, knocking her unconscious—but where had she been and where had she been going?

She could recall running away from her aunt and uncle just before her fifteenth birthday. Her father had written to tell her he would be home before Christmas and would be taking her to live with him.

*I've made my fortune here, Rose Marie,* he'd written. *It is time I came back to England to live and made a home for us both. The ruby will be the icing on the cake, though I have other jewels and money enough. Take good care of it, Rosie my love, for it is special.*

It was two days after her letter arrived that she'd heard her uncle telling her aunt what he planned for her as she went down to have afternoon tea.

*'She is old enough. He wants her and when he's done with her he'll put her to work for her living. She'll not last long enough for her father to find her. If she doesn't die of the whore's disease, she'll be beaten to death.'*

*'Frank, you cannot do it,'* her aunt had protested. *'Rose Marie doesn't deserve to be treated that way.'*

*'She should have given me the ruby when I asked her. It's either the whorehouse or the river—make up*

*your mind. My debts must be paid and that ruby will see us in comfort for the rest of our lives.'*

The past was so clear now. Her name was Rose Marie Pearson and her father's name was Captain Peter Pearson. He'd been an Indian Army officer and then left the service to work for a rich maharajah, first to train his private army and then to teach his sons how to be gentlemen.

When her gentle mother died of a fever, her father had sent her home to live with her aunt and uncle. He'd sent the ruby to her a year or so later with a special messenger he trusted. She had been so proud of being trusted to care for the jewel, but her aunt had seen her admiring it and demanded to know where it came from.

*'Papa sent it to me. He told me to take great care of it, because it is worth a small fortune.'*

*'It is far too valuable to entrust to a young girl. Your father meant me to look after it for you, Rosie.'*

*'No, Aunt. Papa told me to wear it inside my gown always and never be parted from it. If he'd wanted you to care for it, he would have sent it to you. He trusted me, not you and my uncle.'*

*'How dare you speak to me that way?'*

*'The ruby is mine. I shall not give it to you or anyone.'*

Even then, Rose Marie had not trusted her aunt and uncle. They had called her Rosie and she had disliked the name, but they had said her own was too fanciful. She'd known instinctively that if they once had the ruby they would keep it, but she had not dreamed they would kill her to get it. She'd run from them that very moment, clutching the ruby and in fear of her life.

Roxanne's mind was clear now and she recalled that she'd run until she could run no more. After that she'd wandered for days, perhaps weeks, always in fear of being caught, hungry, thirsty and cold. Then one night as it grew dusk a vagrant had attacked her and attempted to rape her. She'd fought him off and run away into the night with no more than a few scratches and bruises, but the smell of him had sickened her and she'd been terrified. She had not dared to approach anyone to ask for food and she had wandered, her stomach aching for want of food. She had fallen and hit the side of her head. After that she had been very ill. As she starved, her mind became hazy and she could recall nothing until Sofia found her and nursed her back to health.

Sofia...Black Bob...Luke.

The memories slotted into place one after the other. Tears trickled down her cheeks as the names came to her mind and everything became crystal clear. Now she remembered both the past and recent events. She recalled meeting Luke and falling in love with him and his grandfather.

She loved Luke so very much, but he did not love her. He did not truly wish to marry her.

What was she going to do? Prince Ranjit wanted his ruby back—but surely it was her father's ruby? Roxanne did not believe that her father would have stolen the jewel from his employer.

There was still a mystery here to be solved.

* * *

Roxanne seemed to have vanished into thin air. No one had seen her. Luke was met with shakes of the head and blank faces wherever he enquired for her. With each day that passed he grew more desperate. If she were lost for ever, he did not know how he would live with himself. He must search and search until he found her.

'No, sir,' one innkeeper told him. 'We did have a coach stop to change its horses on the day you mention. I recall it particularly because of the odd clothes the servant was wearing. They were foreigners, your lordship. The servant who arranged everything was wearing a white turban and inside the carriage I saw two women, but they were wearing odd clothes, too, and had veils over their faces. One was enveloped in a thick dark cloak, though it was a warm day. I did think that odd—also that she never moved or spoke.'

'I see…' Luke frowned as icy chills crawled over his body. 'You did not notice anything else—any sign that one of the women was captive?'

'I wasn't allowed to speak to either of them, sir—but I did think that the one in the cloak seemed to be sleeping heavily; at least, that's what it looked like from a distance.'

'You have no idea of where the carriage was heading?'

'I think one of them spoke of London, but I couldn't say for sure, sir. It's a while ago now. I doubt I'd have remembered anything if it hadn't been for their clothes.'

'Thank you, you may have provided a clue,' Luke said and gave the man a gold sovereign.

He was thoughtful as he left the inn. If the men who were searching for the ruby had captured Roxanne, they would know by now that she did not have it with her. What would they do next? Pray God they would not harm her.

His search had widened the last few days and this was the first clue he'd discovered, but it was of little real worth to him. If Roxanne had been taken to London, it would be like searching for a needle in a haystack. He must certainly make enquiries, but a team of agents would do that far more efficiently than he could, especially in his present state of mind. He could not concentrate long enough, his thoughts wandering to her smile, the touch of her hand and the knowledge that he felt devastated by her loss.

He might do better to return to Hartingdon to discover whether or not a ransom had been demanded for Roxanne's safe return. Luke was praying hard as he made his decision. He would retrace his steps, make certain that he hadn't missed anything, but first he must send word to the agents who had worked for him on various occasions and instruct them to search for the mysterious owner of the carriage. Surely such a man and his servants could not hide themselves completely. If they were in the vicinity of London or its outskirts, his agents would find them.

Luke saw the gypsy camp gathered on the common at the edge of Hartingdon woods. Suddenly, he recalled that Roxanne had been frightened of the man called Black Bob. It was possible that he had taken her. He might have been following the wrong theory all this time.

Dismounting, he tied his horse to a bush and approached a woman who was stirring something in a large black pot on a trivet over a fire. She glanced at him suspiciously and called out to someone. A man came down from one of the caravans and stood looking at Luke as he walked up to her, his arms crossed and a menacing look in his dark eyes.

'Good day, mistress,' Luke said politely and doffed his hat to her. 'I mean you no harm. I am looking for someone and wondered if you might help me?'

'It depends whom 'tis you want, sir.' The woman spoke in a voice that surprised him; looking closely, Luke was certain she was not a gypsy, as he'd first imagined.

'The man I seek is named Black Bob and he leads a troupe of players—actors who perform all over the country.'

'And what would you be wanting of him, sir?'

'You're not Romany,' Luke said. 'Your voice has a good resonance. I believe you are an actress—am I right? Did you know Roxanne? She lived with Sofia until her friend died.' He saw a startled look in the woman's eyes and knew that he'd touched a raw nerve. She did know Roxanne—or she had once. He moved towards her, taking hold of her arm. 'You do know her. Is she here? Has he got her?'

'Leave me be.' The woman cried, a look of fear in

her eyes now. 'I don't know this woman you speak of—leave me be.'

'Leave her be.' The man who had come out of the caravan moved towards Luke threateningly. 'You take your hands off my woman or you'll be sorry. You damned aristocrats think you own the world. If you persist, I'll thrash the life out of you.'

'I mean your lady no harm,' Luke said and let his hand drop from her arm. He was armed with a loaded pistol, but had no wish to use it, for he would lose all chance of discovering Roxanne's whereabouts then. 'I do not fear to fight with you, sir—but I came here in peace. I am searching for Roxanne and I thought you might know of her.'

'Clear off or I'll bash your head in,' the man said fiercely, but another man had come up to them and the first moved back out of respect or fear. 'We've told him nothing, Bob.'

'Quiet, fool,' the tall dark-eyed man grunted. He scowled at Luke. 'Run away from you, too, has she? She's an ungrateful wretch and a thief. Has she taken something of yours?'

'No. Roxanne is not in trouble with me. I am afraid her life may be in danger. Why do you call her a thief?'

'*He* told me she had something that belonged to him.' Black Bob's eyes narrowed. 'I saw it once before Sofia hid it—a huge ruby bigger than a pigeon's egg. Stands to reason a girl like that weren't the rightful owner of a valuable jewel. *He* told me if I knew where she was he would pay me so I gave him the direction of the house she was living in. Followed you, I did, out of curiosity.

When they come looking for her I knew something didn't smell right. There alus was somethin' odd about the girl.'

'Where is she? Have you got her?'

'I ain't got her. She's got the mark on her—I wouldn't have her now if she came crawling on her knees.'

'What are you talking about?'

'She's cursed. *He* told me that whoever has the ruby is cursed. Until it is returned to its rightful place the mark of doom is on anyone that touches it.'

'Whoever this man is, he meant to scare you,' Luke said scornfully. 'Roxanne is not a thief. She was given the jewel to keep for someone. Tell me, was the man who offered you money for information an Indian?'

'I reckon he might be. He were dressed much like you, a wealthy man—but his servants were dressed strange and their faces were darker than his. Some of them wore turbans on their heads and one had a curved sword hanging from his belt. They looked a strange lot and I didn't trust them, though he paid me my money.'

Luke inclined his head. He believed Black Bob was telling the truth. It tied in with what the innkeeper had said and pointed towards the ruby. Roxanne had been kidnapped because of that damned jewel.

'If this man speaks to you again, tell him to come to me at Hartingdon. I shall give him what he wants, but first he must release Roxanne. If anything has happened to her I shall punish him—and you.'

'All I done was tell him where he could find her.'

'Roxanne was once one of your people. If you cared for her at all, you would have come to us and told us about this man instead of betraying her.' Luke's eyes flashed scorn. 'You are a greedy rogue and deserved to be punished. I cannot prevent you from camping here, but I would not advise you to return once you leave.'

He was furious as he mounted his horse and rode off. It had taken all his strength of will not to go for the man and give him a good hiding. Only the knowledge that there were more than a dozen men watching him prevented him from seeking physical revenge. The whole tribe would no doubt have set him on and it was more important to keep searching for Roxanne than to make a fool of himself by indulging in a fight merely for his own satisfaction.

Feeling frustrated by his inability to discover Roxanne's whereabouts and afraid of what might be happening to her, Luke rode towards his grandfather's house. It was six days since he'd last visited. Perhaps there might be some news. The earl might have received a ransom note. He must speak to his grandfather before going out to search again, though he did not truly know where to look next. He'd tried every posting house, every inn and every village within a thirty-mile radius of the estate. He was beginning to think she must be in London—or, worse still, on a ship bound for India. Her beauty would be appreciated by certain men who thought nothing of holding women captive in their households.

No! It must not be. The thought was so terrible that it tore him apart, a groan leaving his lips. Rumours and tales of the white-slave trade passed through his mind. Roxanne was so beautiful. Once this man had her, he might think she was of more value than that damned ruby.

* * *

Roxanne looked at the clothes Shulie had brought her and smiled. She had wondered if she would be given something similar to the clothes her nurse wore, but instead she was being offered a beautiful silk gown of French design and make. As she slipped it on, her heart raced wildly. She had remembered more about Prince Ranjit and she seemed to recall that he was charming, but a little selfish, inclined to lose his temper if he did not get his own way. Yet as a child she had admired him, following him about and hanging on his every word. He had grown up to be a handsome man with an exotic and slightly dangerous air.

What did he want to tell her himself? Why had he not allowed Shulie to tell her about the ruby?

She decided to fasten her hair back in a severe knot at the nape of her neck, but, glancing at her reflection, Roxanne knew that it did not make her look any less attractive. The gown was so very elegant and flattering that she needed no jewels to appear to advantage.

'The memsahib is beautiful,' Shulie said and looked at her oddly. 'My lord has always admired you—and I think he looks for another wife. I have been his wife for nine months and I have given him no sons.'

'Nine months is not long,' Roxanne said and smiled. 'You do not need to fear me, Shulie. I would not seek to take your place. I am grateful for all you have done.'

'My lord does not acknowledge the word no,' Shulie replied and looked doubtful. 'If he wants you, he will take you for his wife.'

'At home Prince Ranjit may soon rule in his father's

place,' Roxanne said. 'This is England and he cannot take me as his wife against my will. Besides, I am already promised to another man. I am betrothed. I do not think Prince Ranjit would take the wife of another man.'

'No, perhaps not, if you belong to another.' Shulie's face cleared and she handed Roxanne a spangled drape to wear over her head and shoulders. 'If my lord wished you for his wife, I think I should not mind too much. You are lovely of nature as well as face; there are some who look for the honour who do not deserve it.'

'Perhaps the prince will be satisfied to have just one wife.'

Shulie shook her head sadly. 'It is the custom for a man to take several wives. If I had given him a son, my place as his chief wife would be assured, but now he may put another in my place.'

'You must make him understand it would hurt you. If he loves you, you will remain the first in his heart even if he takes other wives.'

'Perhaps.' Shulie beckoned her. 'We should not keep my lord waiting, memsahib. I know he will want you, but if you belong to another perhaps he will not insist that you become his wife.'

Roxanne's heart raced as she followed Shulie out of the room and along the hall. There was no point in thinking of trying to escape. She had no idea of where she was being held and the prince's men would be watchful. They had not gone to the trouble of kidnapping and then nursing her when she was in a fever simply to allow her to escape. The prince wanted something. Roxanne must pray that it was only the ruby he required from her. She knew that Shulie believed he wanted her for his second wife, but Roxanne had no intention of being taken off to India to live in a harem as one of the prince's wives.

'Nothing,' the earl said and shook his head. 'I cannot understand it, Luke. How could she have disappeared so completely? Had she been seen walking the roads we should have heard. She has not visited an inn or attempted to buy food at the markets or someone would have reported it to us for the reward money. I fear that she is either dead or kidnapped.'

'From what I now know, I think she was taken by the servants of a wealthy Indian man,' Luke said, his mouth pulled into a grim line. 'I believe they want the ruby. It may have some religious significance, but that is merely a guess. Why they did not simply come and ask for the damned thing I do not know. I would willingly have given it.'

'That gypsy fellow told you it is cursed,' the earl said and his hand trembled. His eyes held an urgent appeal as he said, 'You don't think…she's not dead, is she? Our girl's not gone?'

'No, Grandfather. I'm sure she is still alive. I would know if she were dead.' Luke ran tormented fingers through his thick hair. He had dark shadows beneath his eyes and his face looked haggard from lack of sleep. 'She can't be dead. She must be a prisoner somewhere. I'm certain she would have written to you otherwise. It is too cruel to just disappear like this. I do not believe

Roxanne is that careless of another's feelings, especially someone she cares for. If she could have got word to us, she would by now.'

'We must pray for her safe return,' the earl said. 'Have your agents heard nothing?'

'I shall ride to the village and ask if there is a communication for me,' Luke said. 'Do not look so distressed, Grandfather. I shall find her. I swear to you that I will never rest. She shall be brought home…' The words he added in his own mind were not meant for his grandfather's ears.

*Even if she is dead I shall find her body and bring her home to us.* His throat closed and the agony in his mind was fearful. *Roxanne, my love, please be alive. Your death will kill him...and me.*

'Come, sit here near me,' Prince Ranjit said and captured her hand, leading her to an elegant little sofa. He took the gilded chair just opposite and waited for her to sit before sitting himself. She recalled that his father the Maharajah Jankara had had impeccable manners and he, too, behaved as a gentleman should. 'Please tell me what happened to you, Miss Pearson. My father has been trying to find you for many months. Your family had no knowledge of your whereabouts and believed you dead.'

'Some years ago I found myself in danger and I ran away from my aunt's home. I became very ill and was rescued by a wonderful lady; she cared for me and became like a mother to me. Her name was Sofia and she lived with a band of travelling players. She had been a lady and the mistress of aristocrats and princes and we travelled together until she died.'

The prince nodded and Roxanne realised he already knew this part of her history. Somehow he or his agents had managed to trace her, not only to the camp, but also to the Hartingdon estate. He wanted to know the things his men had not already discovered about her life.

'My father gave me a ruby to keep for him, your Highness,' she said. 'He said I must keep it with me always because it would make our fortune. He was returning to England to set up a home for us. However, my uncle and aunt coveted the jewel and they planned to sell me to a revolting man—a man who meant to use me in a way I cannot bring myself to mention. This was the reason I ran away.' She paused, then, 'Can you tell me where my father is living, please? Has he been looking for me?'

'Forgive me, Rose Marie,' the prince said and leaned forwards to touch her hand. 'Your father believed you dead—a letter came from your uncle saying that you had run away and were believed to have died of a fever in the poorhouse. They said you had the ruby with you when you left—did you?'

'Yes, I took the ruby when I fled—but my father?' Roxanne's throat tightened. 'Please tell me, sir.'

'Your father *had* planned to return to England and make a home for you. However, when he believed you dead, he decided to remain in India. He left my father's employ and lived in solitude doing good works amongst the poor and sick. He died of a fever about eighteen months ago.'

'My father is dead?' A single tear trickled down Roxanne's cheek. For years she had forgotten the tall handsome man she'd adored as a child, but the last few days had brought him back to her. It hurt to know that he had died not knowing that she was alive and well. 'Then I shall never see him again.'

'I am so sorry to be the bearer of this sad news,' the prince said and touched her hand again. 'When he knew he was ill, Sahib Pearson left you a letter and also a small inheritance, which I have placed in a bank in London for you. You see, in the last months before he died, he had begun to believe you were not dead, though his reasons for this belief are not clear. He sent the letter with another of explanation to my father and asked that you might be searched for. It was then that he told my father of the ruby he'd given you. It was only at that time that my father learned yours had possessed the eye for a time. My father sent his men to England to search for you, but it was many months before we traced you to the camp of the travelling players and by then you had disappeared once more.'

'You did not begin your search until eighteen months ago?'

The prince shook his head. 'Until we had your father's letter, the eye was thought lost and you were believed to have died.'

'The eye? Was it stolen? Surely my father would not have stolen from yours?'

'No, the ruby did not belong to us—it is the eye of the goddess Bersheira and it was stolen by thieves who raided the temple. My father believes that your father bought the eye in good faith. He did not know that it was stolen from the goddess, for he would never have bought it and given it to you. Until the eye is returned to its rightful place, all those who touch it are cursed. Since it was stolen the people of our province have suffered in many ways: sickness, fires in the villages, mysterious deaths and other evils. They believe that they will be cursed until the eye is returned and it was for this reason that my father decided to send me to discover you and the eye. I arrived in England only a few weeks ago. Our men had failed and it was I who finally discovered the man who revealed your whereabouts to me.'

'Black Bob—was it he who told you?'

'The leader of the travelling players, yes. I had advertised with posters for a missing girl who disappeared five years ago and offered gold for information of her whereabouts. We had heard vague whispers of a girl travelling with the players, a girl who had lost her memory, and I wondered if it might be you. But until he came to me I had no idea of where you might be. Then I saw the advertisement for a lost jewel and I began to link the pieces together. When that rogue told me you had a fabulous jewel I was sure it must be you.'

'Why did you not simply come to me and ask for its return? Was it necessary to kidnap me?'

'You must forgive me, Rose Marie. It was not my men who attacked you—though we took you from the aggressors and brought you here.'

'Not your men? I do not understand.'

'My father has a brother—my Uncle Sangyo,' the

prince said and looked angry. 'He is a ruthless man and covets my father's throne. Sangyo believes that, if he finds the eye and returns it to the goddess, the people will place him on the throne when my father dies instead of me.'

'So it was your uncle I saw in the tower—it was he who tried to break into the earl's strong room and he that hit the bailiff?'

'I fear this may be so,' Prince Ranjit said. 'I was in London for a time on other matters and, when I was informed of your whereabouts, did not immediately send men to the earl's estate to watch for you. When I did, they reported to me that Sangyo was lurking, intent on mischief. I decided to let him make his move and then punish him. Until he tried to abduct you I could not prove he was guilty of anything. He has been made a prisoner and sent home, to be punished by my father. It was necessary to do this or he would have remained a threat to us all.'

'Yes, I understand,' Roxanne said. 'Though I cannot help wishing that you'd acted sooner for you might have spared me an unpleasant illness, sir. Had you asked for the ruby it would have been given to you.'

'I have suffered for your suffering,' the prince told her. 'I must beg your forgiveness and shall do what I can to make reparation for your pain. I am sincere in my regret, Rose Marie.' He hesitated, then, 'Do you still have the ruby?'

'No, I gave it to my fiancé. Lord Clarendon has placed it somewhere for safekeeping. He will, of course, give it to you if you take me to him and offer him proof of your identity. I remember my friend Prince Ranjit, but the years have changed us both, sir. I think Lord Clarendon would require proof that you are the prince before giving you the ruby.'

The prince frowned. 'It is easy enough for me to supply proof of my identity, but this man—Lord Clarendon—he is truly your husband?'

'Yes—at least, we are legally betrothed and intend to be married soon, sir.'

'I see…then it is my duty to take you to him,' the prince said. He gave her a brooding look that told of his displeasure in the discovery that she was betrothed to another. It seemed that Shulie was right to suspect the prince had entertained ideas of making her his second wife. 'I am disappointed. I had hoped we might renew our friendship—the warm affection we had as children, Rose Marie.'

'I am called Roxanne these days,' she said and smiled at him. 'You are right to think I remember you with affection, sir. You were as a brother to me when I lived at the palace and we played as children. I have to thank you and Shulie for your care of me, Highness. I believe that your wife saved my life. She is both beautiful and wise. I think she will give you handsome and clever sons.'

'We have no sons yet,' the prince said and frowned.

'You will have sons, I am certain of it,' Roxanne said. She hesitated, then, 'Perhaps it is the curse of the eye that has prevented you from having a son thus far, sir. When you return it to the goddess, she will favour you and your wife will give you healthy sons.'

The prince looked struck by her words. He took her hand, bringing her to her feet, then bowing to her before placing a kiss on the back of her hand.

'The Lord Clarendon is a fortunate man,' he said. 'I envy him his wife, Rose Marie. Your words are wise and I am sure that you speak truly. It was my destiny to find the eye and restore it to the goddess. When this is done, Shulie will give me sons.'

'Yes, I am certain this is your destiny, sir.' Roxanne smiled at him. 'If you would please take me to Hartingdon, I shall arrange for the eye to be returned to you.'

'I shall escort you myself,' the prince said. 'It has been a privilege to speak with you, Rose Marie. If things had been otherwise…but a betrothal is sacred and I must follow my destiny.'

# *Chapter Eleven*

Luke sighed as he dismounted and gave the reins of his horse into the hands of a waiting groom. He was tired and hungry and, as he noticed the carriage and horses waiting in the courtyard, resentful of whoever had come calling at such a time. He was in no mood for visitors. What he needed was a hot bath, food and some sleep. His search had once more been in vain and he was beginning to think he would never see Roxanne again. The thought was like a heavy weight, dragging him down.

'My lord…' the groom began, but Luke waved him away in frustration. 'But, my lord…'

Ignoring the man's attempt to attract his attention, Luke walked into the house. He was heading for the stairs and his own room when Mrs Arlet came rushing into the hall.

'Thank goodness you're back, sir,' she cried. 'She's

home, my lord. Miss Roxanne is in the back parlour with the earl this very minute.'

'Home? Roxanne is here?' Luke stared at her in disbelief. A great wave of euphoria and relief rushed over him, making him weak. He had been at the end of his tether, afraid that she must be dead, and now he could hardly believe she was here. He must go to her at once, tell her how sorry he was for the things he had said to her. If need be he would beg for her forgiveness.

Flinging open the parlour door, Luke stopped abruptly on the threshold as he saw that his grandfather and another gentleman were in conversation but there was no sign of Roxanne. Luke instantly recalled the stranger as being the rich Indian he'd seen in the jeweller's shop in London. Where was Roxanne? Had she run off again?

'Where is Roxanne?' he burst out as his heart suddenly plummeted in fear. 'I was told she was here.'

'Luke,' the earl said and both he and the stranger stood up. 'This gentleman is Prince Ranjit and the son of the ruler of a great province in India. He saved Roxanne from rogues who might have taken her life. His wife has nursed our girl through a severe illness and now he has brought her back to us.'

'Then where is she?' The question came out of Luke in a rush of agony.

'I am here, my lord.' Roxanne's soft tones made him swing round to discover that she was standing a little way behind him in the hall. 'I went up to change my gown, for I wish to return this to the prince.' Luke saw she was carrying a rich silk gown that looked as if it had come from Paris. She was now wearing a simple grey gown that he'd purchased for her in London. His eyes ran over her, seeing her as pale and tired, a shadow of the girl he adored, and his heart caught with pain. 'I am sorry to have caused you so much trouble. Grandfather says that you have been searching for me. Had I been able I would have let you know where I was. It was not possible.' Her eyes conveyed a message that silenced him.

Luke inclined his head, standing back to allow her to enter the parlour before him. He followed and took up a position between the prince and the door, standing rather than sitting, his manner one of belligerence that seemed to say he was prepared to throw the intruder out if he attempted to take Roxanne with him.

'Perhaps someone would explain,' he said in a carefully controlled tone, his hands clenched at his sides. 'You seemed to have disappeared from the face of the earth, Roxanne.'

'Yes, I think the prince wanted to keep our whereabouts a secret until he was certain that his uncle's men were all taken and rendered harmless. It was Prince Sangyo that attacked our bailiff and his men that tried to abduct me. I was fortunate that Prince Ranjit was able to rescue me, otherwise I fear I might have died.'

Luke's brow lowered. He glared at the prince, but resisted the impulse to throw himself on the man and strangle him. How dare he sit there looking so pleased with himself—and why did Luke get the feeling that the prince wanted more than the ruby?

'May I ask why that ruby is so important that your life was at risk in the first place?'

'It is a sacred thing—the eye of a goddess—and Prince Ranjit's people have been cursed since it was stolen. My father bought it from the thief. He did not know that it was stolen and I have agreed that we should return the ruby to Prince Ranjit so that he can take it back where it belongs.'

'What proof do you have that he will return the ruby and not sell it?'

At a movement of anger from the prince, Roxanne held out her hand. 'I know you are angry, Luke. Please save your anger for later. Prince Ranjit is my friend. I knew him as a child and he has letters for me from my father and others from his own father. He is the man he claims to be and I trust his word. He is an honourable man, as is his father. I know that the ruby must be returned to the goddess and I beg you to arrange it with your bank, Luke. Please do this for me as soon as it may be arranged. We shall speak of other things later.'

Luke clenched his teeth. She claimed the man was her friend and the accord between them was obvious. From the way the prince looked at her, he admired her, wanted her—and she seemed dazzled by him.

After the way he had treated her it would not be surprising if she preferred the exotic prince to a man who had bullied and insulted her.

Prince Ranjit rose to his feet. His manner was haughty as he approached Luke.

'May I assure you that my father was willing to pay

the price asked so that the ruby could be returned. He would have paid twice its worth to a jeweller—but Rose Marie has given it of her own free will.'

'Rose Marie…?' Luke's gaze went over her, his heart catching. She was so beautiful and she deserved so much more than he could give her. He loved her, but he had discovered his love too late and she must hate him. 'Is this what you truly want, Roxanne?'

'Yes, of course it is. You know that we always meant to give it back if we could discover the rightful owner. My father has left me an inheritance and the prince placed it in a bank in London for me. I have ten thousand pounds, which is more than sufficient for my needs.'

Now that he had had time to look at her, he saw that Roxanne looked different. Despite her pallor she was confident and sure of herself, with a glow in her eyes that he had not seen before. She no longer needed his help. She had a fortune of her own—and an ardent admirer in the prince. Luke had no claim on her. If she wished to be free, he must let her go.

He inclined his head to the prince. 'Very well. If you will come to the library with me, sir. I shall write a letter to my bank and they will release the ruby into your care.'

'As you wish, sir.' The prince bowed to the earl. 'I thank you for your hospitality, sir.' He took Roxanne's hand and kissed it. 'Should you wish it, my father would welcome you to our palace, Rose Marie. I myself have a deep admiration and warmth for you; it would be my pleasure to serve you if you came to me. May the gods watch over you and keep you from harm.' He shot a look of dislike at Luke and then followed him from the room.

Roxanne stood undecided for a moment, but the earl shook his head at her. 'Let them settle it between them, girl. Sit down and tell me again what happened. Is that rogue truly what he says—and do you believe that it was his uncle's men that attacked you?'

Roxanne smiled, drew her chair close to him and reached for his hand. 'Yes, Grandfather, I do,' she said. 'Prince Ranjit is a terrible liar. When we were children he often lied to us to get his own way, because he was spoiled and a little selfish. We always knew when he was lying and I'm certain I would have known this time. His uncle wants to rule in Prince Ranjit's stead after the present ruler dies. If he could have found the ruby and taken it back to the temple, the people might have rejected the prince and placed him on the throne.'

'Yes, I understand that part of it,' the earl said. 'But why could he not have told us that he had you? You said you were ill?'

'I lay in a fever for some days and then I was weak and unable to rise from my bed. Shulie nursed me and the doctor helped me to recover. When I was well enough to leave my bed, Prince Ranjit told me the truth. I think…' She hesitated, then, 'I believe he may have hoped to make me his second wife. Shulie seemed to fear it, but when I told him I was Luke's betrothed wife he brought me back to you.'

'Where you should always have been,' the earl grunted. 'It was foolish running off the way you did, girl. I shan't demand that you marry Luke if you'd rather not—but your home is here with me. I need to see your pretty face, Roxanne. If you're not here, what is there to look forward to in the mornings?'

'Forgive me,' she said and reached for his hand once more. 'I regretted running off as I did and I think I might have returned sooner had the kidnap not happened. I was distressed, but it was foolish of me. I know that Luke does not love me, as I love him—but I did give my word that I would marry him and I should like to live in this house with you, sir.'

'What about my foolish grandson?'

'Luke must tell me what he wants,' Roxanne said and her eyes shone with the tears she was too proud to shed. 'If he still wants me, I shall marry him.'

'My grandson is a very mixed-up young man and a part of that is my fault,' the earl said. 'I resented him because of his father and I blamed John Clarendon for not loving my daughter.' He sighed deeply. 'I pushed them into the marriage and I almost did the same to you and Luke. Please forgive me and stay with me, Roxanne. You are as a granddaughter to me and I hope you will make this your home—whatever you and Luke decide.'

'I shall be glad…' Roxanne's words trailed away as the door opened and Luke entered. The look on his face was so harsh that she caught her breath. 'Has the prince gone?'

'That damned fellow,' Luke said in a haughty tone. 'He had the effrontery to tell me that he would be happy to wed you if I no longer wished for the connection.'

'I'm sorry he made you angry,' Roxanne replied. 'I believe he had some idea that because we had been childhood friends he would like to make me his second wife.'

'Insufferable.' Luke fumed, his eyes glinting with temper. 'You may think yourself fortunate that you did not have the ruby with you, Roxanne. You might otherwise have been left in a ditch to die.'

'Luke, that is despicable. You should not talk about him in such a disrespectful manner. I believe the prince honourable in his own way,' she replied stiffly. 'I know his father sent him to recover the ruby, but they gave me my father's fortune even though they might have withheld it had they wished.'

'Your father bought the ruby in good faith. It was yours by right, Roxanne, and worth twelve thousand pounds if a penny.'

'I did not want it. Such a jewel could only bring ill fortune to anyone who kept it, knowing its history. The prince will return it to the goddess and perhaps his people will prosper again. They are a superstitious people and the curse may only be in their minds, but with the ruby back in place they may be happier.'

Luke threw her a smouldering look. 'I was merely thinking of your rights. Since you do not choose to take anything I gave you…' He glanced at her left hand and saw that she was wearing her emerald ring. 'You are wearing your ring, yet you left it behind—why the change?'

'I did not wish the prince to think I had lied to him concerning my situation. I believe that he wished to marry me and I wanted to make it clear that I was not free without hurting his feelings.'

Luke frowned. 'I shall not keep you to your promise, Roxanne. I can see that you no longer need me. Marry your prince if that is your wish. I have no right to hold you here.'

'Luke, how could you? You are too cruel.'

'Luke, do not be a fool,' the earl said. 'Roxanne has just come back to us. You should not quarrel with her. Besides, she has decided to stay with me—whatever the pair of you decide between you, Roxanne's home will be here with me.'

'How very convenient for you both,' Luke snapped and turned on his heel, striding from the room without another word.'

Roxanne's eyes filled with tears. 'He is angry again. I did not mean to make him angry. What did I say?'

'He is a pig-headed fool,' the earl said, making a sound of exasperation. 'I fear we are too much alike. It is his pride talking, Roxanne. He will apologise to you when he has cooled down and beg you to marry him.'

Roxanne felt the prick of tears and blinked hard. 'I fear Luke no longer wishes me to be his wife, Grandfather. He never did truly. The engagement was make believe—I would have been his wife only for as long as you lived. Then he would have asked for a separation.'

'Stuff and nonsense. Luke is in love with you, girl. When you were lost he searched for you constantly. He was like a man possessed. He neither slept nor ate and I think, had you not returned, he would have gone mad with grief. Why should he react so strongly to a rival if he is not in love with you?'

'You cannot mean it?' Roxanne stared at him in disbelief. 'He is so angry. Surely...was he really in distress because I was lost?'

'I would never lie to you,' the earl told her and smiled. 'Go after him, girl. Sort it out between yourselves—but please do not run off again. My heart won't stand it.'

'I promise I shan't leave you again, sir—though I think you a fraud. I am certain you will live many years yet.'

The earl laughed. 'You may be right, especially if I have good news.'

Roxanne bent and kissed him and then went hurriedly from the room. Where would Luke be? She prayed that he had not gone off to London in a temper.

His grandfather was right to call him a fool. Luke left the house with his pride in tatters and his temper still raging, but he had not gone farther than the rose garden when he realised that he was in the wrong. Why must he always quarrel with the woman he loved? The desolation that had come over him when his search for her had proved in vain was surely enough to tell him that his life would be empty without her. He should have taken her into his arms rather than raging at her, but the interview with Prince Ranjit had not improved his temper, and Roxanne's defence of her old friends had made him snap at her once more.

Yet his honour would not allow him to force her into

a marriage that she might regret. The prince had made it clear that she would be honoured in his country and she had changed since meeting him. Had she rediscovered a lost love? Why did she have that new glow about her? She had always been vibrant and beautiful, but now there was something more—a certainty that had not been there before.

He was a fool and he did not deserve her. No wonder she'd decided that she did not wish to marry him. Why should she? He'd asked her to enter a make-believe engagement, spoken of a convenient arrangement, seduced her and then lost his temper with her. No woman with any pride could accept such treatment. It was not surprising that she'd walked out on him. Now she was back and he had insulted her again. He was a damned fool and he was very much afraid that he'd lost her for ever.

'Luke, please wait for me.'

Turning, he saw Roxanne walking towards him and his heart took a flying leap. The gown she wore was simply cut, but she looked like a queen, regal and proud. In the sunshine her thick luxuriant hair was touched by fire and she was so beautiful that he felt weak with longing. If he lost her, he would have no reason to live.

'Roxanne,' he began hurriedly. 'I know what I said was unforgivable. I had no right or justification for speaking to you so harshly. You have every right to do exactly as you wish.'

'Yes, Luke, I do.' Roxanne raised her head and met his eyes with a cool frank look. 'I am very fond of

Grandfather and I shall not leave him here alone again, though I believe his health is more stable than you may imagine. It is true that he has bouts of illness that could be his last, but he has a very strong will. For as long as he has something to live for he will fight to live.'

'What are you saying?' Luke's gaze narrowed as he tried to gauge what was in her mind. 'Are you suggesting that we should go ahead with our marriage to please him?'

'Perhaps.' She took a deep breath. 'When I left this house that day I felt that your harsh behaviour towards me made a marriage between us untenable. However, after my distress eased, I came to realise that I did not wish to leave Grandfather—or you. I believe I should have returned to discuss the matter with you in a sensible manner had I not been kidnapped.'

She seemed so calm, so in control that Luke hesitated, not knowing what to believe. 'I am not certain what you mean,' he said. 'Are you intending to go on as before—or is this to be a genuine marriage?'

'That is up to you,' she replied. 'My own preference is for a true marriage. I wish for children and—I am very fond of you, Luke. I like you when you are not in a temper and I believe we could go on very comfortably together.'

'You like me when I am not in a temper?' His hands curled into balls at his sides, tension creeping into his voice. 'The evening of the ball you said…I thought there might be more to your feelings than mere liking.' His gaze was intent on her face and he was pleased to see a slight unease dawn in her eyes. She was not truly as calm as she pretended. Roxanne might be a superb actress, but she could not quite shut her feelings out. Making a giant stride towards her, Luke took hold of her, one hand on each of her upper arms, staring down at her fiercely. 'Supposing I want more than mere liking? Supposing I want passion and love—the kind of love that blazes out of control and takes over your life?'

He felt her tremble and she caught her bottom lip between white teeth. Luke smiled, the despair inside him beginning to give way before a new certainty and hope.

'Is that what you want from me?' Roxanne asked, a tremor in her voice now. 'I thought you did not wish to commit to such feelings? You said you did not believe in romantic love, only passion.'

'It was my belief that I could never truly love,' Luke said and smiled. 'Grandfather speaks the truth when he calls me a fool, Roxanne. Everything I ever wanted was there—mine for the taking—but I did not have the sense to see it. Only when I thought you lost, perhaps dead, did I begin to understand how deep my feelings for you actually were. I love you, Roxanne. Not mildly or with fond affection, but with a passion I hardly know how to control. I find the idea of life without you appalling. I want to see you every day, to wake up and find you beside me in my bed—to know that you are mine and always will be.'

Roxanne held back a sob, her face pale and tense. 'Luke, I do love you. You must know it. Surely you must have known that night?'

'I discovered something so sweet in your arms that night,' he murmured huskily, his arms going about her waist as he pulled her close. 'Yet I feared it. I fled from you before you woke because I was terrified of letting you discover my vulnerability. I was uncertain whether you truly loved me.'

'You must have known when I clung to you and held nothing back? Surely you knew then?'

'Yet you so rarely let your feelings show. You are a clever actress, Roxanne. It might have been an act—and it was not all fear that you did not feel as I did; I was afraid that I would hurt you, destroy you, if I allowed myself to offer you a true marriage. I believed my father shallow and thought I might be as he was, but I misjudged him. He lost the woman he truly loved and married my mother just to have an heir for the earldom. He could never love his wife because his heart was in the grave with his one true love. When I thought you might be dead, I knew just what my father felt, Roxanne. Even had I married for an heir in years to come, I should never have loved another woman. You mean everything to me; if you leave me, I shall have nothing left to give anyone.'

'Oh, Luke…' Roxanne's voice caught and a tear escaped, sliding down her cheek. He wiped it away with his fingertips and then bent to kiss her lips. She gave a little moan and pressed herself against him, melting into him so that he felt as if they were one person, one being. 'Luke, my dearest. When I recovered my senses I knew all that I had lost and I feared I might never see you again. Shulie believed the prince meant to make me his wife and for a short time I feared he might take me with him whether I wished it or not.'

'But you admired him. I saw it in your eyes—and there is something different about you…'

'I know who I am now, Luke. Before I wondered if I might be a thief or worse. I was not sure that I was good enough to be your wife and the mistress of this house.'

'Grandfather knew you were a lady born. He saw quality—as I did had I the sense to realise it.'

'Yes, but I did not know. I wanted to be worthy of you, Luke. Now the shadows of the past have gone and I know who and what I am.'

'The notion of India was more true than you knew?'

'My father was the prince's tutor. When my mother died of a fever my father brought me home to live with my aunt and uncle—but her husband was a greedy rogue. When Papa sent me the ruby to keep for him, my aunt saw it and her husband was ready to give me to a man who would have used me for his pleasure and made me work as a whore until I died of some disease. I heard him telling her it was either that or he would kill me himself.'

'Damn him! If I'd known, I would have killed him myself!'

'My aunt pleaded with him, but she was frightened of him. I ran away that night. I was afraid he would catch me and I ran and ran for a long time…then I was attacked by a vagrant and after that I became ill and I must have wandered in a daze. I remember now that I told Sofia some of the story when I was ill, just little things about India. I cried for my mother and my ayah.'

'Why did she not tell you later?'

'Perhaps because she knew it distressed me to try to remember. She invented the game to try to jog my memory, but it did not work and so she decided that it was best to forget the past. She loved me and wanted to keep me safe. Because she feared for me she tried to keep my past a secret, and that is why no one found me for a long time, even when the prince's men began to search. When she was ill she told me she was sure I was a lady and that I should sell the ruby and set up with a companion. She hoped I would marry well.'

'She thought you enamoured of the prince,' Luke said, a hint of jealousy in his voice.

'I was but a child when we were friends,' Roxanne said and smiled at him. 'Sofia asked me about the prince once, but I could not recall him, though I must have said something to her when I was rambling. When she spoke of him I thought she meant one of her lovers, because when I recovered from the fever I had no memory of anything.'

'He remembered you. He wanted you.'

'Then why did he not simply take me? I should have found it difficult to escape had he decided to keep me.'

'He wanted the ruby more,' Luke said. 'He knew that I would never give it up while he had you and that's why he brought you back to me.'

'Yes, perhaps, though I believe he understood that I belonged to you. I know he made you angry, but his father was always an honourable man and the prince did what was right in the end.'

'You may think so, but I cannot excuse the fellow. He had the effrontery to offer to buy you from me,' Luke said, a grim look on his face. 'He said that he would pay my price whatever that might be. I told him that you were a pearl beyond price and not for sale.'

'He tried to buy me from you?' Roxanne was stunned, incredulous. 'Is that what made you so angry?'

'What would you expect? He said that if I was making a marriage of convenience, he would make it worth my while to give you up.'

'How could he?' Roxanne felt a surge of anger. 'He had no right. I am not your property. I am not anyone's property.'

'That is the gist of what I told him, though perhaps not quite in those words,' Luke said. He hesitated, studying her face and trying to read her mind. 'Can you forgive me, Roxanne? Will you give me another chance?'

'Are you asking me to marry you?'

'Yes, of course.' Luke suddenly dropped on one knee before her, gazing up at her in earnest. 'Roxanne, will you do me the honour of becoming my wife? I love you and your agreement will make me the happiest man alive.'

She seemed to hesitate for one instant and Luke's heart sank; then she smiled and inclined her head.

'Yes, of course I shall, Luke. Please get up. There was no need to kneel to me. All I want is to know that I am truly wanted and loved. I do not require homage, nor shall I tie you to me. You may live as you wish, visit London as often as you choose. I ask only that you love me and return to me when you are ready.'

'Unless forced by business, I shall never want to leave you for more than a few hours, my darling.'

Luke was on his feet, drawing her into his arms. He crushed her against him, knowing that she must feel the heat and force of his arousal and he held her pressed into his body. He wanted her to know how fierce was his need and his desire.

'I wanted you from the first moment we met,' he said hoarsely. 'At first I thought to make you my mistress, but…' His hold tightened as he felt her stiffen, pressing her even closer. 'For a long time now I've known that making you my mistress would not serve. I suspect that even when I first asked you to enter a make-believe marriage, I knew somewhere deep inside me that once I had you I should never wish to let you go.'

'Luke…I hoped, but was never certain…'

'You do care for me a little? I know I am far from perfect—but you do truly love me?'

Roxanne smiled tenderly. 'I think I fell in love with you the moment you opened your eyes and looked at me, but I did not admit it until much later. I was afraid that you would never love me—afraid that if you sensed my feelings you would feel trapped.'

'I did for a short time,' Luke admitted honestly. 'I did not want to feel love, because I know that it can bring so much pain. I saw my mother's misery and my father's chafing at the bonds that tied him to a woman he did not love. I was a coward to run from love, Roxanne—but I swear I shall never give you cause to doubt me again.'

'Then we shall be married as soon as it can be arranged,' Roxanne told him. She offered her hand, her eyes bright with love. 'I believe we should tell Grandfather. He cares for us both so much, Luke. Before we came here he was lonely and unhappy. The breach between you was too wide for either of you to cross. Now I think you have reached an understanding?'

'Because of you the breach has closed and we are a family once more.' Luke reached out to touch her cheek. 'While you were missing, our mutual despair drew us together and we realised that we loved each other. Grandfather told me I was a fool and he was right. I had no idea how fortunate I was that day my horse took a tumble in the woods.'

'If I had not run away from Black Bob that day, we might never have met.' Roxanne shuddered and moved closer to him. 'How much we might both have lost, Luke.'

'I think it was our destiny.' He leaned down to kiss her once more. 'Come, we should put Grandfather's mind at rest, though I am certain he already knows.'

'I think the old rascal is truly content now,' Luke said as he took Roxanne's hand. The earl had retired to bed after eating supper with them in the parlour and they were strolling in the moonlight, enjoying the warmth of a summer night. 'He seems much better now, though at times I see that he is still frail.'

'We must make his life as full as possible,' Roxanne

said. 'We shall live here for most of the time, Luke, though I know you have other estates and a house in London.'

'Once I thought the country boring, but it cannot be so when you are here, my love. It may be that I shall have to tend to business at my own estate from time to time and if you cannot accompany me I must leave you here—but I shall return as soon as I can.'

'Perhaps one day we shall spend more time in London or at your own estate, but for Grandfather's sake we must be here as often as we can, dearest.'

'You are as caring as you are beautiful,' Luke said and drew her near, bending his head to kiss her mouth. 'I want you so much. I can hardly bear to wait for our wedding night, Roxanne.'

'And why should you wait?' she whispered against his mouth. 'I do not think you need to consider my modesty or my reputation since the servants all knew what happened on the night of the ball.' She gurgled with delicious laughter and pressed herself against him. 'Take me to bed, Luke. I am as impatient as you—and it is only another ten days to our wedding.'

'Wicked seductress,' he murmured and touched her cheek. 'Since it is too late to save either your reputation or mine, I believe I shall take you at your word.'

'You look beautiful, Miss Roxanne,' the housekeeper said when she brought up the posy of white roses and lilies tied with red ribbons. 'It's a shame that you've no family to share your special day.'

'My family is here,' Roxanne said and impulsively

kissed her cheek. 'You are as a friend to me, Mrs Arlet. Everyone has made me welcome, right from the first moment I came here. If I have no mother, I have my memories and I have my friends. Grandfather is to give me away. Why should I need anyone else?'

'You're a proper lady, miss, and no mistake,' Mrs Arlet said. 'We're all so happy that you and his lordship intend to make this your main home.'

'We shall honeymoon in Paris and we shall spend a few weeks in London sometimes, but I love this house. Lord Clarendon knows that and it is the reason that he has agreed to live here.'

'We are all so excited, Miss Roxanne. His lordship was telling us about the plans he has for bringing the house and estate up to modern standards.'

'Yes, I know. Grandfather had allowed things to stagnate a little, but Clarendon will change all that—and that is as it should be. I know the earl is delighted with the way things have turned out.'

'Is there anything I can do for you, miss?'

'No, thank you. I am almost ready. I shall come down in a few moments.'

'I'll leave you with Tilly then.' Mrs Arlet nodded as the maid entered bearing some floral tributes, gifts and cards. 'We all wish you happiness, Miss Roxanne.'

'Thank you,' Roxanne replied and nodded as she went out, closing the door behind her. 'So many people have sent gifts,' she said as her maid laid the packages on the dressing table. 'Where have all these things come from?'

'Some were delivered by hand, miss. I think his lordship sent this one.'

Roxanne took the small package she offered and opened it, smiling as she saw the diamond-and-pearl earrings, which would go with the pearls he had given her and the bracelet of pearls and diamonds that the earl had sent her earlier that morning. She read the card, smiled and then slipped them into her ears. Looking at her reflection, she nodded in a pleased way. She picked up a posy, held it to her nose and smiled, then indicated another small parcel.

'What is the other package?'

'That came from London this morning, miss.' She picked it up and handed it to her.

Roxanne opened it and gasped as she saw the huge pearl. It was pink, flawless and shaped like a teardrop. Set in gold at the pointed end, it could be worn as a pendant. She picked it up, looking at it as it lay in her palm and thinking that it must be very valuable, then saw the card that had lain beneath it.

*For a pearl beyond price*, she read and frowned as she saw the signature. *This comes from Prince Ranjit on behalf of his family.*

Replacing the pearl in its nest of black velvet, Roxanne fastened the pearls Luke had given her about her throat.

'I shall go down now, Tilly,' she said. 'Please finish packing my things for me. There are only a few trinkets for my dressing case. Everything else we have not already decided on can remain here. Clarendon says that we should not take too much, because he intends to buy clothes in Paris.'

'Very well, miss.' Tilly couldn't keep the note of excitement from her voice. 'I've never been to France, miss.'

'I visited with friends when we travelled as a group,' Roxanne said with a smile. 'I liked it well enough then, but I think it will be wonderful this time.'

Picking up her posy, she walked from the room and negotiated the stairs with care, her train flowing behind her. The earl and most of the servants had gathered below to greet her. She kissed the earl and then turned to a young woman whom she had met for the first time and immediately liked the previous evening.

'Mrs Fox, I am so glad you could come to us—and I hope you like the gown we chose for you. Luke has told me so much about you. Your husband was his dearest friend and I am so pleased that we are to be friends.'

'It is a lovely gown and it was kind of you to invite me to be one of your attendants,' Beth Fox said. 'Please, you must call me Beth. I owe so much to Luke, as you know. After my darling Harry died and I was left alone with a child and no money, Lord Clarendon found me and provided me with a house of my own. I believe you stayed there for a short time before I moved in?'

'The charming house in Hampstead? Yes, I stayed in your guestroom for a short time. Luke told me your story recently,' Roxanne said with a smile. 'Your father and your husband's family rejected you because they did not approve of the marriage. It was unkind of them to leave you to fend for yourself with a young child to bring up alone. I am glad Luke helped you and I want you to visit with us whenever you choose.'

'Luke is fortunate in his choice of a bride,' Beth said and kissed her. 'Many would have believed the whispers and thought me his mistress—though it has never been so, nor could it be. We both loved Harry and felt only friendship for each other.'

'Luke is an honourable man and those who think otherwise malign him,' Roxanne said. 'Now that you are here for our wedding people will see that they were mistaken. Luke ought to have told Grandfather the truth before, but his stubborn pride would not let him defend his honour. It made him angry because the earl believed the tittle-tattle that you were his mistress.'

'You are all so kind. I was not sure I should be welcomed by the earl, who was a close friend of my father-in-law, but I have been invited to bring my son and stay whenever I wish. The earl is so generous, Roxanne. I am not surprised you are so fond of him.'

'Grandfather has made me welcome here from the beginning,' Roxanne said and went to his side, taking his hand. 'Shall we leave? I should not wish to keep Luke waiting.'

Luke turned his head as the organ began to play. Roxanne had just entered the church, standing at the far end of the nave with his grandfather, Beth and some young girls as her bridesmaids. She was so beautiful. His heart caught with pride as she walked towards him. As she reached his side, he offered his hand and she took it. He smiled and whispered, 'You look lovely, my dearest one.'

'Thank you.'

Her hand trembled slightly and he pressed it as the ceremony began.

'Dearly beloved. We are gathered together to see this man and this woman joined in Holy matrimony…'

The words droned on and Luke gave his responses in a firm strong tone. Roxanne's voice was clear and light, carrying to the rear of the church. Luke reached out to lift the white veiling that fell from her satin bonnet and leaned forwards to kiss her softly on the lips.

They advanced towards the high altar to be blessed and then to the vestry where they both signed their names. Then the bells rang out joyously and they were walking into the sunshine. A small crowd awaited their coming and rushed forwards to shower them with flower petals and rice.

After receiving good wishes and small tributes from the villagers, Luke took his bride's hand and hurried her to the carriage drawn up in the lane. He helped her inside, waiting until the door was closed fast before drawing her into his arms to kiss her.

'My sweet love,' he murmured huskily. 'I was afraid this day might never happen, but it has and I am the happiest of men.'

'Thank you for my surprise gifts,' Roxanne said and touched the magnificent earrings she wore. 'You have given me so much…'

Luke smiled, touching her cheek with his fingertips. 'The earrings are just one of many gifts I intend to make you, my darling. I have others for this evening when we are alone—and in Paris I shall buy you all the clothes and trinkets you could desire.'

'You are intent on spoiling me,' Roxanne said and leaned closer to kiss him. 'I love the gifts you've given me, Luke—but it is your love I prize more than any jewel.'

'My love is yours for ever,' he murmured huskily. 'I shall show you later how prized you are, Roxanne.'

'This is the happiest day of my life.'

She reached up and kissed him.

'My beloved.' Luke drew her close as passion surged between them. 'How fortunate I feel.'

The large reception hall was overflowing with guests. They spilled over into the parlours and out on to the terraces in the sunshine, the sound of laughter and chattering voices resounding throughout the house.

The bride and groom stood together to welcome all their guests. It was a glittering occasion, for friends and relatives had come from all parts of the country to stay and witness the wedding.

'I never thought I should see this day,' the earl said to Roxanne when she brought him a slice of rich fruity wedding cake with thick white icing. 'I don't know when I've ever seen Luke look this happy, girl. I never expected to see him head over heels in love, but there's no doubt of it. It's a transformation and one that gives me a deal of pleasure.'

'We are both very fortunate,' Roxanne said and took his hand, holding it to her cheek. 'I owe this to you,

Grandfather. Luke told me what you said to him—the way you made him realise that he was in danger of losing everything he truly wanted.'

'I told him the truth about things he should have known long ago,' the earl said, shaking his head. 'If it made the difference, I'm glad.'

Music had begun to play. Luke came to Roxanne and took her hand, leading her out to the middle of the floor. They danced together, a slow stately performance, then suddenly the music changed and he swept her into his arms as they waltzed.

'I want to take you somewhere quiet and make love to you,' he whispered against her ear. 'How much longer must I wait?'

'Luke…' Roxanne drew back, her mouth soft and seductive as she smiled. 'Be patient, beloved. We shall be together very soon now—and we have the rest of our lives to make love.'

'Hardly enough,' he murmured throatily. 'I want you for ever. Eternity is not long enough for all the things I want to tell you.'

It was as if Luke had suddenly discovered a well of emotions and feelings that he'd never known existed and they spilled over, engulfing her in a tide of love and desire.

'Well, I shall go up and change very soon,' Roxanne told him. 'You could follow me if you wish and…' She left the words unsaid, but her eyes told him all he wished to know.

Roxanne slipped out of her wedding gown and put on a soft silk wrap. She took the brush in her right hand

and began to stroke it over her hair, letting the dark red tresses fall over her shoulders and down her back.

'Come back when I send for you, Tilly,' she said. 'I want to rest for a little while before I change for this evening.'

'Yes, miss—I mean, my lady.' The girl blushed and bobbed a curtsy. 'Ring when you need me.'

Roxanne nodded and smiled. She was dabbing a little light perfume at her wrists when the door opened and Luke entered. She stood up and moved towards him, a smile of invitation on her lips.

'I told Tilly I wished to rest before I change for the evening,' she said huskily. 'I am not tired, but the sheets have been turned back. Shall we rest for a while together?'

Luke moved in closer and reached for her, his arms sliding about her waist. 'Those of the guests who are staying have gone up to change for the evening and the others are departing. I do not think we shall be missed for an hour or so, dearest.'

'Luke…' Roxanne lifted her face for his kiss, melting against him as his lips took possession of hers. 'I love you so very much.'

Then she was in his arms, responding to his kiss, and the next instant he was carrying her to the bed, placing her carefully amongst scented sheets.

Going to him without reserve, Roxanne shuddered with delight as his hands stroked up the arch of her back. Luke reached for her wrap, slipping it back off her shoulders to kiss her soft skin. The touch of his warm mouth on her breasts and then the inside of her thighs made her whimper with pleasure and she trembled, arching to meet him, lips parting as his kiss swept her away on clouds of exquisite pleasure.

Luke removed his own clothes and she saw the urgency of his need as he lay down beside her and drew her into his body. She felt the burn of his desire next to her thigh and then her legs were parting and he was between them, thrusting up into her. She gave a cry of pleasure, opening to him, wanting him deeper and deeper inside her. Her back arched and her hips thrust forwards to meet him as the desire pooled and grew into a raging need.

Together they reached for and found that wonderful place that is known only to true lovers. Luke gave a great shout of joy and triumph as he came inside her and she found her climax rolling through her as it came and came again in waves.

Afterwards, he lay with his head against her breast, their sweat mingling as they held on to each other, replete and content.

It was some time later that they left the bed. Roxanne sat at her dressing table and began to brush her hair.

'I must go and change,' Luke said and lifted her hair to kiss the back of her neck. He moved round to look at her and watch as she brushed her hair, perching on the edge of the dressing table, reluctant to leave despite his avowal that he ought to go. He picked up a small box casually and opened it, then stiffened as he saw what lay inside. 'Where did this come from?'

Roxanne looked and saw the magnificent pearl.

'Oh—that arrived just before the wedding. Tilly brought it up with some other things. Prince Ranjit sent it on behalf of his family.'

'It must be almost priceless,' Luke said and frowned, taking it out so that it lay on the palm of his hand. 'You did not choose to wear it today?'

'Of course not. I wore the gifts you gave me—and Grandfather's bracelet. Why should I wear that pearl, Luke? It is lovely, but I think we should send it back. I have no need of such gifts from the prince.'

Luke's expression eased, anger and tension gone. 'I would return it except that to do so would cause offence. I shall acknowledge the gift, Roxanne. There is no need for you to do anything.'

'I shall not wear the pendant, but if you think it rude to return it…'

'It can stay in the strong room. Perhaps one of our children or their wives will take a fancy to it in the future.' Luke smiled and leaned forwards to kiss her lips. 'He said you were a jewel of rare value. I replied that I did not need to be told. I was well aware of your value to me. I was so angry that I wanted to kill him for daring to think you could be his for a sum of money.'

'You have no need to be angry, my love.' Roxanne stood up and put her arms about him. 'No jewels could buy what we have, Luke. Love such as we feel for each other is a gift from God. It is all that either of us need now or in the future.

'I am so happy,' Roxanne said. 'Paris will be wonderful, but all I truly need is to be at home with you and Grandfather.'

* * *

'So you're home again,' the earl said and nodded with satisfaction as Roxanne came to kiss him on the cheek. 'You look happy, girl. Paris was a success, then?'

'Paris was exciting and I enjoyed the experience,' she said and pulled her elegant satinwood chair closer to his. It had a shield-shaped back, spindly legs and was one of a set of fourteen from Mr Adams's workrooms scattered throughout the house. 'However, I am glad to be home again, sir. Luke will be down shortly. He thinks he must go to London for a few days soon on business, but he will not be away for long.'

'You must neither of you feel tied to my coattails, girl. As long as you visit often I shall be content.'

'Well, I dare say I shall go to London or Bath for a visit sometimes, but not just yet.' Roxanne smiled, hardly able to contain the delight she felt inside. 'Now, I hope you will not think this too soon, Grandfather—but Luke and I…' She paused to watch his face, saw his frown and then a look of enquiry in his eyes. 'Yes, I am to have a child. I know it may seem too soon to be sure, but I think…it may have happened before the wedding. We did anticipate our wedding a little. I hope I have not shocked you?'

'A child…' The earl looked at her eagerly, a hint of tears in his eyes. 'You're certain, girl?'

'I saw a doctor just before we left Paris and he was sure that I was with child, perhaps two months or a little less. If I take good care and do not rush about all over the place, I believe you may have your first grandchild sooner than you had anticipated.'

'An heir…' The earl grinned at her. 'I thought I might have to wait months, years even. You're a clever girl, Roxanne. I knew you were just what this place needed when Luke first brought you here.'

'I may have a daughter,' she cautioned. 'But if I do we shall have to try again. I must confess that I shall not mind if we have a brood of children, both sons and daughters, to fill this big house with laughter.'

'You've already done that,' he said. 'The house has not been empty since you left for France. Your friend Beth Fox brought her son to stay for a few days and I gave him a pony of his own to keep in our stables—so I think we can be sure they will visit regularly. They might find a home here on the estate if you wished it, somewhere close enough for you to visit each other often. Besides, I've had a stream of visitors, neighbours and friends I hadn't bothered with for years—even Luke's godmother stayed on after the wedding—and guests are what this place has needed since Luke's parents died.'

'The tragedy was a terrible thing and it blighted all your lives, but the past has gone and we have a future filled with love and happiness to look forward to.'

'Luke knows of the child?'

'He is delighted. He thought I should tell you alone, but he will be down soon and then we can all celebrate together.'

She glanced up as the door opened and Luke walked in. 'Here you are, dearest. Grandfather is pleased with our news.'

'You've done well by me, sir,' the earl said. 'I'm

proud of you—proud of you both. And this is one of the happiest days of my life.'

Luke looked at Roxanne, his eyes warm with love. 'We both hope there will be others as happy, sir.'

'Yes.' Roxanne stood up and went to him. She glanced back at the earl. 'We have decided that you shall name our first child—boy or girl, the choice shall be yours.'

'Emily for a girl or Selwyn if it's a boy,' the earl said. 'To tell the truth, I have a fancy for a little girl first, but we must wait and see what the good lord sends us.'

'Yes, I do not think even Roxanne can arrange that, though she leaves little else to chance,' Luke said and laughed as his wife pulled a face at him. 'For myself I care not whether the child is male or female—as long as Roxanne is well after the birth I shall be quite content.'

'I have decided we should have at least two boys and two girls,' Roxanne said and smiled. 'But as long as we are all well and content together little else matters.'

'We should send for champagne,' the earl said. 'I want to toast my new grandchild—and the staff must share in our good fortune. We shall give a fête for the people, Luke. I'll leave it to you to organise the affair, but I shall attend if the day is fine.'

'I shall set it all in order before I leave for London—and I'll be back within a week so you need not pull caps with me, Grandfather. My home is here with the people I love and I have no wish to stay away an hour longer than I need.'

The door opened to admit Mrs Arlet. A few words from the earl and she left, face wreathed in smiles, to communicate the news to the rest of the household and order their champagne and lemonade for Roxanne.

'You know that they will be counting back the weeks after the birth,' Roxanne said. 'I think we shall shock our neighbours a little, sir.'

'Nonsense,' the earl replied and winked at her. 'Have you never heard of a babe coming early? My Emily had our son a month sooner than expected—big bonnie boy he was, too.'

'Grandfather,' Roxanne said and laughed. 'You are a rascal.'

'I was a bit of a rascal when I was younger,' he agreed and glanced at his grandson. 'It might be that Clarendon is more like me than any of you thought…'

# *Afterword*

'So, Selwyn Luke John Arnold Hartingdon, future Lord Clarendon and one day heir to this old pile,' the earl said, looking down at the child in the cot beside Roxanne's bed. 'How does it feel to be the first-born of a clever girl like your mama? I dare say you are pleased with yourself and will lead us all a merry dance one day.'

'Grandfather,' Roxanne scolded with a smile of affection. 'He is but a day old and interested only in feeding and sleeping.'

'He is my great-grandson and will take after his father and his great-grandfather,' the earl replied with satisfaction. 'He is going to be a fine big chap and will make us all proud of him. I dare say he might be the Prime Minister or a famous general if he chose.'

'I think he may have some of Roxanne's qualities,' Luke said and raised his brows at her. 'I certainly hope he has more sense than either of us ever had.'

'Well, yes, of course—but he's got my nose and his mouth is just like yours, Luke.' The earl chuckled. 'And I am an old fool clucking over him as if I'd never seen a babe before. Roxanne, I am proud of you, girl. I wanted to tell you that I love you and make sure you were well—but there never was such a beautiful child.'

'Thank you, dearest Grandfather. I love you, too.'

'Well, I'll leave you together for a while—but you should let Roxanne rest, Luke. She needs to get her strength back.'

'I shall do so in a moment, sir.'

Luke grinned as the door closed behind him. 'I've never seen him look so happy and proud. Anyone would think the boy was his son.'

'He loves us all,' Roxanne said. 'Are you proud of me, Luke? Are you pleased with your son?'

'You know I am,' he said and perched on the edge of her bed, reaching for her hand. 'I am the happiest man alive—except perhaps for Grandfather. He looks younger and I begin to think he is an old fraud. He will live for years.'

'His health is not good,' Roxanne said and held his hand tighter, 'but he is content and will have some time with us yet.'

'Yes, I know.' Luke bent his head and kissed her. 'Now I must do as Grandfather bid me and leave you to rest. Beth will be here later and I know she will be eager to see you. Rest now and you will feel better when she arrives.'

'I am perfectly well, you know,' Roxanne said. 'I

shall rest, but only for a little time. Come and see me soon, my love.'

'Of course. I have no intention of going anywhere else,' he said, blew her a kiss and went out.

Roxanne lay back against her pillows, a smile on her lips as she closed her eyes and slept.

* * * * *

Harlequin® SuperRomance®

# ...there's more to the story!

Superromance.
A *big* satisfying read about unforgettable characters. Each month we offer *six* very different stories that range from family drama to adventure and mystery, from highly emotional stories to romantic comedies—and much more! Stories about people you'll believe in and care about. Stories too compelling to put down....

Our authors are among today's *best* romance writers. You'll find familiar names and talented newcomers. Many of them are award winners—and you'll see why!

If you want the biggest and best in romance fiction, you'll get it from Superromance!

**Exciting, Emotional, Unexpected...**